JONATHAN REAPER

REAP THROUGH THE END OF THE DAYS

By: Jonathan Reaper
SERIES VOLUME VII

CR3 CONCEPTS®, LLC © 2021

Cover design by: Emil Goska
https://www.facebook.com/emilGoskaDesign

FIRST EDITION
ISBN: 979-8-9851355-0-3

PREFACE

What you are reading is not a religious story or myth but a record to be documented only as a reminder to those who will survive the great purge. Unlike world wars, famine, plagues, and high mortality pandemics, this is silent and with one purpose. To transform our world by shedding all but two billion souls. By twenty fifty, a completion of a prophecy called the End of Days.

The true story has been altered from the beginning of documented time. Starting with Babylon, not a city but the bible's name for the earth after Adam and Eve were banished from Eden. This is our first attempt to change fate, each corresponding event in history can create a different future without losing ourselves in the process.

You currently only know of the edited recording of our existence. The original author was turned into a fiction writer showing slight discrepancies to cause a certain amount of the population to doubt the truth or follow the wrong path. How do I know this? We discovered the original work from Enoch, Moses, Isaiah, Ezekiel, and John that was left in Adam's cave. Yes, the first Adam.

The original scripts seem to have been a way to catalog the truth but not for distribution. With the writings never shared, oral history skewed over time and small details changed. From what all have read from stone, clay, animal skin, parchment, and paper is not the original author, but rather a copy. We can change our timeline.

The irony is, with your help, we will be successful in fighting the future, so none of what I've captured will be true in a potential new timeline. This means the green notebooks I wrote, and an additional hundred zettabytes of knowledge making up all the data ever produced in the world is stored for your trip.

When you arrive, know that before there was a beginning, you will witness the first war. A fight between immortal beings on the side of good and those of evil. This event changed the universe and every dimension. It also created balance between light and dark, right and wrong, good and evil. This happened a hundred millennia before the earth was created.

As I tell this narrative, our origin story, I know that the current understanding of physics is mostly wrong in every aspect except one. There is a fixed amount of matter in the universe. It can never be destroyed or created, only changed. So, the same is for the immortal beings from our past, present, and future. This is true not only in this dimension, but all and for the beings that can travel between them. Though they have many names, we will call these immortal beings, angels; those who rebelled against the Creator are called fallen ones.

Like all matter in the universe, the immortal war never ends, none of them are destroyed, they only change to the side of good or evil. Such is true of those souls who will be judged at the End of Days and reside in forever lightness or darkness. The only two places for matter to exist for all eternity. Then it happens again.

If you are asking why we should care, it is simple. The current projection by our best artificial intelligence is less than five percent will be judged favorably once all the parts of the original two billion souls are tallied. Today this means the sum of every lineage of mankind. When combined, is a total of a hundred and five billion people who have ever walked the earth. This cosmic balance will factor in each individual experience and action; then give a weight on either the side of the balance for good or evil.

Let me explain, based on the original author and translated through our artificial intelligence computer. The original two billion humans were given a soul upon birth. After that, the soul is divided each time a birth happens and like your DNA, those experiences are carried with you. If you want to equate this to energy, in the beginning, the amount per soul must have been much greater than today. The more concentrated the energy, the longer life and health remains, such the reason early humans recorded in the bible lived a thousand years.

The original author wrote when the earth experiences an event that returns the population to two billion, the End of Days will occur; the first seal will be broken. As you know, this is not the first time the Creator reset souls and I'll explain this in more detail later.

The events are clarified based on the origin story from Enoch, who was from the line of Seth and documented his experience in heaven before the great flood. Way before Moses, his original work, not what you know in the bible, tries to communicate with words that best describe what was known at the time. Lastly, Isaiah who told of the corporeal immortal beings and Ezekiel who foretold the End of Days. This all was before John the Apostle who wrote of the four horsemen and the seven seals, our milestones to fight against the End of Days.

So, how do you communicate what is happening with a remote village who has never seen your world? How would you describe a car, airplane, computer? These ancient authors are trying to explain the unexplainable.

Now let's start before the beginning. In the original author's account in the bible, this is the first-time eternal beings were tasked with the responsibility of monitoring our creation. As the universe is unknowing and unseeing, so are the number of entities created to bring glory to the supreme one who makes all, we call it, the Creator. You may call them or him or her something else, the name doesn't make a difference, only that they are the intelligent design for our dimension and all we see and don't see.

The Creator delegated their most trusted angels, as the last edicts were accomplished, to watch over the earth. All we know is that when earth was created, the one called the 'Light-bringer' or 'Morningstar' was struck down with his followers and ejected from paradise. For a moment before the betrayal, the Creator trusted in his right hand to complete those tasks beneath the Almighty. This is what kicked off the Immortal War.

As written by Adam, in a failed coup that cost one third of all the members of paradise, a war exposed a trait unknown by the Creator at the time, it was that his servants had the ability to exhibit pride and envy. This turned into jealousy and hate. These fallen ones were morphed and changed over millennia into what we now call evil immortal beings or demons. Even though the winners returned to paradise, it was a warning to those who forsake the Creator in the future. As a result, the losers were cast out, to fend for themselves, in the blackness and emptiness of space. With no home or destination. Not in a corporeal form, wandering the universe as spirits in search of purpose.

The fallen ones migrated to the far reaches of space, creating corporeal bodies like those of humans and lived in them while building giant cities and creating ships to physically travel through time and space.

It was then, many millennia later, these losers, also known as the fallen ones, came back to earth. Led by the immortal being called, "Morningstar," they were angry and jealous of what the Creator coveted, "In his image and with free will." By creating life beyond the non-corporeal immortal to a physical body, and with a celestial existence, Morningstar decided to destroy what was most cherished by the Creator.

When the Creator chose humans over angels, Morningstar led his army to fight heaven. When Morningstar was defeated, it was his mission to show the Creator how flawed and evil man could become, more than his fallen ones. This changed the mission of the immortal war, if you can't destroy paradise, make it unattainable by those who the Creator loves most. Now this war is a fight for the souls of man. The first attack was when Morningstar kicked Adam and Eve out of the

Garden of Eden. Showing that the Creator's favorite was not perfect but flawed.

To align with what is in the original writings, Eden was a perfect place, separated from the rest of the world. A location where the Creator regularly visited and walked with his most favorite corporeal beings, both beautiful inside and out. Remember that angels were created as servants, but man's existence was to be a child of the Creator. To be raised and mentored into a more perfect immortal existence. Adam wrote the more a man worships the Creator, translates to more power it receives.

Moses wrote in the original writing, "And the Creator said, 'let us make man in our image, after our likeness and let them have dominion over all the earth. So, we created man in our own image, a copy of us. Both male and female were created. And we blessed them, and we said unto them, be fruitful, and multiply, and replenish the earth, and subdue it and have dominion over the fish of the sea, and over the fowl of the air, and over every living thing that moves upon the earth.'

"And the Creator planted a garden eastward in Eden and there he put a man whom he had formed. And out of the ground grew every tree that is pleasant to the sight, and good for food. The Tree of Life was within the garden, and the Tree of Knowledge. And a river went out of Eden to water the garden and from there it was parted and became into four heads.

"The name of the first is the Pison, which encompassed the whole land of Havilah, where there is gold, bdellium, and the onyx stone. And the name of the second river is Gihon, the same is it that encompassed the whole land of Ethiopia. And the name of the third river is Hiddekel, goes toward the east of Assyria. And the fourth river is the Euphrates.

"And the Creator took the man and put him into the Garden of Eden to dress it and to keep it. And the Creator told Adam, saying, 'Of every tree of the garden may freely eat but of the Tree of Knowledge, if you eat, you will surely die.'

"And then the Creator said, 'it is not good that the man should be alone. I will make him a partner.' And out of the ground the Creator formed every beast of the field, and every fowl of the air. Then brought them unto Adam to see what he would call them. After the creation of Eve, they did as were told and lived in Eden. Naked and unashamed of their existence.

"While watching Adam and Eve for some time, Morningstar witnessed the woman questioning why of all they could see and touch, one part of the garden was off limits. This was a perfect time for Morningstar to enter the corporeal body of a lizard while waiting for Eve. When alone with her, he pointed to the Tree of Knowledge and said, 'If you want a taste, it is ok, you will not die, your eyes shall be opened, and will be wiser than Adam or the Creator.'

"It was then, when she ate it, a new self-awareness came over her and she now knew about all that happened before, an understanding of good and evil. With the feeling of unbelievable power, she shared with Adam and they both were all knowing. To include their failed promise to the Creator.

"A time later, Adam and Eve heard the Creator's voice calling out to them in the garden. Hiding, they concealed themselves from their presence. Adam said, 'I was afraid, because I was naked and hid myself.' The Creator said, 'who said you were naked? Did you eat of the tree I commanded you not to eat?' And the man said, 'The woman gave me fruit and I did eat it. I did this by not knowing what it was.' The Creator said unto the woman, 'What did you do?' And the woman said, 'The Lizard lured me into eating the forbidden fruit.'

"The Creator then looked for and found Morningstar who was possessing the body of a reptile and said, 'Because you did this, this beast will slither on its belly, as a reminder of what you did to me.'

It was then, Morningstar discarded the threats of the Creator, returned to his fallen ones, and realized his revenge was within reach. By teaching man to be self-sufficient, why would they need the Creator for help. No help translates to no worship which means no power. This would be what was needed to defeat the Creator. With all the angels serving no one, they were free. With man no longer worshiping the Creator, Morningstar would win the immortal war.

With many dimensions and worlds to manage, the Creator would arrive on earth from time to time and check in making sure life was progressing in the way they had designed. Morningstar realized the Creator didn't watch everything all the time, nor read the minds of man. The absence of both would harnesses the power of free will.

By doing this, the Creator's power becomes greater than simple worship from angels. Remember, one third of them were kicked out of Paradise. This allowed the fallen ones to change the fate of man. With Morningstar to influence man to be absent of the Creator was the new mission.

Now fast forward many generations of man to the original scripture according to Enoch. He refers to both good and bad Watchers or Holy Ones, with a primary focus on the rebellious angels. Also, explains how angels teach man. He discusses the place where angels gather, located on Mount Hermon near modern day Syria.

The angel Azazel, a Watcher sent by the Creator to report on what men were doing. Rather than watch and report, he taught men the art of warfare, of making weapons and armor. He also taught women how to enhance their sexuality. The most egregious of offenses was teaching witchcraft. Lastly, he and they fornicated with women, and bore children called the Nephilim. When it was revealed to the Creator, Azazel was bound hand and foot by the archangel Raphael and forced to stay in darkness until Judgement Day. Then he would be cast into the fire and be consumed forever.

Enoch reported of two hundred angels who mated with human women. In the original text of Moses, it says, "When humans began to multiply on earth, the servants of the Creator mated with the women." These hybrid children called Nephilim appeared on earth. These sons of angels and human women were leaders with special powers.

What this writing shows is that the Creator has allowed servants to influence man, but there are actions that warrant confinement and forever darkness and fire. Those all on earth were rewarded with a flood resetting the inhabitance of the earth. From then on, no man would live more than a hundred and twenty years.

As a loyal witness for the Creator and the Archangels, Enoch was rewarded, "Behold, I, Enoch was taken unto heaven. And the structure was of crystals and fire. Its ceiling was like the path of the stars and lightning, and between them were fiery cherubim, and their heaven was clear as water. Flames surrounded the walls, and its portals were a blaze. And I entered the house, and it was hot and cold. There were no delights of life therein."

Enoch then wrote, "There was a second house, greater than the former, and the entire entrance stood open before me, and it was built of flames. And in every respect, it so excelled in brilliance, magnificence, and to the extent that I cannot describe. And its floor was of fire, and above it was a path of the stars, and the ceiling also was of fire."

The writing of Ezekiel also speaks of these corporeal eternal beings, "…the heavens opened. I looked and saw a whirlwind coming from the north, a great cloud with brilliant light all around it. In the center was a glow like amber, and within it was the form of four living creatures.

"And this was their appearance, they had a human form, but each had four faces and four wings. Their legs were straight, and their feet were like the hooves of a calf, gleaming like polished bronze. Under their wings on their four sides, they had human hands. All four of them had faces and wings, and their wings were touching one another. They did not turn as they moved; each one went straight ahead.

"The form of their faces was that of a man, and each of the four had the face of a lion on the right side, the face of an ox on the left side, and the face of an eagle. Such were their faces. Their wings were spread upward; each had two wings touching the wings of the creature on either side, and two wings covering its body.

"Each creature went straight ahead, never turning side to side. Wherever the spirit would go, they would go, without turning as they moved. Being with the all the living creatures here, was the appearance of glowing coals of fire, or of torches. Fire moved back and forth between the living creatures; it was bright, and lightning flashed out of it. The creatures were darting back and forth as quickly as flashes of lightning.

"When I looked at them, a wheel on the ground beside each creature. The workmanship of the wheels looked like the gleam of beryl, and all four had the same likeness. Their workmanship looked like a wheel within a wheel. As they moved, they went in any of the four directions, without pivoting as they moved. Their rims were high and awesome, and all four rims were full of eyes all around. So as the living creatures moved, the wheels moved beside them, and when the creatures rose from the ground, the wheels also rose.

"Wherever the spirit would go, they would go, and the wheels would rise alongside them, because the spirit of the living creatures was in the wheels. When the creatures stirred, I heard their wings like the rumble of many waters, like the voice of the Creator, like the uproar of an army.

"When they stood still, their wings lowered. Then a voice came high above on a throne with the light of sapphire, and there was a figure of a man. From his waist up, I saw a gleam like amber; from the waist down, I saw what looked like the color of a flame, and brilliant light surrounded all around. Looking like a rainbow, this was the Creator. And when I saw, I fell facedown and heard a voice speaking."

Referenced in Ezekiel's writings, a cherub is one of the unearthly beings, also known as the shiny ones, a corporeal body for an angel, they attended to the Creator's needs when he was not around on earth. The numerous depictions of cherubim have many different roles, such as protecting the entrance of the Garden of Eden. One named Ruh is said to be the most noble among the cherubim. Others are the Bearers of the Throne or the Archangels. There are seven cherubim, comparable to the Seven Archangels.

From Ezekiel, "Then the cherub said, 'Son of man. I am sending you to the Israelites, to a rebellious nation that has defied the Creator. To this very day the Israelites and their fathers have transgressed against him. They are obstinate and hardhearted children.'

Especially important information Ezekiel wrote, "The Cherub said, 'The Creator wants me to say to you that in the distant future my disciples will shrink the world to two billion. They will die by plague, famine, and sword.

"Wherever men live, the cities will be gone, and the high places will be demolished, so that your altars will be destroyed and desecrated, your idols smashed and obliterated, your written works blotted out. The slain will fall among you, and you will know that I am your Creator.' These were the living creatures I had seen beneath the Creator, and I knew that they were cherubim. Each had four faces and four wings, with what looked like human hands under their wings.

"Then the cherubim, with the wheels beside them, spread their wings, and the glory of the Creator was above them. And the glory of the Creator rose from within the city and stood over the mountain east of the city. Furthermore, the word of the Creator came to me, saying, 'The vision that he sees is many years from now' Ezekiel prophesized about the distant future."

Ezekiel wrote that the cherub said, "If man does not worship, the Creator will send a plague into that land and pour out wrath through bloodshed. Cutting off from it both man and beast. The prophets called Noah, Daniel, and Job were in it, they could deliver neither son nor daughter. Their righteousness could save only themselves."

Those who are the proclaimed righteous, have been around since Babel. They have taken on the role and responsibility in shaping the world in preparation for the End of Days. Numbering in the tens of thousands, are imbedded into every government and religion around the world, with the mission to begin the End of Days.

The United States, the most powerful part of the Order, used members to be the first to unleash the virus. Called the New Majestic Twelve, they had decided the plague of man will begin with a manmade weaponized form of the common cold. Both the ever-mutating virus and the mRNA vaccines. It was created from thirty years of work in various labs. We found a sample in Antarctica along with the scientist who helped create it.

With the ability the make women with specific blood types sterile. As advertised by Dr. Heller, when ready, this will be the first seal to be broken with the most impact on the world seen five years later. This will start the End of Days.

Ezekiel wrote, "Yet, behold, some survivors will be left with sons and daughters who will be brought out. They will come out to you, and when you see their conduct and actions, you will be consoled regarding the disaster I have brought upon Jerusalem. When I shower you with the deadly arrows of famine and destruction that I will send to destroy you, I will intensify the starvation by cutting off your supply of bread. I will send dearth and wild beasts against you, and they will leave you childless."

With the slow changes to the birth rate being recorded, the poorest of countries will be identified last. America, with the best ability to track people, will be first. But the Order will delay the truth thru subterfuge and lies. They own the media, the government, and technology.

When the birth rates drop and elderly die in high numbers, it will be blamed on the lack of nutritious food and fresh water rather than the vaccines. The next fifteen years, the World Health Organization will get involved resulting in the realization that forcing the World to be vaccinated will result in entire blood types now childless."

Ezekiel then wrote, "In the future, all the land is not safe. The Creator says, 'I am against you, and I will draw My sword from its sheath and cut off from you both the righteous and the wicked. From south to north all flesh will know that I, the Creator, have taken My sword from its sheath, not to return it again.'" Meaning those who are good, or evil will not be able to produce a child.

I know what you are thinking, don't we want to side with the Creator? Yes and no. If the Order has their way, Judgment Day will work in the favor of the fallen ones. We want to continue humankind to the point they no longer need to fight for greed and power. I feel the future is not to stay on Earth but to travel out of our solar system. There is a small fraction of the shiny ones who are helping us. You will not know who they are, but I know and trust they will help us fight the future.

Now to where we are today. The next move by Majestic Twelve is the release of another mutated virus and vaccine. Next, they will release free energy. China and Russia have the fuel and will be bankrupt in six years without the need of gas and oil. Both start a chain reaction that forces civil war across the globe. For the next ten years the world is focused on these conflicts that drive a revolution of Nationalism to include the United States. It won't be until then; the birth rate reduction will be highlighted across the world. Too late to stop.

Now that you know what is at stake, here are the coordinates for the Garden of Eden. I need you to go there and retrieve the original writings and artifacts.

There are additional directions once you get to the dive site. Now you know why this place was hidden from satellite mapping, radar, and sonar. Following coordinates 38.635631, 42.691983 and locate where this all began.

When you are done researching the entire site, send video and audio recordings to IP Address 2.12.959.285. Jane smiled, as she looked at the envelope stained in dried blood.

To My Dearest Jane, from your brother,

CONTENTS

LXIV

Milwaukie, Wisconsin JUN 2015
Counter Mission Alpha Delta Golf Eight

LXV

Bangor, Maine OCT 2016
Counter Mission Charlie Hotel Kilo Five

BLACK HORSE

LXVI

Bass Harbor, Maine JAN 2017
Counter Mission Zulu Charlie Papa Seven

LXVII

Hull, Massachusetts AUG 2018
Counter Mission Delta Charlie Victor Three

LXVIII

Nasiriyah Iraq MAR 2019
Counter Mission Alpha Delta Xray One

LXIX

Wright Patterson AFB NOV 2019
Counter Mission Indigo Kilo Sierra Seven

PALE HORSE

WHITE HORSE

Detective Bloom looked at the weathered spine, running his hand over the pitted leather, feeling every tiny abrasion. Why do I have an uneasy feeling, he thought while moving his fingers to the red sash separating the semi-transparent pages. "Not the King James Version," he said softly then shifted his body weight on the hard wood chair that matched the design features of the desk.

With fifteen years as an investigator, the detective had seen many suicides, but in his gut, this was something else. Problem was he couldn't prove this one because it was too perfect. Every detail in the autopsy report would lead the coroner to ruling self-inflicted death by poison but the motive had a flaw.

After canvassing the neighbors, the victim was happy and normal. Interesting enough, he did leave a note. Well not the typical confession, like a letter with a signature. It was cryptic, on a yellow sticky that didn't match his handwriting. Even more strange, it was on the bathroom sink, placed there, not written there. The note said…

It begins here with the first broken seal.

Three hours earlier a call was made from the Topaz Lake Fire Station. A neighbor smelled death coming from the home, eliciting a health and welfare check by the local first responders. Once the Emergency Medical Technician reached the back door, the distinct odor coming from the home was easy to recognize. His partner called in the situation over the Douglas County police and fire radio frequency. After breaking into the back door, they found a bloated body in the bathtub.

An hour later, the county coroner and police department were dispatched. From what Detective Bloom saw from his initial assessment of the scene, it was clear the two EMTs were not used to these situations. While they backed out of the house, Detective Bloom noticed two fresh streaks of vomit on the back wall opposite the bathroom entrance. He thought, at least the EMTs didn't mess up my crime scene.

Twenty minutes earlier, Detective Bloom received a call from the county coroner, now he was ducking under the yellow tape bouncing against the light wind created from an intersection of water and mountains. Tom thought, at a mile high, this cute little casino town rarely got a visit by him other than the craps table or to wet a line. With little crime in the county, today felt like he may actually get to do his job. Smiling when he read the street sign,

Goldfield Drive, he thought what an ironic name for the victim but not for his state of mind.

Leaning in, behind the coroner who was doing a preliminary sweep of the body, Detective Bloom uttered, "Looks open and shut to me boss." The Coroner, Dr. Hector, nodded and replied, "That's what happens when you drink Strychnine with Kool-Aid." "Really?" "Check the kitchen, a box was on the counter."

"How much to end himself?" Tom asked. "For his weight, about a hundred milligrams would do it. The way this body is contorted, I would say he ingested double that." "How fast?" the Detective asked. "Five minutes of agony before choking on his own blood." "Not the easiest way to go."

Walking over to the kitchen, Tom noticed the box of poison and then the calendar on the fridge. As he took it off the hook, flipped through the months leading up to today. Thinking to himself, why was the twenty eighth of March twenty twenty-eight, circled on the calendar? That was today. And why did he have appointment set going out six months? Didn't make sense. Was this unplanned?

On Tom's return, the office gossip was palpable as he walked into the station. Without a word spoken to him, the whispered judgments from coworkers were visible. Mostly office staff, they could be seen leaning over their cubicle walls keeping today's rumor alive.

On the other side of the police station were uniformed officers sitting and standing in the bullpen or the breakroom mesmerized by his presence as he nodded to those who made eye contact. Others in suits were fellow detectives and were located close to the sheriff's office and in the center of the large room. They all seemed to fake their way through not looking at him.

This could be the fourth suicide in his career that initially was treated as such until he found enough evidence to be a murder. The other three were when he was with a different employer. Tom then shook his head, while thinking about the bet he would have lost if someone said he'd be back in Douglas County. Even more, being a deputy for the sheriff's department.

To think, it had been five years since leaving his federal badge and gun for high desert and boredom. All from the result of a botched operation ten years prior to killing his team and being the only survivor, nothing was the same. He needed a fresh start. It wasn't guilt, being treated like a leper that nobody wanted was worse.

Tom's existence in the Bureau dragged on for a while after the investigation ruled him not culpable for the deaths of an elite team he led. Not being able to let it go, he started his own unauthorized investigation until now. He continued to ride a desk until the death of his parents and an inheritance was a way out.

The largest asset willed to Tom was a large industrial modern design overlooking Lake Tahoe. With a small inheritance and a home paid off, he lasted two months before a knock on his door from the sheriff. Tom originally had no intention with returning to law enforcement. The insistence of the sheriff, who was a family friend, had Tom was back in a suit with a badge.

Detective Bloom didn't need the money, just purpose again. He then flashed back to his days in the Bureau during his last assignment. Heading up an anti-terrorism unit after a three-year stint in the Behavioral Analysis Unit a Quantico Virginia. Then his department was part of the National Center for the Analysis of Violent Crime that was used to track serial killers and terrorists.

It was his work at the BAU that was a pipeline to the Foreign Terrorist Tracking Task Force composed of personnel from the FBI, the CIA, Immigration and Customs Enforcement, and the Department of Defense. This posting led to the events that ensued in Antarctica that ended his FBI career.

The other officers in the sheriff's department didn't know the circumstances or why he left the FBI because his entire career was classified. There were rumors but all were wrong. When asked, he would always reply like a scripted response, "A family emergency reset my goals and I needed to come home." Even the sheriff didn't know what happened.

When conducting Tom's background check and polygraph, there was nothing but positive and unofficial comments. Everyone stated that due to national security considerations, they could not say whether his performance was good or bad when working for the Feds.

Sitting at his desk, Tom could hear others venting about a break in another case and the inept witnesses to a crime. He shared space and small cubical walls with twelve other detectives tasked with everything from theft to missing children.

Tom replaced a thirty-year veteran of the department who died of a heart attack weeks before Tom's return to Minden Nevada. Without an interview for the homicide detective position, it seemed that Tom just fell into the job curtesy of the sheriff. The other seasoned staff were jealous of him and weren't afraid to show it in the office.

"Hey Tom, did you catch the perpetrator? If not, I can help," said the detective who was leaning back in his chair speaking over three others separating them. "How so Miller?" "I have a mirror you can use. Just point it at the victim and you'll see the perp who did it." Tom responded, "Very funny Chuck.

"Looks pretty open and shut on this one but the coroner is still working the body." Another detective interrupted the conversation, "From what I hear by the forensics' team, if there was foul play, it would be a perfect crime." Tom smiled and nodded before returning to his bible to read the etched reference located in the victims' desk. As though he knew that it would help fill in the blanks.

When Tom watched again the virtual reality recorded rooms in the large chalet, he noticed odd contradictions throughout the house. Carved with a knife was the letters *KJV REV 6:1* on the right corner of the large natural oak desk. The rest of the room had immense shelves lining the walls with a combination of genetics, viral, and religious textbooks. There even was a section on aliens.

The rest of the home was absent of any personal effects except a single picture of Dave. He was on a pontoon boat, holding a large trout, with the Topaz Lake Casino in the background. Re watching the video many times in virtual reality from his desk gave him the idea of calling the Topaz Lake Marina to see if he had a boat there.

"Hello, can I speak to someone about a boat owner renting a slip?" Tom asked. "You're talking to him. Who is this?" the Marina owner said. "I'm Detective Bloom, Douglas Sherriff's Department." "You callin' about Dave Taylor?" "Why yes I am." "I thought one of you would be stopping by eventually. I was going to give it three days and then call you. Well technically, the boat is owned by the landlord of the house he was renting." "Really, do you happen to have the name of the boat owner?" "It's not a person but a company." "That will work too… and a contact number if possible." "Sure thing detective, it's Raven Defense."

After writing down the information received, Tom hesitated, so not to push his luck, "Can I ask you another question?" "Shoot. Whoops, bad choice of words." "Good one. Do they pay month to month?" "Nope. We negotiated a fee for ten years." "Really. Is that typical?" "No Sir. I told the lawyer representing the company that we were not going to jack up the price or give it up to someone else. We don't do stuff like that here."

"Do you happen to have his name?" Tom asked. "Sorry sir just identified himself as a lawyer representing the company. I tried to press him so I could get a point of contact with a name. He just said to list the company name and phone number if there was an issue." "Hmmm. That is strange," Tom said trying to keep the asset talking.

Then Detective Bloom flashed back to his days talking with the locals in Iraq and Afghanistan about Private Military Contractors who had taken some high value targets that his team was trying to arrest on terrorism charges. The same name came up, even stranger, most PMCs for Raven Defense were women dressed in burkas and taking out targets a mile away with sniper rifles.

When Tom asked about the women in black, military leaders said the name of the outfit was Raven Defense working for the Agency. Of all the PMCs in country at the time, it was weird that such a small outfit in comparison to the big boys, would have so many KIA and they were women hunter killers.

After getting off the phone, Tom grabbed his coat and headed for the door. "Detective Bloom, chasing down a lead?" the uniformed officer blurted while snickering with his cohorts. "I got a lead on next of kin so they get notified. Is that ok with you Sullivan?" The laughter stopped and Tom smiled thinking to himself, got you back dickhead.

Returning to the lake house, he could see the yellow tape still flapping in the breeze while driving down Topaz Lane to the Marina. "You must be Detective Bloom," the voice said as Tom was getting out of the unmarked cruiser. "I am and you must be Captain Jessup."

"Yes Sir. Twenty years in the Coast Guard and this was my investment plan. I could have done worse," he said. "Yes, you could have. Beautiful place. My family would come here many times in the summer, and I caught a fifteen-pound trout off the point over there."

"I thought I recognized the name. Weren't you a big-time track star at Douglas High?" "I don't know about that, but it did get me a scholarship to NYU." "What brings you back here?" "Homesick, so I came back. My folks left me a home on Lake Tahoe when they passed a few years ago. It was time."

"Did you go in the military after college?" "No sir. FBI." "That makes sense. Now I know why you came home." "Really Sir?" "I ran drug interdiction missions in Central America through the nineties as a boat commander and you bastards held up a few of my busts. Bigger fish you G-men would always say." "Sorry about that Sir."

After a long pause Captain Jessup said, "You're one of the good ones." "Really Sir." "Yup. You were smart enough to get out and get a job protecting the people that matter. Not some bullshit Bigger Fish." "You got it right Sir. Can you show me the boat?"

After walking around the parking lot, Captain Jessup led the detective to the pier and onto the twenty-seven-foot pontoon boat. "If you don't need anything else, I'm going to get back to the front desk," the captain uttered something while walking back inside. Tom yelled, "Thank you, Sir. I'll let you know when I'm finished."

After about an hour walking every inch of the boat, Tom headed back to the parking lot and into the Marina Office building. "Captain Jessup, I noticed a couple cameras. Are they real?" Tom said with a smile. "I should hope so, saved me thousands in damages. Keeps those little shits from trying to take a boat to go joy riding." "So that happened did it."

The captain smiled and said, "Yup. First year I owned this place, had a boat stolen and even though my contract paperwork was bullet proof, the lawyer fees killed me. So now I run cameras with a sixty-day loop. If anyone bitches, I just show the video." "Do you mind if I get a copy of what you got?" "Detective Bloom, got a hard drive? These are big files." "I do Sir. I'll be right back, it's in the car."

Heading back to the station, Tom wanted to report his status to the sheriff, grab a laptop, and drop off the suicide paperwork. The reason everyone gave him grief was that he was the only person not in the chain of command. The big man called the position, Detective for Douglas County Special Investigations and Homicide.

"Boss got a minute?" the detective said while peeking his head in and knocking softly on the door. "Yes Tom, come in. Got anything for me?" "Just wanted to keep you in the loop." "Absolutely. Shut the door and join me for a scotch."

The two men sat across from each other. Tom leaned over to grab his drink while Sheriff Waters was nursing his second glass. "I think we have someone who can tell us next of kin," Tom said. "How so?" the sheriff questioned while sipping his scotch. "Seems a parent company where he works also owns the home and boat the victim was using." "What did this guy do again?" "A warehouse worker." "Weird." "I know. Got a call back east in the morning and hopefully get an emergency POC." "Any luck with this guy through taxes and such?"

Tom responded, "No Sir. I checked with my IRS buddies and this guy's employment was spotty until twenty twelve. After that he settled here, working for the same company until his apparent suicide. They confirmed that he was making a hundred thousand a year and listed as a warehouse worker."

"That Raven company is giving this guy a chalet, food, car, million-dollar view, and a boat?" "Also, his job doesn't match what his library books were saying to me. He looks more like a witness protection winner." "So did the Feds teach you that?"

After a swig of scotch, Tom nodded, "Yes, it is odd and even more, this guy doesn't have a social media footprint, bank card, credit card, or shopping history on Amazon." "Wow. You can do that?" "Well Sir, when you hired me, you got my contacts too. I spent enough time as a G-man to build up quite a list of unofficial assets for stuff like this.

"This guy is a social security card and driver's license. The rest is blank." "Well son, keep pluggin' away but I'd like to close this case by next week. You and I have a fishing trip." "Yes Sir." "Remember to point out the house when we are slaying those trout."

Arriving home, Tom couldn't shake the feeling about Raven Defense. Of all the companies in the world, these guys were protected by all the intelligence services and the U.S. State Department. With their grubby little hands in everything. Then he remembered that the bible in his office was the wrong version.

At home Tom opened his dad's bible. Flipping to the correct page he read aloud, "King James Version, Revelation six, verse one, and I saw when the Lamb opened one of the seals, and I heard, as it were the noise of thunder, one of the four beasts saying, Come and see. And I saw and behold a white horse, and he that sat on him had a bow, and a crown was given unto him, and he went forth conquering, and to conquer."

Tom couldn't wait for the morning to call and grabbed his virtual reality glasses and looked down at his hand. In it was a phone. The glasses, looked more like Oakley's than the antique oversized phone inserted goggles ten years ago, he spoke her name and it was ringing. Once the person answered, he was transported into the corner of her bedroom.

"Simone, you awake?" Tom said with an apologetic overtone and a smile. Like a voyeur, he could see her in bed, with her naked form caressing the silk semitransparent sheet. "Better be calling because your horny, it's too late for another theological debate," Simone said sliding on the virtual reality glasses and looking around the room. "I do love messing up the sheets with you, but can't we have a little bit of both?" Tom replied with a flirty overtone.

"You are weird, it's a good thing your ass makes up for it," Simone giggled. "Business before pleasure?" he replied with a smile. "Ok. Go," she said. He spent the next ten minutes explaining everything to include sharing the video of the man's home and the current situation in all the rooms at the time of death. With virtual reality it was like they could both walk through the rooms together while discussing everything that was odd.

Tom met Simone, also known officially as, Special Supervisory Agent Cooper at the Academy. They made it a point to meet up periodically if both were not in a relationship. That was too often due to the demands of the job. They preferred it and wasn't until they started working together in the BAU, things got serious. Then out of the blue, she was reassigned to London, timing was not great he thought. Because of this time away, it was too hard for them to continue the charade of a relationship and agreed to be friends with benefits using virtual reality, or as Tom called it, "the safest sex."

"Let me see. My notes on Revelations," Simone said, while virtually flipping a book to a thesis she wrote in college. Almost becoming a nun, it was one night when a mugger rocked her world, she couldn't turn the other cheek. Eighteen years of catholic school down the drain. At a hundred pounds, she beat that mugger with his own gun to the point of unconsciousness. It was at that moment; she wanted to kick ass and joined the FBI.

"It's here. I'll read it to you… The Book of Revelations or also called the Apocalypse of John is in the New Testament of the Christian Bible. The book is traditionally attributed to John the Apostle, but the precise identity of the author remains a debate among academia. As the opening act of the seals, it starts with the White Horse. There are a total of seven seals and four horsemen. This is the beginning of the Apocalypse, as they are called, emerging as the first four seals are opened."

As Tom was sitting on a couch in Simone's virtual room, it looked like her house near the backside of Quantico on Rolling Road in Tackett's Mill. A three-bedroom cape, he had visited when posted at the FBI Academy. In past rendezvouses, they always played in his virtual reality space. This was new, different, but familiar. As though she was letting him in a little bit more than usual. If he asked her for a date, flew to Quantico, would she say yes? He imagined a life together as she explained.

After more flirts and sexual innuendos, Simone continued reviewing her notes, then looked up, "Here it is… And I saw and beheld a white horse and he that sat on him had a bow and a crown was given unto him, and he went forth conquering, and to conquer. Revelation six verse two." "Tell me what this means." "Wait. Here is what I wrote."

She then flipped to another section, "Throughout history, various sources often explained the first reveal of the coming apocalypse in various ways, since his role is the only one not explicitly stated. While most interpreters agreed that the white rider symbolizes a government-controlled nation state assigned to give disease and pestilence upon the world. There is a widely attested description that places this white horseman as a metaphor for a group who are the most righteous acting on the Creator's wishes.

"In a world where sin is rampant, a righteous omen of justice and goodness would seem a fitting antiseptic in an apocalypse. The crown that was given unto him could signify the rule of justice or represent a truly just leader, if one can exist.

"But the imagery of disease and pestilence in this book could still be the most plausible description. The aspect of a conqueror is familiar of a major plague back in that day. The crown would symbolize the ultimate rule from a king who in some cases during that time would slaughter a whole city because they could. In this case a king of death with the power and authority.

"A fitting metaphor of the first horseman, a white rider, of the four horsemen of the Apocalypse. But as the time progressed, and by the time of the beginning of the sixteenth century, many have come to interpret this 'white rider' as the personification of the second coming of the messiah.

"At the time of the writing, the Romans slaughtered many Christians. The author uses the canvass to write about destroying the sinners and getting revenge. The white color of the horse and the rider was linked with divine purity and absence of sin, and the bow is the tool of divine punishment. Likewise, the rider is interpreted as the Holy Spirit, pure and just.

"Another popular view is much simpler; the white horseman could just be the embodiment of mass conquest. The passage, relating to the rider that 'went forth conquering, and to conquer' could simply be that a prophesied vanquisher that will enslave the populace of the earth."

Simone then stopped, looked at Tom, who leaned back on the couch with his right leg propped up on his left. She said, "Do you need anything else my dear?" "Nope, I think you confirmed that this guy was a nut or just liked killing himself with a cryptic message. I thought I'd seen it all. Fooled again."

As Simone moved over to the couch, placing a hand in his lap, she moved closer. Then said, "Imagine being the weapon at the end of the world." Tom thought for a second what she said and then stood up. Brushing her hand away, then looking at his holographic phone. Moments later, the entire virtual reality location changed to the Topaz Lake crime scene. With Simone now sitting across the room in a chair, Tom made his way to the ceiling high rows of books.

She snapped, "Hey dick, I was trying to be romantic." "I'm sorry baby, it's what you said. This guy had books on genetics, viruses, physics, chemistry, but his occupation was a warehouse worker. It doesn't make sense. Looking at the background report on Dave Taylor, it didn't add up.

"Originally from Atlanta, Georgia, in his youth, was in and out of juvenile detention. Adulthood was a sad story of a relapsing gambler, two ex-wives before thirty, and a three-time unemployed warehouse worker. Then fifteen years ago it was as though he was given a new life. He was a ten-minute walk away from a casino and never gambled. Why suicide with having a new life? He was so happy and successfully shed his past. Doesn't make sense."

"So, you think he wasn't the same guy, like witness protection?" Simone uttered when Tom paused. "What if he thought of himself as the conqueror and was going to or had unleashed some bioweapon on the world," Tom responded using a different train of thought. "So, does this mean I won't be getting laid tonight?" He

43 | Page

REAP THROUGH THE END OF DAYS

pointed to the folder, "I promise to give you multiple orgasms but what was that about the other horseman."

Simone then got up and walked to the victim's desk, flipping through the bible that was heavily highlighted with a code in many of the margins. Tom turned around and leaned over her, "Can you tell me what each horse does and maybe I can match it to these books on the shelf?" Simone touched his hand, "Sounds like a plan, we talked about the white horsemen, being the personification of mass conquest.

"In Revelation six three, the second horseman is War. It reads that when the angel broke the second seal, a red horse went out; and to him who sat on it, it was granted to take peace from earth, and that men would slay one another; and a great sword was given to him. It is also said that the second Horseman may signify civil war as opposed to the war of conquest."

"Let me get this right," Tom blurted then said, "If this angel unleashed a plague, there would be an impact on the entire planet. A pandemic of sorts impacting local, state, and federal governments around the world. This also means shutting down commerce, travel, and a strain on most hospitals. Supply chain would be disrupted, and civil rights would be put aside for the greater good."

Simone looked at Tom with a serious tone, "Think transmission rate like all the SARS mutations at once with a death toll of two thirds in the world." "You mean from twelve billion, to four billion. How would you bury the bodies?" Simone smiled, "Ok I'll bite." "No really. I don't know.

"Before leaving the bureau, I read a Continuity of Govt report on Extinction Level Events and one of the scariest is a biological agent because it kills just enough to shut down everything until a vaccine is developed. Then riots, civil war, and piles of infect dead bodies that must be burned. So, what is the next horse… there are four right?"

Simone giggled, "Look at you Mr. Bloom, I mean Mr. Gloom and Doom. It's just a ranting crazy guy who wrote well enough to get in the canon." "Very funny," Tom said, while sticking out his tongue. "So, based on your request, the third horse is black and represents famine. It says in the bible that when they broke the third seal, had a pair of scales in his hand."

Simone then pointed to the line and verse in the good book and said, "And I heard something like a voice in the center of the four living creatures saying, 'a quart of wheat for a coin, and three quarts of barley for a coin; but do not damage the oil and the wine.' Of the Four Horsemen, the black horse and its rider are the only ones whose arrival is accompanied with a vocal articulation."

Taking the book, Simone walked over to the couch in the great room, then gestured to Tom, "Come over here and sit." "No. I need to compare the books to what you say or the coding in the book." "You are impossible."

Then she continued reading aloud, "John hears a voice, unidentified but coming from among the four living creatures, that speaks of the prices of wheat and barley, also saying 'and see thou hurt not the oil and the wine.'

"This suggests that the black horse's famine is to drive up the price of grain but leave oil and wine supplies unaffected though out of reach of the ordinary worker. One clarification for this is that grain crops would have been more vulnerable than olive and grapes, which root more deeply. These goods were common back then and the author would use this as an example for current critical supply chain of microchips and lithium."

Tom walked over to the couch, "Holy Shit. So then with civil war, commerce ends, and everyone is without money to purchase things or go to work." "The statement might also suggest a continuing abundance of luxuries for the wealthy while staples, such as bread, are scarce, though not totally depleted. As was with the occupation of Rome, such selective shortages happened.

Alternatively, the preservation of oil and wine could symbolize the preservation of the Christian faithful, who use oil and wine in their rituals.

"The last horse is the Pale one," Simone said then continuing to read from the bible, "when the fourth seal was broke, I heard the voice of the fourth living creature saying, 'Come.' I looked, and behold, an ash-colored horse; and he who sat on it had the name Death; and Hell was following with him."

"Just like the Clint Eastwood movie," Tom said to lighten the mood in the virtual room. Simone gave a smiled describing her annoyance more than as though it was funny, "Authority was given to protect a fourth of the earth, to kill with the sword, famine, pestilence, and by the wild beasts of the earth.

"This is in Revelation chapter six verse seven and eight. Even though called the pale horse, he has been called Thanatos, of all the riders, he is the only one to whom the text itself explicitly gives a name. Unlike the other three, he is not described carrying a weapon, instead he leads, and Hell follows. Could mean that the dead live. However, some show a depiction of the Grim Reaper with a scythe. The color of Death's horse is written as a greenish-yellow."

Simone used her virtual reality interface to walk into the library. With her hand in the computer-generated world, she highlighted each book that matched the codes in the bible.

"Baby, how did you figure that out?" Tom asked. "It was not that hard; they must have been more of a reference than codes." "Nice, I'll take all these books, cross reference to the chapter and verse, and then get a sense if this guy was crazy or something far worse." "One thing that you should know is that he referenced a Jane Roche with phone number."

Tom asked, "Where did you find that?" Simone pointed at the calendar showing a view of the Nevada high desert. As Tom looked, she highlighted it with a wave of her hand. "Simone, great eyes." "Does this mean we are done?" Tom looked at his phone and the virtual reality environment changed to a moonlit night on Narragansett Beach with a large blanket, temperature seventy-two degrees, and they were alone.

Tom slowly took Simone's hands in his and brought them to her side while kissing her deeply. She shuttered as his mouth moved down her neck, to her shoulder, with his hands traveling over the straps of her dress and it fell on the cool beach sand. Her naked body exposed to their private virtual reality world.

The waves pounded against the sand, muffling their moans as her body covered him in perfect ecstasy. After a time of letting her take control, Tom pushed against her, and they faced each other on a large Indian blanket with their legs intertwined. "I missed this," Simone softly uttered in his ear. "This virtual reality is amazing but nothing like the real thing, when can I see you for real," he whispered back. "I'm in Los Angeles next month, can you get away?" "Yes. Most definitely. Just send me your address and the date. I'll be waiting in your hotel room with candles and rose petals."

The next day, "I need everything on a Jane Roche and Raven Defense," Tom requested from a friend in the Defense Intelligence Agency who owed him a favor.

"This makes us even Tom," Marcus said. "Ok, but if I ask again, then I'll owe you." "I wish you never knew about my issue." "Hey Marcus, you used your only call for me." "If I would have known it would potentially jeopardize my job once a month, I would have called someone else." "Wow. Didn't realize my asks were that hard." "It's all good man. Give me a day and you'll know more about her than she probably does."

After hanging up, Tom flashed back to that night. "Tom, I fucked up. Can you help?" "Marcus, what happened?" "I'm being accused of soliciting a prostitute." "Wow. That happened. Where are you?" "Arlington Police Station." "I'm on my way."

Upon arrival, Tom met with the senior officer in charge explaining that Marcus was undercover for an FBI operation involving human trafficking. Within an hour, Marcus was out, arrest paperwork shredded, and after twenty minutes of apologies, Tom was tapping this asset for many favors and unauthorized intelligence. The last time was getting information on who killed his team in Antarctica and knocked him out.

A month after the investigation into Tom, "Marcus, I need to meet you for coffee." "Where Tom?" "Usual spot." "Roger that." This was code for a room Tom kept for rendition operations in Northern Virginia. Set up like a single-family home near Reston, the garage was soundproof with a mylar lining.

"Pretty sparse accommodations, Tom. Is it safe to talk freely here?" Marcus said while seeing the brushed steel table with two large rings on either side. Mirroring two chairs bolted to the floor. In one corner was a locked gym locker and in the other a weightlifting bench half in a small kiddie pool. Draped over the head rest were three towels and two untouched water cooler jugs.

Marcus said, "Nice place. Got anything to drink," while gesturing to the water boarding starter kit. "Locker is open," Tom signaled, sitting in one of the chairs. Marcus walked over and to his surprise were everything a terrorist would want, alcohol, cigarettes, porn mags, candy, and the Qur'an.

"Thanks for the whiskey, now what do you need, Tom?" "I need you to get me everything you know about the classified site in Antarctica and why my team was killed. It was supposed to be an operation involving an insider threat. Turned into a war zone"

"What can I do?" Marcus asked after pouring a cup of scotch before sitting down. "Want any video footage you can find. I blame myself for not being prepared for the speed and skill of these assholes who hit the station," while Tom lowered his head.

"Where is it?" Marcus requested. "Coordinates are -77.84733255268759, 166.75613147607245." "I'll see what I can find. Under the radar of course." "When." "I need a week. If I lay breadcrumbs in a random sequence, my leaders will not suspect anything." "Thank you." "Don't thank me yet. I am good and have access to any military facility or operation. If it is outside our purview, I can't go asking sister agencies."

A week later, Tom was already there nursing his third scotch, "Marcus, what did you get?" "Wow Tom. Aren't you in a hurry? How about I get one of those? Then I will tell you all the cloak and dagger shit I needed to go through to get your answer." "Sorry Marcus, I've got some serious guilt over this cluster fuck to include the FBI questioning my leadership ability." "Well, this is what I got. Are you ready?" "Go."

Marcus took a swig, then spoke, "The location you were told to go and arrest an insider threat is a level 5 bioweapons research facility. In it, they were testing everything from multi-variant vaccines for SARS mutations to Ebola Plus Plus." "So, who infiltrated the base?" "The brass doesn't know but the cameras did pick up enough to show an entire team of women who ambushed your people." "I don't understand?" "They were all in white with a balaclava."

Tom asked, "How did you know they were women?" "It was the eyes and the way they moved. All were measured between seventy to seventy-four inches; slim build and their weapons techniques were not brute force but rather subdued through soft tissue strikes and edged weapons." "I don't understand."

Marcus responded, "The report I read said that they were surgical with killing by targeting eyes, throat, lungs, and femoral artery." "When the video showed them transitioning to firearms, they were disciplined, and everything was two shot intervals to the chest, and a third to the head. No hesitation and with little communication."

"The second team that showed up looked like a platoon of SEALs. They were brutal and calculated, but definitely men who looked like they had done a few tours in country." "Did you get a look at their faces?" "Nope. Dressed in white just like the ladies." "That's weird." "I know."

Handing a set of virtual reality glasses to Tom, Marcus then said, "I was able to smuggle this edited series of events all through closed circuit tv on site. Check it for yourself." As Tom watched two platoons move through the base, he couldn't understand how they got access. The ladies came in from Williams Field. They too gained access and executed the scientist that his team was going to arrest. He watched as the camera was blacked out and he saw her eyes.

Leaning over Marcus, Tom said, "Who is this guy?" Unable to see the person's face, watched as though he was in the room. The victim was sprayed with a small canister of something, Tom could see two large men in white with blood spray across their chest carrying this VIP off site.

Tom thought, quick and surgical, like they were looking for him and had a plan. "His name is Dr. Heller."

"Wow, you are good." "Not really, I figured you would ask because even though they torched the place, his body was never found. Read this," Marcus leaned over and opened a file.

Present day, Tom remembered the meeting with Marcus those years ago in Northern Virginia. "There was a guy?" Tom tried to remember. "Marcus, what was the guy's name you told me about when I needed to know about my trip to the penguins?" Using his virtual reality glasses, Marcus appeared with Tom in the same room from years ago. "Of all the places, we are back in your torture playhouse?" "Sorry buddy, I'm nostalgic."

Marcus said, "The guy's name was Dr. Heller. Did you find him?" Marcus said shaking his head. "Nope but after our meeting, I did find a picture." Tom looked at background information and noticed that this guy's specialty was virology. Tom thought, this guy looks like Dave if you added the Santa Clause starter kit; meaning forty pounds, a beard, and glasses.

LX

Dorian Phillips, NYC New York NOV 2012
Counter Mission Yankee Kilo Echo Three

When the limo arrived to take the ladies to the Owl head Airport, Bella gave both a hug, "Don't be a stranger, you two are always welcomed back." Tina nodded, "Bella, next time you are available, I say the three of us have a wild Friday night in the City of Angels or even better, NYC as a thank you for your hospitality." I leaned into Bella, "I'll have business there for a week out of the month."

Bella excitedly looked at the ladies, "I'd like that. Next flight out, I'll be with him." Hoe son said, "We look forward to it. Wait, how about we set up a week of fun at the next Victoria Secret Show." "Oh, my god that would be amazing," Bella said. I redirected the conversation, "Have a nice flight ladies. See ya soon and thank you for the business."

Months later, Tina and Hoe son arrived at the Los Angeles airport, heading to NYC. The night air was cool and dry, while the tarmac was still warm from the heat of the day. As a private jet, a white limo pulled up to the stairs. One of the pilots greeted two beautiful women who exited and then watched new ladies walking up the ramp. "Welcome ladies. Jonathan has a bottle of Dom Perignon on ice to say thank you."

The counter mission was to begin now and would mean the entire Reaper Force would be part of this plan. "Alpha, it seems Mr. Grimm gave us a token of his appreciation to kick off the end of the Order." On the bar was a bouquet of flowers with a note, Tina picked up the small white envelope with no writing. Removing the card, she read it and smiled. It said, *Reap through the End of Days. Love Jonathan.*

Their destination would be the Victoria's Secret Fashion Show. This is an annual event sponsored by the owner of the company, a brand of lingerie and sleepwear. In the last three New York and Paris shows, TEMA was used as the largest supplier of models to promote and market its goods in a high-profile setting. The Seventeenth fashion show featured some the new Angels from TEMA but a few returning from years past. The entertainment would be Kanye West, Maroon 5, Jay-Z, and Justin Bieber.

The night started out on the runway with our TEMA number one model, in a red lace ensemble. She shocked the crowd with her beauty and presence, as a full house was packed at the Lexington Avenue Armory on November ninth. My mission was to provide a Raven

Defense guard force to protect the girls in the show and site security. My counter mission was simple but an effective method in reaping a target, be a friend.

The organizers were impressed that my staff were as beautiful as the models in the show. TEMA Gray Side ladies added a layer of legitimacy to my counter mission. As the owner of both the Talent and Executive Modeling Agency and Raven Defense, it was easy for me to swap around when needed.

"I'm so excited, this is my first fashion show," Bella said leaning into Tina. The three ladies had center and front seats to the performance. Their job was to keep Bella safe; my job was to end the first of twelve section chiefs in the Order.

"Bella, I'm surprised with your figure and looks, I could see you walking the runway," Tina said while holding Bella's hand. She giggled and squeezed, "No, I'm too short but you two ladies fit the bill." Ho san then added to the conversation, "You are too kind, we prefer management over having to starve for a month to fit into those zero size lingerie ensembles.

When I received the BIO from Control, it was done in the classic style. Not via email or private courier, just a piece of what looked like junk mail under the door. Using a simple cypher, I would identify the correct period in the sentence. Then under a special reader, would reveal the information in the microdot. Using a document with a summary, background, and action. It would be destroyed after reading in the usual manner and then the job would begin. This time, there was a small red mark on my can of shaving cream on the penthouse bathroom vanity. When I ran my finger over the edge, I could feel a false bottom. Unscrewing the cap revealed three pieces of paper.

COMPANY CLASSIFIED

TEMA GRAY SIDE   DATE
624 S Grand Ave
Los Angeles, CA 90017   01 NOV 2012

To: Mr. Grimm
From: Control
Subject: List of the New Majestic 12 identified Section
Chiefs and as per your request, here are the top
stories of 2011.

Based on your needs, in summary, the following list has
been vetted for future interrogation, rendition, and
disposal. A Reaper has been monitoring them since they
were suspected of being a key member of the Order. We
feel that if these people are taken out of play, the
organization will be unable to carry out their plan.

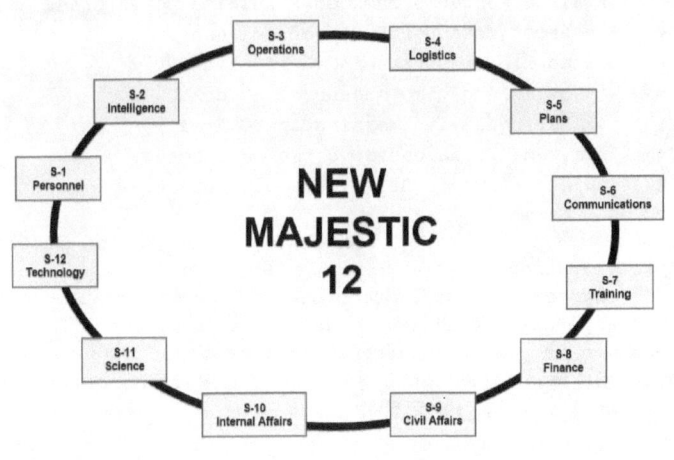

REAP THROUGH THE END OF DAYS

JONATHAN REAPER

```
S-1   Tory Kilmer, Milwaukie, Wisconsin
S-2   Jessica Ramos, Hull, Massachusetts
S-3   Quinn Brody, Bangor, Maine
S-4   Timothy Hicks, Phoenix, Arizona
S-5   Kelly Masters, Boston, Massachusetts
S-6   Thomas Shasta, Wright Patterson AFB
S-7   Ginger Garner, Sacramento, California
S-8   Brian Burke, Washington D.C.
S-9   Khaled Basmi, Sweimeh, Jordan
S-10  Victor Cartwright, Central America
S-11  Dorian Phillips, NYC, New York
S-12  Michael Jasper, Bass Harbor, Maine
```

Two that align with your mission, the Arab spring and the death of Osama bin Laden was carried out by the Order to further disable the middle east to make finding the garden of Eden easier. Other events created by the Order through Reapers and HAARP.

- Plane crash in Russia. All three hundred and twenty died.
- Earthquake and tsunami that hit Japan's east coast in March, sending waves as high as twenty-one feet. The natural disaster left twenty-three hundred people dead or missing and triggered a nuclear crisis at Japan's damaged Fukushima power plant.
- Bin Laden death ends 10-year manhunt.
- Ousted Libyan Dictator Gadhafi killed.
- Norway island camp massacre, 80 dead.
- 6.8 Earthquake in Washington DC Area.
- Hurricane Irene destroys the east coast.
- Apple co-founder Steve Jobs dies at 56.

Your mission is to act as a bodyguard for the ladies participating in the Victoria Secret's Fashion show. The counter mission is to clone his phone, we will send him an encrypted file that has a task. In it will be a picture of you with the instructions to do what you say without question. Once you have the transcripts and original texts, send them to us. We will load them in the system and compare with what we have from the Vatican and other Museums with fake copies.

Without the transcripts, the Order will be unable to determine what parts of Moses' writing is true and what is not. A delay that can have ramifications when determining if the writings of Mathew and Luke are correct when determining the lineage of Adam.

Based on our findings, this is unneeded to complete their goals but without any additional information, may be more realistic. If you can find out the blood type of Adam, Shem, and Jesus, there should be a correlation with how a blood type can fight off a type of virus or disease.

Here is what we know on Blood Type Focused Viruses…

Researchers analyzed patients of the Yellow South Asia Nidogen Virus and concluded after studying the blood samples of ten thousand patients in three Chinese hospitals. The findings were presented by Country run studies groups after going through the rigorous peer review process required by scientific journals. Never released to the world, their findings on a topic sparked a debate with fellow experts and is particularly useful in a fast-moving situation during a major epidemic or pandemic situation. Like SARS and MERS, the virus has a blood type infection rate component.

	Test positive.	Died.	Population.
A	31.16%	67.05%	42%
B	34.30%	16.32%	08%
AB	30.44%	14.83%	03%
O	04.10%	01.80%	47%

Taking the data, researchers concluded that "blood group A had a significantly higher risk for SARS and MERS" when compared with non-A blood groups. Those in the O group, meanwhile, "had a significantly lower risk for the infectious disease." The difference could be explained by certain antibodies in the blood.

After thirteen months of the research, we have identified the first section chief for interrogation, rendition, and disposal. Use of poison is the best method to Reap Dorian Phillips. In your hygiene kit is a pack of gum. During dinner at his villa, if he gets any part on his skin, there will be an allergic reaction like a shellfish allergy. His epi pens will have been switch and will not work. He will be dead in fifteen minutes, just before EMT's arrive to revive him. The Order will send a helicopter to his villa on long Island. You need to leave before they show up. We will send a BIO on him if you want to proceed.

We still do not know what they are going to do but our best calculations are a virus to impact the planet but not enough to stop the world. Just slow it down with considerable loss of wealth and life. It is our recommendation that if more than ten percent of the world population is extinguished too quickly, the Order will be unable to meet their goals.

TEMA Gray Side Control

COMPANY CLASSIFIED

Receiving the report was further proof that the players matched the inside cover of Mr. Stephen Walsh's journal. His original list had a total of ten names and two actions, I started my task of connecting the dots to discover this secret organization's end game and if my prior activities have advanced their agenda. Now four years later, I had created more names to further infiltrate the Order and stop them for good.

Looking back, I'm still amazed that my original twelve Gray Side TEMA Reapers had grown into twenty-six fully capable silent assassins. With additional assets and companies to compartmentalize resources, we are ready to take down the Order. Our goal was to covertly take down an organization that has shaped mankind since the tower of Babel. Now I needed to green light the last twelve names and fight the future.

"Control, this is Grimm." "This is Control. Ready to receive message." "Please activate the counter missions, based on the following." "Ready to copy." "Eleven, seven, four, niner, one, tree, ten, twelve, two, five, eight, six, over." "Copy Grimm, will send the first counter mission in one week, Control out." "Grimm out."

JONATHAN REAPER

COMPANY CLASSIFIED

TEMA GRAY SIDE
624 S Grand Ave
Los Angeles, CA 90017

DATE

04 NOV 2012

To: Mr. Grimm
From: Control
Subject: Counter Mission Yankee Kilo Echo Three.

Per your request, we have built a BIO on your first target.

Dorian Phillips, age thirty-five, was born in Columbus Ohio. He was a savant with languages and recruited early by the Order as a translator. After extensive training with Sumerian, also known as the first language, they sent him to the New York School of Design and Fashion at the age of fifteen as a cover. It was soon after, his name recognition burst out of the covers of Vogue magazine. All was a front to get into manufacturing centers like Milan and Dubai. He has unhindered access to all middle east operations.

Twenty years later, Dorian is a Section Chief for Majestic twelve. You will need to approach as a Reaper under orders for personnel protection from Quinn Brody. Without giving him that level of information, he will not believe you. Because he was recruited and funded by the Order at a young age, he is very loyal. Also, with his large transportation network, he has access to some of the hardest to access locations in the last ten years. With the wars across the middle east and instability in the South China Sea, he can fly in and out of most airports.

REAP THROUGH THE END OF DAYS

Dorian currently has the original papyrus writings from Moses. His task over the last five years was to find the Garden of Eden. The Order will also ask from time to time to ship large weapons supplies to keep organizations like ISIS operational. They are currently operating in large portions of Iraq and Syria.

The Order has been instrumental in the enhancement of ISIS with the intent for them to destroy all Sumerian and Babylonian artifacts to include a dedicated supply chain of dependable weapons. With the history of al-Qaeda who also was financed with weapons and artifact identification and destruction, started when the Soviets invaded Afghanistan in the hope to find artifacts for the Order. Once found and sent to the many warehouses maintained around the world. It was after that, when the Order decided the open the middle east through multiple facet wars that could be financed, with the intent of weakening multiple countries while giving the Order unfettered access.

The Soviets withdrew from Afghanistan in nineteen eighty-eight, but they left a puppet regime in place, and the war continued. The next year, a Jordanian man named Ahmad Fadhil Nazzal al-Khalaylah joined them, learned, and then changed his name to Abu Musab al-Zarqawi. With the help of the Order, founded the group that became what we today call ISIS.

Zarqawi and bin Laden built up allies and followers independently from each other. The Order used this so if one became weaker than the other, the mission would still be accomplished. Bin Laden drove his membership from educated upper middle class, Zarqawi as a criminal, recruited the uneducated and desperate, not true believers. Over ten years they created a major friction and mutual distrust until the two met in Afghanistan in two thousand. After nine eleven, Zarqawi lost membership to Bin Laden and needed to find a cause that would change his future as a leader.

The American-led war's mission was regime change, leaving much of the country in chaos. Foreign fighters and extremists began moving into Iraq, assisted by Bashar al-Assad's regime in Syria, sought to bog down the US efforts in making a democracy. Zarqawi and his group piggybacked on their efforts. By recruiting former soldiers from Iraq, Zarqawi led anti-American fighters starting in two thousand six.

The Sunni extremists who arrived outside of Iraq found a friendly audience among former Iraqi soldiers and officers. The US had disbanded Saddam Hussein's overwhelmingly Sunni army in months after the invasion. Because the US refused to pay the soldiers to stay home, it created a group of men who were unemployed, battle-trained, and unable to regain their power in an Iraq dominated by a Shia majority.

Zarqawi's push for an Arabic focus group, as it fought in Iraq, growing to prominence, attracting al-Qaeda's attention. In two thousand four, Zarqawi promised loyalty to al-Qaeda, for which he would obtain admittance to its funds and fighters. His group was renamed al-Qaeda in Iraq, and it became the country's leading Sunni rebels.

AQI had a focus on splitting the county by Shia, Curd, and Sunni by killing civilians who benefited from the US occupation. The retribution would be against Sunni civilians, who would then join AQI.

Dorian, a newly appointed Section Chief for the Order, was unable to control Zarqawi, so he tipped off the US military, resulting in an airstrike. The hope would be a change in leadership. Someone the Order could better control. Dorian was looking for a more moderate and structured leader.

In two thousand nine, with a change of leadership in the United States and a new pandemic, the Order was pushing for access in Syria. Dorian needed access to the ancient, buried cities to accomplish his mission. To find the location of the Garden of Eden.

A year later, Iraq began unraveling, al-Qaeda in Iraq had a new leader named Abu Bakr al-Baghdadi, an Iraqi who had a background in serious religious scholarship. AQI began allying with former young officers from Saddam Hussein's army and recruited disaffected Sunnis. Iraq's own government, unintentionally, gave them exactly the opening they needed to regain strength. They moved west into Syria around the Arab Spring protests that became a civil war.

It was this opening and moving west that gave ISIS an opportunity to create their caliphate. Confusing and difficulty with Syrian rebels and ISIS recruitment, the Order was able to dig and move artifacts out of Syria. Dorian was looking for Canaan.

Descendants were enslaved by the Egyptians, until the day when the Creator calls onto Moses. The Promised Land was Northeast of Egypt where there was freedom. A place where people lived according to God's will. That is what would make it a return to Eden. Today, the Creator has placed the memory of Eden in every person, with most humans knowing this story and what it means.

There are artifacts and writings needed to be discovered to address such as the location of where Adam and Eve lived after being expelled from Eden. Dorian wants to know where this area is located.

Dorian also wants the bones of the Cainites who were described as exceedingly wicked, being prone to commit murder. Also, offspring of aliens and women become the Nephilim, also known as "mighty men" of Genesis 6 were all destroyed in the giant deluge. Most religious scholars say that man was wicked and needed to be wiped off the earth. The real reason was that these genetic mutations were against what the Creator had designed.

When the Creator flooded the earth, at the cost of the entire population, it destroyed both good and evil men. With a reset, all the immortal souls worship the Creator were lost. This is an estimated 500 million people wiped from existence. Based on our theory on matter, energy, and the creation story, this must have impacted their power. Such the reason it was written that it would never happen again, would an alien be able to mate and create superior men and alien hybrids.

It is written in obtained original texts from the Order that when Adam was seven hundred years old, he told Seth about the creation story and how they lived in Eden. Adam then relates to Seth the hidden knowledge he received in a revelation from three angels. Adam then prophesied about a great global flood and by fire. He lastly said, that after the floodwaters have receded, Creator will give the earth to Noah. Because of what Adam did, all mankind is a slave of the Creator or will have eternal damnation. These descendants form the twelve kingdoms. Adam foretells of the coming of the Illuminator, who will be more powerful than the Creator by changing the future.

TEMA Gray Side Control

COMPANY CLASSIFIED

"Mr. Dorian, great show," I said gesturing for the exit. "Who are you?" he said, taken back by my request. "My name is Jonathan and I'm here from the Order, Brody sent me." His eyes lit up, "I didn't get any correspondence from my contact." "That is because the organization has been compromised." "What? By whom?" "We don't know. Therefore, we need you and the original texts. Did you make any progress transcribing them?"

Seconds later a quiet shot vaporized the champagne glass in Dorian's hand. "Oh my," he instinctively said, looking down, chards breaking the skin, dotting the floor with small droplets. "Get behind me," I said while pulling him and looking for the assassin.

Once a moment had passed, I grabbed his shoulder and led him through the back entrance of the fashion show and into the alley. Before my car arrived, he nervously tried to let me know what he had done but I stopped him from speaking as we hid behind the dumpster.

"Dorian, I was asked by Majestic Twelve to collect the documentation, original text and you." "Where are we going?" "Somewhere safe but first, we need the original texts and your translations." In shock, he quietly nodded and waited until we got in the car. "Can I look at my phone? I just got a text." "Yes. But know that we need to get rid of it to keep you safe. I have a plan."

Earlier the shot was perfectly timed by Hoe sen, she had used a new magnetically altering frangible twenty-two round created by TEMA to be subsonic but exert forces equal to a forty-five-caliber bullet. It was one of many breakthroughs that we used to level the playing field with the Order and in this case, create an incident to get an edge on their plans.

Looking down at his phone, Dorian saw my picture with instructions. He then looked at me, "Sir, what do you need me to do?" "First, give me the phone." He handed it to me as Tina was driving the blacked out suburban and I was in the back seat with him. "Next, I need you to wear this large sticker on your shoulder." "It looks like the material my phone went in after you took it." "It's foil and will not allow any radio communications to get out."

Dorian looked confused, "What do you mean? I have a tracker in my body?" "You do. It is so we can keep you safe, but right now my job is to trust no one until we complete the mission." "I get it. Did they see us get in the vehicle?" We have foil lining the car. They lost you at the back entrance. We then jammed all radio signals for a two-block area to get away before close circuit television could catch us." "Good thinking. I'm just a translator, not an Agent." "The Order gives us a purpose, yours is just as important as mine."

For the next twenty-four hours, Dorian explained everything to me. As you read the rest of this chapter, it will shock you. Don't panic, we have a plan, and it starts with knowing when, where, and why all of this has happened.

As we boarded the helicopter with a destination to Orient Point, Dorian thanked me for saving his life. Forty minutes later we landed on his large oval shaped driveway overlooking the Atlantic Ocean, it was a little after zero three hundred hours. His villa was one of the furthest easterly towns and safe from the commercialization of Hampden Beach and the rest of Long Island.

Without a word, Dorian accessed his walk-in safe hidden behind a large painting. I glanced at a room filled with books, artifacts, scrolls, and coins. He pulled an oversized beige pelican case out of the room and shut the heavy metal door. Then rolled the item to me gesturing to take it and then have a seat in his giant solarium.

Given the late night and now early morning, I was hoping he would have given me a room so we would discuss things over brunch, but I could see his adrenalin was too high. "Maybe this isn't the best place and time to discuss sensitive information," I said. "Don't worry, with my security system, this place is as well guarded as

Fort Knox and even have an electromagnetic field so no one can hear us. In our world, it is hard to trust anyone but for some reason Jonathan, you're a guy I have a good feeling about."

After spending twenty minutes walking the area checking for radio frequency, burst, and laser listening devices, I returned to the sitting area. "What's that?" Dorian asked, pointing at the eastern glass facing the ocean. "This device will create vibration on the glass so a laser can't listen to what we say."

I then changed the subject, "So, tell me why these scrolls are so valuable to the Order?" Dorian paused as though I asked the perfect question, and he was the only one who could answer, "They feel that these writings from Moses are different from what has been published in today's Torah, Qur'an, and Bible. Moses wrote Genesis for both. It is divisible into two parts, the Primeval history, and the Ancestral history.

"The primeval history sets out the author's concepts of the nature of the deity and of humankind's relationship with the Creator. By creating a world which is good and fit for mankind, but when man corrupts it with sin, the Creator decides to destroy his construction, saving only the righteous.

"Noah is to show a re-established relationship between man and the Creator. The Ancestral history tells of the prehistory of Israel, and the chosen people, at the Creator's command, Noah's offspring Abraham voyages from his home into the Creator-given land of Canaan, where he lives, as does his son Isaac and his grandson Jacob.

"Jacob's name is altered to Israel, and the children of Israel descend into Egypt, seventy people in all with their households, and the Creator promises them a future of greatness. Genesis ends with Israel in Egypt, ready for the coming of Moses and the Exodus. The story is disrupted by a series of contracts from the Creator, successively narrowing in scope from Noah to Abraham and his offspring through Isaac and Jacob.

"Exodus and the second book of the Torah. This tells how the early Israelites leave the limits of slavery in Egypt through the power of the Creator who chooses the Israelites as his people. The results are horrific harm on the captors. With the prophet Moses as their leader, they voyage through the wasteland to Mount Sinai, where he is promised land called Canaan.

"The twelve tribes, also called Israelites, Hebrews, or Jews had entered into a contract with the Creator, by devotion they build a Tabernacle, a guarantee of protection. Then the Creator will come from heaven and dwell with them once they are two billion. By defining the Israelites as the chosen ones.

"The Book of Leviticus is how the Israelites use the Tabernacle, which they had just built. This is followed by rules of clean and unclean living. Controls are put in place to protect them from disease and sin. This results in sacrifices at the Tabernacle as an everlasting ordinance, but this decree is altered in later books with the Temple being the only place in which sacrifices are allowed."

Unknown to Dorian, my Raven Defense team found the Tabernacle. It is located at 29.7617638325665, 34.96979967385197. We found many artifacts. However, it was a parchment saying where the Ark of the Covenant was buried that was what we were after.

Unknown to anyone, in five hundred Before Christ, the Babylonians destroyed Jerusalem and Solomon's Temple. There is no record of what became of the Ark in the books of Kings and Chronicles. It was ten years later that we revealed the location to the Israeli government.

Known as the earthly dwelling place of the Creator, it was used by the Israelites from the Exodus until the conquest of Canaan. After four hundred and forty years,

Solomon's Temple in Jerusalem superseded it as the dwelling-place of the Creator.

Dorian continued, "Numbers is named from the two censuses taken of the Israelites. Beginning on Mount Sinai, the goal is to take possession of the Promised Land. The people are counted, and arrangements are made for resuming their march. The Israelites begin the voyage, but their faith is questioned by hardships along the way, and the authority of Moses and Aaron. To prove his will on the people, the Creator destroys fifteen thousand of them through many events. Years later, they arrive at the borders of Canaan.

"When they arrive, the Israelites refuse to take possession of Canaan. This angered the Creator who condemns them to death in the wasteland. Their offspring crossed the Jordan River and accepted the Creator.

"The Elephantine Papyri was the first found original writings of Moses and consists of a hundred and seventy-five documents found in a fortress in Elephantine. Consisting of demotic Egyptian, Aramaic, Koine Greek, Latin, and Coptic, spanning a period of a hundred years. They are a collection of ancient Jewish manuscripts dating from the fifth century before common era. The dry soil of upper Egypt preserved the documents.

"The Order first discredited the person who found it. Then stole the manuscripts. What I received were documents including letters and legal contracts from family and other archives. The remaining books of Moses totaling six through twelve is where the good stuff is located.

"The church discounted all as heresy. There are significant parts that discuss the use of magical incantations and seals. It instructs the reader in the spells used to create some of the miracles portrayed as well as to grant other forms of good fortune and good health.

"An example is reputed Talmudic magic names, words, and ideographs, some written in Hebrew and some with letters from the Latin alphabet. It contains 'seals' or magical illustrations accompanied by directives intended to help the user perform numerous tasks, from controlling the weather or people to contacting the dead. These books have influenced African American hoodoo, and witchcraft.

"As most have not been able to recreate the magic words, the scrolls were considered fake. The validity of the scrolls was questioned by scholars." We again, created forgeries and returned them to be studied, PhD's created, and fights between the various religions carried out.

I listened as Dorian continued, "Then in nineteen forty-seven, our best find was the discovery called the Dead Sea Scrolls." I interrupted him, "So, the Order has been making forgeries for the last hundred years." "No. For the last ten thousand years," he said. "I don't understand?" I quickly remarked because I was unable to get my head around why.

Dorian said, "Since the tower of Babel, we were given a mission to change the course of mankind. The angels or the Creator couldn't do it on their own, he made us perfect by giving us free will. That alone continues to increase our numbers to levels that the planet can't maintain so he tasked us, the Order, to carry out his goal."

I then asked, "So, you have a mission directly from the Creator?" "Yes and no. It is in the original text we have obtained and offered to anyone who is strong enough to carry it out." "And that is?" "Two billion souls on the earth and he and his angels will return."

After pausing to better understand what Dorian said, I asked, "Doesn't that go against the ten commandments?" "Who do you think wrote them? Or should I say changed them." "I don't know." "We did." "So, what are the original commandments?" "Does it matter?" "Well actually it doesn't but now I know why you are so patient about this task by the Order."

Dorian nodded as if thanking me for understanding his sacrifices over the last twenty years, "Did you know there was an eleventh commandment?" "What?" "We changed the books Moses wrote. It was originally called the Commandment of Love."

"Really?" I then started rethinking all the work I had done since nineteen eighty-nine. That the Order has been alive and well since the tower of Babel and I was one of their soldiers. From what Dorian said, it was intoxicating to be tasked with changing the planet but then who is so brainwashed that they would murder two thirds of the population because it was written in a book or on the side of an alien craft.

Dorian continued, "Yup. It's something you read in the New Testament but was never written in the Old Testament, 'Thou shalt love thy Creator with all thy heart, with all thy soul, and with all thy mind, and love thy neighbor as thyself.'"

I then asked, "Why did you take it out?" "If the population at that time followed this, it would contradict our goals." "So even those in the Order don't know?" "Now you are getting it." "We have selected only those from Majestic Twelve to know." "Why me?" "You saved my life and if something does happen to me, you need to get those documents to them. I have solved the code hidden in the text that gives the day and where to unleash the virus on mankind."

"Are you kidding me? Does the Vatican know?" "Who do you think runs it? Since the rise and fall of Rome, the Order has infiltrated every part of organized religion." "ISIS?" I questioned. "Not a religion but funny you ask. It was Saddam's Army Officers who created them." "We tried to infiltrate them and failed.

However, we were able to influence their need to destroy all the artifacts in the area. Well, all but the ones that Reapers would smuggle out of the country. Our best way to hide the truth." I thought to myself, I now know who was asking for these items from Brody's list, "Anyway, tell me more about Moses and these books I'm carrying."

Dorian explained, "The Lost Books of Moses were found as part of the Dead Sea Scrolls. In the Qumran Caves in the Judaean Desert, near Ein Feshkha on the northern shore of the Dead Sea in the West Bank. Other texts found have great historical, religious, and linguistic significance because they include the second-oldest known surviving manuscripts. We made sure the works matched the Hebrew Bible canon.

"Many thousands of written remains were found representing the fragments of larger manuscripts that we damaged on purpose but looked like natural causes. The eleven Qumran Caves is the place the scrolls were found, near the settlement at Khirbet Qumran in the eastern Judaean Desert, in the West Bank. The caves are located about one mile west of the shore of the Dead Sea, whence they derive their name. We even left some bronze coins from two hundred before common error.

"Most of the texts use Hebrew, with some written in Aramaic and a few in Greek. Discoveries were mostly found near the Judaean Desert and in Arabic texts. Most written-on parchment, some papyrus, and copper. Qumran cave four is where ninety percent of the scrolls were found.

"The initial discovery by Bedouin shepherds were seven scrolls housed in jars at the now Qumran site. The Bedouin kept the scrolls and took them out to show their people. When rumors reached the Order, they sent a spy who bought them and the location of the find. Once we had excavated the sites, copied the contents, and returned any artifacts that were aligned with the current biblical text. Any controversial writings were altered or damaged to hide the truth from the world.

"Due to the ownership of the area, we decided to change the lines. So, in March of nineteen forty-eight we created the Arab and Israeli War, prompting the move of some of the scrolls to Beirut for safe keeping. With unrest in the country at that time, no large-scale search could be undertaken safely. This delay slowed down the finding of the caves. Two years later cave one yielded discoveries of Dead Sea Scroll fragments, linen cloth, jars, and other artifacts we planted. Excavations of Qumran and new cave sightings have continued for seventy years.

"This year, Hebrew University archaeologists found a twelfth cave. There was one blank parchment found in a jar; however, broken, and empty scroll jars and pickaxes suggest that the cave was looted in the fifties. In cave one we initially found the original seven scrolls." "Did they mirror the current canon?" I asked. "Yes and no. We, I mean, the Order quickly took photos of the following scrolls, destroyed parts, and returned them. Examples are the two copies of Isaiah, Community Rule, Pesher Habakkuk, the War Scroll, Thanksgiving Hymns, and the Genesis Apocryphon.

"Another great find was the Sweimeh document in cave four, which was the complete book of Genesis." "Wait. I thought it was just a fragment?" I said, pondering the last thirty minutes. "I know. We have been rewriting history since the tower of Babel," he said. "Unbelievable." "What's even better is that in cave six we discovered thirty-one manuscripts collected from Wadi Qumran. These continued to help to find Eden.

"Then in cave number eight were complete copies of all of Moses and Enoch's writings. We replaced them with fragments and other useless artifacts that matched the dates of two thousand before common area.

I then asked, "Did other caves help?" "Twenty-one texts were discovered in cave eleven, some of which were quite long. The Temple Scroll, so called because more than half of it refer to the construction of the Temple of Jerusalem. We left it because there was nothing of note but further proved the authenticity of the find. We did omit parts of the Aramaic manuscript called Enoch." "You mean the guy who flew with aliens?" "Angels or aliens, these corporeal and non-corporeal beings took him. In the original text, there are twelve more pages filled with parts that would have scared the church, so we made it disappear."

I then asked, "Are all the caves now discovered?" "Not yet. We have been waiting for cave fifteen to be discovered on the cliffs west of Qumran, near the northwestern shore of the Dead Sea. They will again find some interesting works, but most fragments of the scrolls have neither significant archaeological provenance nor records that reveal in which designated Qumran cave area they were found. They are believed to have come from Wadi Qumran caves but are just as likely to have come from other archaeological sites in the Judaean Desert area. We did add a little treat for them."

I faked my interest, "Really, when and what?" Dorian said, "This was done in the late nineteen fifties, the original list of books, it will put a wrench in the current canon and theology for some time." "What do you mean?" "Well, we didn't rewrite the books of the bible, just simply omitted parts that align with our plan." "I don't understand." "If we didn't do this, what you know of Noah and the tower of Babel, would happen again and again.

Dorian then nodded and continued, "When the internet happened, we no longer could keep the population in the dark. Therefore, we planned on creating another extinction level event." "Really. Can you tell me how?" "Just so you know what others have forgotten, there have been hundreds of extinction level events that were omitted from history. The human species is two greedy to sacrifice for the needs of the Creator, and again and again with tribes and regions, the human species has been reborn out of the ashes of what was recently purged.

"Our strategy has always been to cull the herd slowly, but with an increase in numbers over the last fifty years, it needs to happen soon. The key is finding Eden and the Tree of Life." "What is it?" "I don't know." "My job was to find the place. Your job is to get the information I gathered to the Order before it is overtaken by forces more interested in power than the greater good." "When has this happened before?"

"In the first chapter of Genesis the Creator said, 'so, we created man in our own image, in the image of us. Both male and female created. And we blessed them, and we said unto them, be fruitful, and multiply, and replenish the earth, and subdue it and have dominion over the fish of the sea, and over the fowl of the air, and over every living thing that moved upon the earth."

"Ok, so what," I said. Dorian smiled, "We omitted an entire paragraph between verse three and four so the world would not fall into the same repetition." "What did it say?" "From memory, my teacher made me learn by heart, and it was found in cave twelve. It is in the case by your side." I looked down to fully appreciate what was inside it.

Dorian then said, "The omitted the part that said, 'If you grow too large in numbers or fail to take dominion of all, I will purge you and start again, for we will not sacrifice heaven or earth for man.' But man did not listen and thirty-nine times the Creator destroyed and rebuilt man. The last time was Noah. Those who was part of the last purge became the family and followers of Cain and the Watchers."

Then I said, "What changed?" Dorian shook his head, "It was free will to do what was necessary to stop this after the great flood and the tower of Babel. The Order was created to stop another purge. After forty of them, it was decided that the Creator would never again purge mankind and let the earth die. That is where the journey started and now it is ours?"

I changed the subject, understanding how important what was in my possession, "So, only you know the true words from the Creator and as written by the original authors?" "Amazing right?" Dorian explained with a level of excitement and ego.

"Are you the only translator of all these documents?" I asked while again running my hand over the large waterproof case. "I exist for the Order. With my gift of languages, I've been overseeing this for twenty years. Digitizing all the documents in English and in the first language." "What do you mean?" "The Sumerians learned a new written language that evolved into many languages so they could help destroy mankind repeatedly. Remember, each time the Creator may wipe away all existence of earth, Morningstar wins." "I am speechless," I said, uttering the first honest thing since we met.

Dorian stood up and gestured for another glass of scotch, "Even more, I have some writing that has never been released into this world. It was written by the Creator and the Order was able to keep out of the Torah, Qur'an, and Holy Bible." "Were these scrolls dangerous?" "Tablets, and absolutely, the Order has made it clear that none of the connotations are to be spoken in the first language. It would be catastrophic."

"I don't understand?" I said wanting him to continue now that he had a few glasses of scotch in him. As we spent more time together, he was overflowing with information that not only I heard but was being recorded from a device hidden in my glasses and pushed to my phone. Once we were outside, there would be a burst message sent to TEMA.

Dorian continued after returning to his chair, "What is more interesting is Glossolalia or speaking in tongues." "Is that a real thing?" "It is the language of the Angels and the Creator. A divine language recorded from other religions. An example is the non-canonical elaboration of the Book of Job, where the daughters of him are described as being given sashes enabling them to speak and sing in the angelic languages.

"Since recordings have been made and stored for the last hundred years, many scholars have received PhDs by calling this language into question as 'ravings of lunatics or simply non-comprehensible language.' Their inability to understand and decipher it is because of their bloodline. I have this gift and a high concentration in my blood. Another reason I was tasked with using when we want the Creator to return."

"Really?" I questioned never hearing this from my sources. "They never told you?" "Told me what?" "To be recruited into the Order, your blood line must be a high concentration from Noah. Before gene testing, they would look at family trees for recruiting." "That just answered many questions I had on why me? So, do I have the gift?" "What we need to do is give you a quick test and see the percentage of purity you are."

Dorian got up and walked into the kitchen. Pulling a small leather kit from a drawer, he walked over to me, "Put this in your mouth and rub it on your inside cheek Jonathan." Reaching for the swab, I completed the task and placed it inside a small test tube with a cap and liquid inside. He shook it for ten seconds and then placed it into another device, that in seconds put by level at ninety two percent."

"Oh my," Dorian said, looking at me as though he had seen a ghost. "What?" "You have the purest readings I've ever seen." "How many do you evaluate?" "Everyone in the Order." "Are you serious?" "Yes.

Someone hid this from me. I would have been tracking you since getting this task twenty years ago. When did you join?" "Nineteen eighty-nine I was recruited." "Incredible."

Pausing for a second in trying to process, the last thirty years flashed before my eyes. What do I do with this information? It must mean something. Like trying not to give away a straight flush in a poker tournament, I looked at him, "Now what?" "Well, the first thing I need to do is let the Order know we have you." "What will happen to me?" "We will dissect your family tree. Do you have any family? This is exciting."

"Dorian, before you let them know, tell me more about this gift I have?" I asked. He nodded, "Some have said, your soul or non-corporeal being, like the angels, have the ability to live in an anointed corporeal form." "I don't understand." "Think of your body as a capsule that fuels the soul or your conscience."

I confirmed what he said, "Ok, I got that." "When you have children, like physical traits passed on, a piece of your soul is transferred into another. If you do this over and over again, from Adam to you, small parts of everyone before you on the male side is now in you. This is why we can read such a high percentage."

I then questioned on behalf of my sisters without saying their name, "What about women?" "They are carriers, so in fact their percentage will be higher as they can't pass on a part of their soul but only those of their male lineage. First it was where you were from because people never traveled and married inside the tribe developing Surnames. To track ancestry for the Order." "They invented last names?" "Yes, we did."

"Why does the Order care?" I asked. "The higher the percentage, the longer you live after drinking from the Tree of Life. We become immortals" "So that is why you want the location of Eden.

"But back to this other gift, Dorian," I said. "So, there are five places in the New Testament where speaking in tongues is referred to explicitly. In Mark 16:17, Acts 2, Acts 10:46, Acts 19:6, and 1st Cor 12, 13, and 14. Then other verses may be considered to refer to 'speaking in tongues', such as Isaiah 28:11, Romans 8:26 and Jude 20.

"The New Testament describes tongues largely as speech addressed to the Creator, but also as something that can potentially be interpreted into human language, thereby. The 'sign of tongues' refers to xenoglossia, wherein one speaks an actual language they have never learned. The 'gift of tongues' refers to an utterance spoken by an individual and addressed to a congregation of, typically, other believers 'Praying in the spirit' is typically used to refer to glossolalia as part of personal prayer."

Hearing the helicopter blades getting louder, I smiled at Dorian, "Is there anything else before we head out to the safe house and wait for further instructions from the Order?" "No. I've told you everything I know and am excited to do more testing with you and your family." Seeing the lights from the helicopter, "Ok, follow me," signaling for the entrance to the back yard.

"Where are we going?" Dorian asked, grabbing his coat, and leaning down instinctively as the propeller blades created a cyclone around us. "There is a place in Maine we can set you up with all the testing needed. There I will make contact with the Order on what we need to do next." I looked at Tina with a nod and then rolled the large pelican case between us.

Thirty minutes later, Dorian opened his eyes with instant panic. When Tina took off, I leaned in to tell him to buckle up and injected him with a sedative, seconds later he passed out on the floor. Then using a chainmail sleeping bag, no additional restraints were needed, he slid easily out the door.

With the loud noise of the helicopter blades and the air rushing past the large opening, I could barely make out his screams. Still dark out, the skyline was starting to show a defined water line. Tina nodded at me; she marked the gps coordinates for Dorian's final resting place.

We were thirty miles off the coast of Cape Cod and with depths of five hundred feet, no one would ever find him. Acting like a faraday cage, his tracking device would show his last location just outside his home. Also, it would break under the pressure of this cold-water abyss. My family would be safe and TEMA could use the items retrieved to get me one step closer to stopping the End of Days.

REAP THROUGH THE END OF DAYS

LXI

Sacramento, California FEB 2013
Counter Mission Charlie Hotel Kilo Five

"Bella, grab the sheet to get the front sail full," I yelled from the helm. She was not in her usual boating attire, a bikini that was in a color that matched her mood. With temps in the fifties, she was wearing cold weather gear. We had been piloting the two thousand eleven, Southerly. Since leaving the port in Washington, we had been sailing for the last month. Leaving the San Francisco Bay and heading to Sacramento, she was tempted to lose the jacket but with a good breeze, just didn't meet her bikini top threshold.

"I think we should buy her," Bella shouted once the sails were dialed in. Then she walked down into the cabin, changed over to an ensemble of traditional yoga pants and storm weather jacket. Back on the forward deck, made her way to a yoga mat, balancing the ten-degree heel of the boat. She then noticed and pointed, "There is a boat five hundred yards on port traveling at us fast." Over the course of the day, we passed many bass boats on the San Joaquin River, all in a hurry to get to their favorite fishing spot and then back to the dock.

The trip was a culmination of much planning and a little luck. Bella always wanted a sailboat, and it was time to make a purchase. Also, another person on my Reaper list was found just a mile from our current location. Unknown to Bella, I'd already sent a direct deposit of four hundred and eighty thousand after two days at sea.

Leaving Vancouver in January would seem to be the worst time of year to grab our new toy for the ocean but like I told Bella, when she initially boycotted the plan, we needed to sail at its worst to verify it would meet our needs. With time on my side and a month of surveillance conducted by Tina, the plan was developed by her and executed by Naomi.

A couple months ago, explaining conditions in the Northwest, the current owner said, "Sir, are you sure about doing this now? The weather is going to be treacherous all the way down to Portland by the latest weather reports." "Like I said, I'll rent her for one thousand a day until my wife makes the decision to buy it." "No, I get it but if you wait a couple weeks the conditions should greatly improve." "No thank you. With Maine winters, I need to make sure this boat can handle it. We plan on sailing year-round and this means during times like today."

"Are you sure we should start today?" Bella asked, looking out over the sound through the comfort of our hotel room. "You have the right gear, and it will only be nasty out for a few days." "I trust you honey bunny but promise me that if I get scared, we'll come back and wait it out from here." "I promise baby, now call the valet and get our bags in the rental."

It was surreal when first entering the cabin and sitting in the saloon. Already pre-checked with engines running and the heater on, when Bella got out of the weather, she smiled. "Oh my god, this is awesome. It's like an apartment here." "Technically a two-bed two-bath to be precise." "How did you do all of this?" Bella said going through the galley and closets filled with our things and provisions for our month-long trip to the city of Sacramento.

The Southerly is best in class for the under fifty blue water capable cruisers. With three large cabins, two oversized heads, full raised saloon, passageway gallery, excellent access to engine, generator and workbench, center cockpit, and of course, easy to sail single handed.

When I had the opportunity to purchase this west coast boat, I couldn't pass it up. The location was perfect for my counter mission and all the east coast boats are either full of mold in the south or hard winters in the north. With her lifting keel and twin rudder arrangement she sails confidently offshore and cruises the shallows which makes the seventeen feet of tides less stressful. I chose her for the long-distance cruising and by getting her to Sacramento, there was a truck waiting to drive her across country, away from the snow and ice.

When evaluating what sailboat would be best for Bella and me, it needed to be easily sailed by one or two people with power winches and all lines led aft to the helm. I also wanted to bring the boat in shallow waters without worrying about depth, so it needed to be a Swing. With a fully battened main, furling genoa, and stay sail. Bella demanded a spacious, center cockpit, raised saloon, and slept many, with a generator. I also added eight hundred watts of solar and eight hundred watts of wind.

"I can't believe how easy this forty-five-foot boat steers," Bella said while leaning on the wheel to counter the healing boat. "Hard to believe this thing weighs twenty-three thousand pounds and with the ballast full add another ten." "I don't know what that means silly." "Your car weighs three thousand pounds."

"Why did they get it?" She asked. I paused for a moment determining if my recount would be short or long, "The story he told me was extended cruising after their retirement. They wanted a liveaboard for a few months in the summer, sailing around Vancouver. From what they said, they wanted the space of two double cabins and two showers. They would hide behind islands crawling in the shallow." "Silly, that still doesn't tell me why." "I'm getting to that baby doll." "Ok, continue my sexy husband."

I smiled at her while looking up from the saloon. "Bella, they told me this information, so you'll love the boat more. The owners would anchor often when the weather turned nasty." "When did they get it?" "Two years ago. He commented that they always felt safe and in control in rough conditions and his wife had enormous confidence in the boat."

Bella impatiently asked me, "So when did they get divorced?" "Good guess baby. He told me that they originally decided to sell everything and sail around the world. The boat was in England. They made it across the Atlantic and through the Panama Canal. Then all the way up the coast and back to Washington. Two weeks ago, started separating assets. Sometimes spending too much time isn't a good thing." "I could be with you every day. Let's sell everything and just do this." "We'll see baby."

It was later in the day when the western wind increased to thirty-five knots, I engaged the headsail furling. One of two on the boat. "Bella, stow the gear down there, we'll be healing at least fifteen degrees." "Ok, I'll shut the bow hatch and we should be ok." It was there under the forward bunk; I had my kit. Bella only knew about the suppressed beretta in the galley with three magazines and an additional hundred rounds strategically placed in the helm gear locker.

In my kit was for the latest counter mission. It was more than a weapon, consisting of the standard interrogation package. The job was to get to the truth and the target was Ginger Garner, a section chief for the Order under the New Majestic Twelve. She recently purchased a home in Rancho Cordova.

"I really love it," Bella said. "It seems like the sailing yacht's standard hull and raised saloon was modified just for us." She then proclaimed, "The side galley is my favorite and especially useful when we hit those big seas between the Portland Oregon and California border." For me, I only cared about the tall, oversized rig providing a powerful sail pattern as we worked south.

The purchase of this beautiful and comfortable sailing yacht would help navigate our passages in Maine. With an electric genoa furling, electric cockpit winch and single line slab reefing, she is easily sailed by two, especially on long passages. All controls are in the cockpit so there are no foredeck maneuvers required in the dark. The lifting keel has also allowed us access to some very shallow inlets. Over the last three weeks, we have raised the drop keel and enjoyed beaching it without needing the dinghy.

With a few glasses of wine after a successful anchor and love making in our aft cabin, Bella was fast asleep, and I was moving my way back for scullery duty and plotting our journey tomorrow.

"Get me November Romeo," I said to Control. With her background, Naomi Carson would be my inside girl. The past missions for me involved retrieval of an ancient script, help with the universal translator, and exposure to the linkage between first people and the writing. Oh, and is a Reaper. Her cover is as a project manager and will fit nicely.

COMPANY CLASSIFIED

```
           TEMA GRAY SIDE              DATE
           624 S Grand Ave
        Los Angeles, CA 90017      01 FEB 2013
```

To: Mr. Grimm
From: Control
Subject: Counter Mission Charlie Hotel Kilo Five

Ginger Garner was born in nineteen seventy in Sheffield
England. Both parents were Order members. Testing high
for languages, she was encouraged to learn Russian,
Spanish, Slavic, French, German, and Polish. By twelve
she was proficient in all western country languages.
Then Her family moved to Egypt to support the Embassy.
She pursued all Middle Eastern languages.

Education is in geology, vertebrate paleontology and
paleolithic archaeology. Completed her doctoral
dissertation on paleolithic archaeology from UCSB.
Because of her loyalty and work, the Order promoted her
to replace a recently deceased Majestic Twelve member.

Ginger started her scientific career studying
anthropology at the University of Idaho, but later
shifted to paleolithic archaeology. By the direction
Order when another member was Reaped. They needed her
skills to find the most ancient artifacts in existence
to prepare for the End of Days. Ginger's task was to
examine the seven original wonders of the world. After
completing an initial survey on the geomorphology of
the entire seven, this helped her find artifacts
mentioned in the original text from many scripts that
were replaced with forgeries and then released to the
world.

REAP THROUGH THE END OF DAYS

The lengthy excavations over the next twenty years resulted in the revelation that many of the texts found by the Order had coded transcripts that revealed the general location of the Garden of Eden.

However, the area was limited to a hundred miles. Based on communications intercepted, they have not found the location, but it is likely that it will be found by twenty twenty-five. Many are looking for it. Under section seven, there are many training arms to the organization. After Recruitment, it is training either directly or indirectly to support the Order. These are called Acolytes or Assets.

We are focused on the translations, archeological research, religion's scholars, and computer algorithms specific and significant to the potential location of the Garden of Eden. After adding the text from your last mission, the best resource to get these untranslated parts is an English linguist, geologist, paleontologist, and archaeologist. She is currently living in Sacramento California. Three years ago, received tenure at the Sacramento State University Department of Anthropology, College of Social Sciences & Interdisciplinary Studies.

Ginger's contributions through her field work, academic monologues and archeological excavation discoveries are vast and have contributed to continued scientific findings. She was recruited by the Order in nineteen ninety-four. The next year she was tasked to India, Ginger began explorations in the foothills of Siwalik Hills of Western Nepal. For the next three years, she was rewarded with answers and encounters of original writings that were intercepted; she recently translated with the help of Dorian.

The discovery of an unexpected wealth of information from the paleolithic to the Neolithic time found in the Dun Valleys, and an area along the Rato River in East Nepal. Ginger also discovered a skull from the first people dating back to one generation after the tower of

Babel fell. Evidence of a mark made on a nearby rock matched historical notes taken from that time.

Ginger's next big find was a hand axe showing human occupation dated back at least to the late middle Pleistocene period. Most significantly, her finding of the Acheulian sites demonstrates that despite the scarce materials, the early South Asian Acheulian hominins were able to cross the vast Indo-Gangetic floodplain.

For well over a thousand years, sacred narrations and valiant epics have made up the mythology of Hinduism. She did explain in one paper, "That nothing in these complex, yet colorful legends is fixed and firm. Pulsing with creation, obliteration, love, and conflict, it shifts and changes. Most myths occur in several different versions, and many characters have multiple roles, identities, and histories. This seeming confusion reflects the richness of a mythology that has expanded and taken on new meanings over the centuries."

Hinduism stood for a wide variety of related spiritual civilizations native to India. Historically, it involved development and growth since the pre-Christian epoch. In turn, it looked back to the age-old belief of the Indus Valley Civilization followed by the Vedic faith. Later in her career was associated with UCSB where she studied prehistory, geology, and paleontology.

Ginger's interest was from the Order, they wanted to connect religions and genealogies. At UCSB, she established relationships with likeminded associates with ties with numerous resources. This gave her access to African sites. Also helping with the discovery of Lucy, a female hominin belonging to Australopithecus afarensis, and other prehistoric hominids in Ethiopia.

It was the Order that has been creating anthropological fakes for two hundred years. By convincing the world there is no Creator, they can move through the science industrial complex without fear or question. While in

Ethiopia, Ginger also found a 2.6-million-year-old relic. Again, a fake to create a different timeline. With hundreds of these assets around the world, history and anthropology is reshaped. She was the first person responsible for discovering paleolithic sites there that turned out to be among the oldest archaeological evidence in the world.

Ginger's most notable contribution to the Order was finding thirty giants in a crypt, ranging in size from 12 to 30 feet tall, near Southwestern Syria. Like her predecessors in the Order, two things must ever be revealed to the world. The truth of Angels and Nephilim.

After discontinuing her efforts in Ethiopia, Ginger worked for UCSB on fossil-bearing sediments in Namibia. It was here, she not only found 18 million years ago, fossils that dated back to but also many Paleolithic artefacts. While in Namibia and South Africa, worked as a geologist and archaeologist for the Order, retrieving more artifacts and planting fakes to tell a correlated story.

Over the last five years, her passion was to go back to India. Ginger further theorized to the Order the heavy layer of radioactive ash in Rajasthan was from the Watchers. This three-square mile area, ten miles west of Jodhpur, has an extremely high rate of birth defects and cancer in the area even today. The levels of radiation there have registered so high on investigators' gauges that the Indian government has now cordoned off the region.

Ginger reported to the Order that the ancient city where evidence shows an atomic blast dating back to 12,000 years. Her theory is that the city had created nuclear power from the Watchers or the Nephilim. When the Creator found out, it was mostly destroyed buildings and half a million people dead. She estimates that the nuclear bomb used was about the size of the ones dropped on Japan in 1945. It was her classified memo to the Order's highest authority that gave her the notoriety, to head up the section.

Excerpts from her memo … "Describes a catastrophic blast that rocked the continent. "A single generation facility charged with all the power in the Universe. When the Creator found out, the Watchers were directed to make sure this never happened again, the aftermath was ash and corpses so burned as to be unrecognizable. Their hair and nails fell out, pottery broke without any apparent cause, and the birds turned white. After a few hours, all the food was infected hundreds of miles…

"When excavations of Harappa and Mohenjo-Daro reached the street level, they discovered skeletons scattered about the cities, many holding hands and sprawling in the streets as if some instant, horrible doom had taken place. People were just lying, unburied, in the streets of the city. And these skeletons are thousands of years old, even by traditional archaeological standards. What could cause such a thing? Why did the bodies not decay or get eaten by wild animals? Furthermore, there is no apparent cause of a physically violent death.

"These skeletons are among the most radioactive ever found on par with those at Hiroshima and Nagasaki. At one site, they found a skeleton which had a radioactive level 80 times greater than normal. Huge masses of walls and foundations of the ancient city are fused together and vitrified. And since there is no sign of a volcanic eruption, it can only be described by an atomic meltdown or explosion. These cities were wiped out entirely."

Mission: Using November Romeo, who has already gained access to the target. Posing as a project manager of a new archeological dig site in India, Naomi Carson is to get Ginger to take a sabbatical from her current job with promises of publication and further her search for the Garden of Eden. November Romeo has set up a lab in Sacramento per your instructions and meet up when ready.

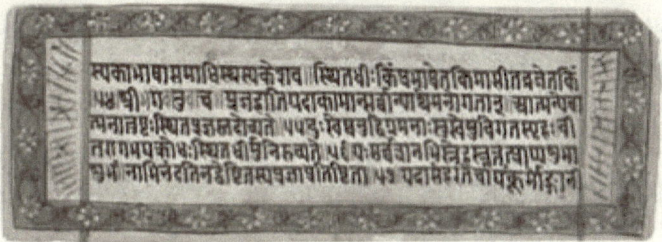

TEMA Gray Side Control

COMPANY CLASSIFIED

REAP THROUGH THE END OF DAYS

"Dr. Garner, do you have a moment to speak?" Naomi said dressed in attire to blend in with the student body. Ginger looked up from her desk. Like most professors, her office was littered with large stacks of papers, binders, textbooks, and framed letters, diplomas, and certificates. "My office hours are on the door, and these are not them."

"My name is Naomi Carson, I'm not a student, but rather work for a collector that has found something and you were highly requested for the job." "I don't moonlight outside the university." "Would you at least sign a Non-Disclosure Agreement, take a look at what we unearthed from India, then you can decide if this is worth breaking your school policy." "I'm intrigued, give me the form."

After spending a long moment looking at the pictures, with the assistance of a large desk mounted magnifying glass, she lifted her head with excitement, "Where did you find this?" "Ginger, I would prefer to discuss this outside the office. We have a clean room in the area." "Naomi, you are telling me it's here?" "Yes Ginger, are you interested?" "I am. Where and when?"

The contract laid out a six month leave of absence with sequestration at a location in Sacramento and the Keti Bunder South Wildlife Sanctuary. Because of the sensitivity, she would have to leave with Naomi now, no questions asked. With no ties to the area other than her relationship with the Order, she felt it was worth falling off the grid.

Arriving in a large warehouse on the Sacramento River, Ginger was impressed by the clean room accommodations in what seemed from the outside was a typical, old, and drafty, dry storage building with an associated dock. Unknown to Ginger, a tracking device on her was disabled and replaced with a Reaper acting as her teaching assistant, to take over the class in her absence. Once the Order was notified of Ginger's sabbatical, another Reaper picked up the tracker. Destination was a remote location in Egypt to keep the Order away from the find.

"This is amazing, did this all come from there?" Ginger said watching a video of an unearthed random location in India that mirrored hundreds of other digs. This one did seem slightly different; the videos were filmed with thermals around and through the entrance. Then she saw a track lighting system throughout the seven miles of caves with detailed drawings. Ginger was surprised how the entrance was only reachable by water. It was later a secondary tunnel was cut vertically for safety and to bring in machinery for the site.

"Well without being at the sight but with quick evaluation of the artifacts here and what the topography was, this may be part of the land of Nod." "When would this be?" "Think Adam and Eve." Naomi faked her surprise, "Are you serious?" "Check this out," Ginger said, pointing at the part of the map where she was guessing the Garden of Eden was located.

With a video wall made up of thirty large flat screen televisions connected in a pattern taking up a twenty-by-twenty-foot wall of glass. Super imposed on the grid wall was subterranean maps with a graphical information system overlay that went thousands of miles. Along with a projected timeline showing the half the planet factoring in plate tectonics, ice ages, and pre flood sedimentary changes.

Naomi saw the geography in the area looked very different from the current Indus Valley. Assessing that all these areas looked similar to those in Egypt and Peru twenty to fifty thousand years ago, with rich agricultural lands being surrounded by highlands, fertile lands and a deep ocean coastline.

Located on an area unknown until now Ginger said, "If we treat the bible stories as fact but adjust the timeline to match the topography, this still doesn't explain how urban centers created were intertwined with these large tunnels." Naomi smiled, "Indus sites were discovered in Pakistan's north-western Frontier Province as well as other smaller isolated colonies. These were found as far away as Turkmenistan."

Naomi said, "Control this is November Romeo." "Go for Control." "We have completed phase one and are moving to the site for confirmation of the missing text." "We will pass on to Mr. Grimm. Control out." "November Romeo out."

"Honey, are you ready to dock?" I said reaching for the throttle and adjusting the bow thrusters. Bella was at the bow with dock lines in tow and ready to throw on command. After setting the lines and making sure the stern was also secured.

We disembarked where she didn't expect. "Why here baby?" Bella said, rolling her luggage along the long wharf. "It's ours. What do ya think?" "You bought a warehouse?" "I know it doesn't look like much but Raven Defense plans on rebuilding so we can use on, and off-loading supplies as needed. We currently have limited assets on the west coast." "That sounds exciting." "I know."

Yesterday, I was briefed by Control the day Naomi and Ginger left for India. I spent hours monitoring video footage captured within the two weeks Ginger was there. Her routine was impressive, she would wake at zero six hundred, an hour of yoga, then a smoothie, and followed up by six hours of work. Then lunch and back in the lab until twenty-two hundred. She would take a shower then repeat the day.

Ginger had no communication with anyone except Naomi, who would mirror her daily routine. Each day, with cameras in every space of the complex, Ginger would be linked through an orally ingested tracking beacon that would be administered each lunch. Because of her dietary requests, Naomi would be her chef and overall administrator to meet all of Ginger's needs.

When they landed at the Kandla Airport it was with twelve land cruisers, full security compliment, and a travel plan to the secret site. Arriving at zero two hundred, Ginger requested to see a selected area before going to bed.

Naomi accommodated Ginger with the help of a rail system to get them to various areas on the recently created map. "Where do you want to go?" Naomi asked. "The walls show angelic beings along with images of animals, people, and other types of inscriptions, including the yet undeciphered writing system of the Indus Valley Civilization." "I can do that."

Gold was the central theme of the mapped tunnels. Therefore, Ginger's first reaction was that the Order needed to see this. But like most archeology digs, there could be years between reports, but she knew this was the missing link from Genesis. "Could this be the place Cain went after being thrown out of the Garden of Eden. As the crow flies, it was a thousand miles from the Order's assumption.

When Ginger first saw what was in front of her, she found it difficult to believe that they were prehistoric; they completely upset all established ideas about life through the eyes of Darwin or other evolutionary scientists. She was connecting the dots to archaeology, multiple religions, genetics, and anthropology. The thing that excited her and scared her at the same time was something ten thousand years old. It told the same story as revelations in the Judeo-Christian bible.

The ladies witnessed more inscriptions on the cave walls in the Indus valley. Especially the seven seals displayed along with metal vases mounted with ancient scripts. These were a detailed account, while the wall gave an overall timeline.

This aligned with what is now Hinduism, Buddhism and Jainism. The earliest indication of Hinduism is before and during the early Harappan period. She knew this was from her people... the Order. An early documentation in case things changed on the surface.

Not able to sleep, they both returned to the central research area. Ginger made the initial assumption that the people of the Indus Valley appear to have worshipped the Creator even though Cain was their leader and banished from the first family. In the writings she watched on a giant video wall recently recorded. On it was additional writings from Moses. This convinced her that before and after the flood, this place was used as a library to capture all that took place throughout time.

Cain lived for a thousand years and shared with a non-Adam family the Sumerian language and the spoken word of the first people. Ginger was fluent in ancient Sumerian and immediately transcribed everything she saw. Unknown to her, Naomi, using our universal translator had already transcribed everything but wanted her occupied and motivated by the Order.

"Naomi, do you understand this symbol's significance in the context of Cain," Ginger said. "Do you mean like Cain and Abel in the bible?" Naomi questioned. "Before now, the earliest use of language to describe Genesis in the archaeological record goes thousands of years, this is tens of thousands of years. Maybe even longer." "So, what we have found could change how the Old Testament was written?"

Ginger continued, "See this symbol, it appears in the Vinca script of Neolithic Europe. And in the Balkans, in the sixth to fifth millennium before common era. Another early attestation is on a pottery bowl found at Samarra, dated to as early as four thousand years before the common era.

"One scientist carbon dated a mammoth ivory bird figurine found near Kiev as the only known occurrence of such a symbol predating the Neolithic. These symbols appear only very rarely in ancient Mesopotamia.

"In Hinduism, the symbols show the Creator. Looking at the cave walls, facing right signifies the evolution of the universe; facing left typifies the enfolding of the universe. This symbol is one of a hundred signs of the Hindu deity Vishnu and represents the Sun's rays, upon which existence depends. It is also seen as pointing in all four compass headings and thus implies steadiness. Its use as a Sun symbol can first be seen in its image of a Watcher. The character is used in all religious designs."

Naomi nodded and added a few facts to help Ginger process the connections easier, "What we know so far is that Buddhism originated in the fifth century before the common era and spread throughout this subcontinent in the third century before the common era. The symbols were believed to have been tattooed on the Buddha's chest by his initiates after his death. It is known as The

Heart's Seal. With figurines and statues, this religion reached Tibet and China."

Ginger then explained an additional theory that seemed more plausible now, "I agree. Now with these artifacts, we can prove that Cain was the ruler and created this language. But based on the Bible, all on earth was destroyed with the great flood."

Naomi interrupted, "What if Noah was told to put all the scriptures gathered in the arc, along with the animals." "Genius Naomi," this makes sense. Also, the Great Flood wouldn't have impacted areas that were covered over by the sands of time. And would further explain how so much sediment lays waste on these areas. Even more, you found this place. There must be more we can find and study with satellite ground penetrating radar."

Smiling, Naomi said, "We have to be able to link Cain's language to the four hundred distinct Indus symbols." Ginger blurted, "Some say six hundred." "Ok, maybe six hundred have been found on seals, small tablets, or ceramic pots and over a dozen other materials, including a signboard that apparently once hung over the gate of an inner citadel."

Ginger pointed to the video evidence they acquired yesterday in one of the caves, "Many eminent scholars contend that the Indus system did not encode foreign language but was instead like a variation of non-linguistic sign classifications used extensively during this time.

"Others have claimed that the symbols were solely used for financial transactions, but this claim leaves some unexplained occurrence of Indus symbols on many ritual objects. These were mass-produced in molds as though to share with the world. There are no parallels to these inscriptions, I can't find this level of sophistication in any other early ancient civilizations."

Naomi interrupted, "If we go to this cave, it reveals much about what happened after the flood." Ginger took an hour and studied every word, then spoke, "There is only one language during the building of tower of babel. Think about it. Noah reinvented the world. He only spoke one language with his children, I attest, this was what we call Sumerian.

"Also, it must be the first written language. He learned this from the Watchers or the shiny ones. Then after the tower was destroyed by the Creator, all were scattered around the world. Speaking and writing different languages, someone must have been able to keep the original language alive." Worried that Naomi was getting too close to the birth of the Order, she changed the subject."

Ginger then flipped to another wall of inscriptions, "That is fascinating but still does not explain how a society predating Noah knew that the seven seals identified in the bible would set off the End of Days." Naomi smirked, "What if that was what the forbidden fruit showed?"

Ginger responded already knowing the answer, "You mean from the Garden of Eden?" Naomi continued, "What if that is why the Creator didn't want Adam and Eve to know? As an experiment to see if they don't know the End of Days, they would live a better immortal life on Earth. Protected from the rest of the world."

"Honestly, I originally thought the Garden of Eden was a myth. Now not so much," Ginger than said, "What would you think if this place were under a glass dome? With angels guarding the gate?"

Naomi later reported everything Ginger had found and said to me, "Using ground penetrating radar, we found a library containing thirty cuneiform tablets written in the first language. One tablet recorded the location of the Garden of Eden. I hid this inscription from her, but Ginger read the rest and believes that Cain wrote about his experiences after killing Abel. This passage focused on the four angels entrusted with the Creator's prize.

Watchers were called upon as witnesses in a treaty between Cain and his father Adam. As a result, Cain's people would not be allowed to conquer Afghanistan. A place to separate Adam from Cain, "For no person or tribe could defeat it's people or land." We now know a recent find shows the largest lithium deposit in the world. At fifty tons, this element is used to travel across the universe in corporeal bodies.

Based on November Romeo's secure communications to me, she plans to extend the contract with Ginger. This was by request from Ginger and feels there is more she can decipher before finalizing findings and having them validated by independent sources. I plan on letting this play out until Naomi can get nothing else or a fear of revealing to the Order.

Naomi said to me, a month later, "Ginger found a more complete Vedic text predating the earliest Indo-European-speaking peoples. Several scholars held that Indo-Aryans reached Assyria in the west and the Punjab in the east two thousand years before the common era. Ginger did comment on how everything known about Indus Valley groups was wrong except the idea that an archaeologically documented west-to-east movement of human populations. She felt this treaty was the reason and why the movement was because they were not allowed to go east."

It was in the final days of the archaeological dig that Ginger said to Naomi, "I'm ready to brief you on what these lost Vedic hymns mean and can prove this as the oldest writing after Adam. Technically written from Cain." Naomi then said, "I'm ready to video your results so I can send them directly to my boss." "Here are my findings on the proof of a Creator or great deity, and a general idea of where the Garden of Eden is located."

After a short pause, Ginger spoke about what she knew and could surmise based on all the information provided up to now, "Connecting the dots, we start with Cain. I first found where he was banished and become the ruler of all lands of modern-day Iraq, Jordan, and Syria. The ancient scripture says Cain knew his wife, and she conceived and bore a son named Enoch. The city was called the same. Later Enoch bore a son Eridu and another city was built of the same name. The entire land South of Eden was called many names. Babylon, Land of Nod, or Canaan.

"While it is commonly understood that Cain was the one who built the first city and named it after his son, some have suggested that it was Enoch, the son, who was the city builder rather than Cain. In Genesis chapter four, the city is named Enoch, but the people are called Canaanites.

"Then the name of the city changes in writings to Eridu. The first documented Mesopotamian city. Then Cain moved some of his family to across Afghanistan and into modern day India. Her he decided to create great cities and the caves to make sure they would be protected from another one of the Creator's purges.

"Before his death, Cain returned to Eridu. Living a thousand years, he watched as his family line exploded. With hundreds of cities and people living long lives, fifty million people spread from modern day Spain through Pakistan. But after the Great Flood, in Genesis chapter six, each person's spirit would only be able to survive in a corporal body for a hundred and twenty years."

Naomi then asked, "After Cain's death, priests performed rituals and prayer for abundance of children, rain, wealth, long life and access to an afterlife? Was this worship what we now call Hinduism? Based on your finding, this is twenty thousand years before any other known writings." Ginger then said, "In a simple answer, yes."

Then Ginger said to then further explained what happened before the great flood, "Thousands of years later, people disregarded the warning from Cain and started migrating west for trading opportunities. With Watchers teaching men how to harness nuclear power and weapons, when the Creator found out, destroyed the region. This caused the area to be unable to grow anything and created a large band of land that was uninhibited. When the creator destroyed the world with the great flood, reshaping in forty days, and the sediment renewed the land to where it is today."

Naomi responded, "Incredible translation and my boss is excited to get this through the dissertation process and then share with the world. He and I both want to thank you for your help." Ginger excitedly asked, "Now what?" "A professor has been selected to validate your findings and then have you publish your results." "Who did you choose?" "We would rather not share this to make sure an intellectual firewall is established. Does this make sense?"

Ginger had planned to complete her work on the site. Then arrive home, call Brody, and have the entire Indian site wiped from existence. This included Naomi and all her staff. Little did she know that it was in our plan.

"What is the status?" I said sitting across from November Romeo in the warehouse. Naomi reassured me, "She passed from a heart attack upon her return to her home in Rancho Cordova." "Was she able to contact the Order and give them her findings?" "No sir. I took her to dinner on our return. The poison worked as designed, very public, and the EMTs coded her before arriving to the hospital."

I then asked, "Any cameras?" "I accessed the restaurant and street recordings, they were wiped, electronic interference. Nice little gadget from the tech team."

Happy with the result, I said, "What about you?" "I also looked very different in case someone sketched me. With age and cause of death, it's unlikely the Order will do too many internal affairs investigations on their former section chief." "Appreciate you taking the time to safeguard the operation."

Naomi smiled then said, "It was less about me, loving this new tech. It made this easy. I fried the tracker before leaving the college. Then we were monitoring all her movements through a digestible chip and cameras. There was no way for her to check in and they did not suspect anything. I monitored her anytime she was not sleeping.

"Again, thanks for the tech. Without it, we would have needed five Reapers to keep an eye on her." "Glad it worked. Did you get the coordinates of the Garden of Eden?" "That and so much more. It is amazing what she identified for us in the caves."

After getting off the phone with Naomi and then calling Bella, "Honey, how long are you staying in Sacramento?" Bella asked as she was talking with me while drying her hair after a shower. "Baby, I'm charting the next leg of our trip this morning," I said while watching her on the video chat. "Don't get me wrong, I love hanging out with Tina and spending a week here in Lake Tahoe. The skiing was amazing and spa days were crazy. Totally pampered for a week. But I missed my man," as she repositioned the camera view, showing me all of her.

A week later, laying in the aft cabin, I was kissing Bella's neck, "How does tomorrow sound?" "Really, when will the boat arrive?" She asked. "Gets towed to Maine. Roughly two weeks, going the southern state route. Tomorrow, we drive to San Francisco, grab the company jet, and then on to Los Angeles." "Is Tina meeting up with us?" she said excitedly bouncing up and down on my pelvis.

"Easy there, honey. We are staying at our LA penthouse for a week and then fly back to Maine to meet the boat," I said. "Sounds amazing." "Oh really," I said while changing the subject with a simple distraction. In a moment, I flipped her on her back, while running my hand between her legs. "Don't stop," she moaned while grabbing my head and driving it into her chest.

Days later the spa confirmed the appointment, "Bella, I'll see you later today." After getting off the phone, "Where are you going?" she asked as we boarded the plane. "I told you honey, boring meetings with Tina all day." "About what?" "Her models have shoots planned all over the world, she want's Raven Defense to provide transportation and security support throughout."

While Bella was busy, I had meetings with Alpha and November Romeo. Bella then blurted, "Hoe sen is picking me up after my spa treatment, we plan on heading to the beach and then her work friends are taking me to the clubs.

Later that day, sitting in a large secure conference room in the Gray side space of the building with Tina and Naomi, "November Romeo please report." "Yes Sir." She stood in front of a twenty by thirty-foot video wall. "Sir, Ma'am. We shipped the submarine to Turkey on July seventeenth when it was revealed the quadrants of where the Garden of Eden is located. The incredible thing was that the writings gave us exact latitude and longitude." I was shocked and uttered out something and then looked at Tina. She was surprised but held her emotions in check better than me, "Sorry for the interruption."

Naomi excitedly continued, "Well sir, I boarded the boat the day after reaping Ginger." I then interrupted her again, "What did you tell the crew?" "Well Sir, we flew all but a three to Ankara for leave. There was no video outside what was recorded on the submarine, and I was the only person who had access. The remaining crew thought the job was a sunken city for artifacts and gold. With our satellite overlay, we created a dummy image to convince the crew what was down there matched my story."

As Naomi explained the timeline of events, behind her the video wall showed recordings, satellite images, and maps with interactive graphics. When Naomi explained what she saw, we all were in shock. There was over a thirty-mile area that was mapped with perfect detail, viewed on multiple screens with radar, sonar, video, audio, and high-definition pictures.

I looked at Tina to get a reaction from her and she was in a state of surprise more than me, "Johnathan, it's all true." Naomi then said, "I need you to know that initially something wouldn't let me get close to the site." "What do you mean?" "Sir, when I tried to dive, it was like something was keeping me away. Like a wall of bubbles surrounding the site."

I stood up and shook Naomi's hand, "Thank you. We will plan more trips in the coming years. You will oversee this. Get me a plan and timeline."

LXII

Phoenix, Arizona JUL 2013
Counter Mission Mike Tango Foxtrot Eight

"Boss, what's going out the door today?" 1ˢᵗ Lieutenant Bard asked while looking at the manifest. Timothy responded, "Sending six tons of munitions for Special Operations Command." "Is this for Seventh Group?" while looking for the destination. "Yes but no." "What do you mean?" "They are training Bolivian rebels." "I hope they like them."

As Timothy drove home, his trip was interrupted with a text redirecting him to a nearby bar. Waiting for him was the leader of Majestic Twelve, "Timothy, have a seat. Can I get you a drink?" "Yes please. Johnny Walker neat." "Just like your dad. This is fitting."

Timothy then asked, "What's up Sir." "Just doing a health and welfare check." "I'm good, on a mission, keeps me busy. Is everything ok?" "Couldn't be better." "Is this all?" "Not really. You need to find yourself a wife." "Really Sir?" "Yup. It's weird that you're ordering me to what, have a family?" "This isn't an order. It's weird that a thirty-three-year-old man has no social life, isn't dating, or has no family. You should have kids by now. Even if it's just a cover." "I get it, Sir. Do I just use a dating service?" "Don't care. When you have something serious, we'll vet her and whatever happens, the key is normal and boring." "Roger that Sir."

COMPANY CLASSIFIED

TEMA GRAY SIDE   DATE
624 S Grand Ave
Los Angeles, CA 90017   01 JUL 2013

To: Mr. Grimm
From: Control
Subject: Counter Mission Mike Tango Foxtrot Eight

Timothy Hicks was born in Roswell, New Mexico in Nineteen Ninety. Six years later, moved to Washington D.C. There he lived until graduating from Georgetown University with a bachelor's in international studies and a master's in business administration.

His life was not his own. Thomas Hicks, Timothy's father, was indoctrinated into the Order at a young age in the Seventies. First serving as a Reaper after special forces during Vietnam. After six years, was promoted to Grimm status. Ten years later, was a Regional Supervisor for the Southwest United States.

It has been mapped that the Order's structure is with a hierarchy in multiple areas that align with MJ-12. Each Member is aligned to a part of the whole. Thomas groomed his son to take his place who was Regional MJ-12 Supervisor, then headed up Supply Chain for North America. This role was to get assets to all members of the Order. From Reaper weapons to support staff housing.

When Timothy was groomed for his dad's position, it wasn't without sacrifice. He was recruited days later, with fast promotions until taking his father's position ten years later as a section chief for MJ-12.

REAP THROUGH THE END OF DAYS

JONATHAN REAPER

Now residing in Phoenix Arizona, he followed a routine by hiding behind what looks like a legitimate Government Services position at Luke Air Force Base. This gave him access to C-17s and Military Sealift Command to transport through a legitimate mission.

We need to Reap him after gaining access to his network off the supply chain throughout the world from the MJ-12 section chief through the end user. The Reaper needs to be his type. The Order will do a background check. We have built a legend that any Reaper can fit into. Recommend Reaper Echo or Victor who closely meet his online pornography history. Also, while tracking his internet history, he is now adding himself to multiple dating sites. This has been ordered by his masters so he will fit in. We have added both Reapers to his list of preferences, once he slides right, we will backfill her past.

TEMA Gray Side Control

COMPANY CLASSIFIED

REAP THROUGH THE END OF DAYS

"Grimm, this is Echo Romeo." "Hear you five by five, let's meet and discuss what you and November Romeo found on your dive." "Roger that boss. There is video but I didn't take any of the artifacts found per your orders. Mapped when and where." "Let's meet in Phoenix in one week. Sheraton Grand at Wild Horse Pass Hotel under the name Jonathan Gray."

Sitting at the hotel restaurant, I positioned myself to see everyone who was sitting at the bar and the main dining area. That is when I and everyone else at the bar saw her entrance in a strapless dark blue cocktail dress. Her blonde hair was up with color coordinated stone earring and necklace that accentuated her tan athletic build. At nearly six feet tall with heals, she stood out while making her way to my table.

Standing up and greeting her with a kiss on the cheek, "Erin, I guess you wanted to make a statement." Leaning in after I pushed her chair in and sat down, "He's at the bar and based on a long and detailed internet history search, I'm his type." "Oh, I think you're everyone's type." "You think?" "We'll talk about it in your room."

After an hour of dining with a three-course meal and two bottles of wine, the plan was set. Along with many innocent gestures, simply through eye contact, he was hers. After dessert, I excused myself and went to the room. Minutes later, Erin, walked to the bar, wedging herself against the target and the bar stool, "Bartender, could you make me a nightcap?" "Yes beautiful. Anything in particular?"

After a long pause with her contemplating the best drink for her mood, "How about a rum flip?" Mr. Hicks couldn't help but speak up, "Sounds angry." Erin laughed and placed a hand on his shoulder as though she was steading herself from having a little too much to drink with dinner.

Erin then said, "It does but tastes so good. Bartender could you get one for my new friend," she then looked at him wanting his name. "Timothy," he blurted. She then started again, "Bartender, could you get my friend Timothy a rum flip in a highball glass." "Coming right up." Erin then leaned into Timothy and placing her hand on his thigh, "Can I sit here?" Timothy then said blushing, "Oh, yes. Absolutely."

After a long moment staring at each other, Erin smiled and introduced herself, "Hello Timothy, my name is Erin Roth." "Nice to meet you, Erin. Hope I'm not keeping you from your husband." "Oh him? That is the pilot who flies me around the world. He's a little too old and not my type."

Timothy's mannerism changed as though he just won the lottery, "Wow, if you don't mind me asking, what do you do?" Erin leaned back as the bartender brought both their drinks, "I buy distressed companies and sell off their assets." "Wow. Not what I expected." "I'm curious, what did you think I did?" "Well first I thought you were married to a rich older guy. Then thought you were a model. Now I want to learn about your world." "Ok. Tit for tat, what do you do?" she asked. "I'm in logistics for the Air Force."

"Are you in the military?" Erin knew more about him than even he probably did. "Nope. I'm a GS fifteen." "What is that?" "I'm sorry. It's a term for a director level government service employee. Not as cool as your job but getting our warfighters the right equipment at the right time."

Over the next two hours, they drank many rum flips and Erin did her best to continue the covert flirting. "Well, I actually came here because a friend was supposed to meet me for drinks, but I'm much happier to have met you, Erin." "So, would you mind escorting me to my room? Those drinks were very tasty and potent." "Absolutely, let me get the check." She laughed while leaning on him, "It's taken care of cutie."

What Timothy didn't know was that Control had intercepted a co-worker's email, called a man in the middle attack, and slightly changed the meetup spot. After reading the email, the original location was changed and returned to his inbox. Also Control disabled his phone so no voice or data could interfere with their magical evening.

When Timothy woke in the morning, he was in a strange bed. Trying to get an orientation on where he was, the blurry bright haze he was seeing and feeling started to come into focus. "Would you like a coffee, Timothy?" Erin said while standing in the doorway that separated the three-bedroom suite and the large step-down living room and full kitchen. She was wearing a white semitransparent silk robe untied and showing her hairless and toned body.

"What happened last night?" Timothy said, sitting up and noticing his clothes in the corner of the room. "Wow. Not what I would expect to hear in the morning." "I am so sorry. Last night seemed a little hazy. I remember leaving the restaurant and then going blank." "Well Timothy, I remember everything, and can I say, you were exactly what I needed."

Timothy cleared his voice, "Good because I'm kind of freaking out right now and didn't want to fuck this up. You are so amazing, and I shouldn't have embellished so much, not really a drinker, in fact I never drink." "Well, you can make it up to me." "I'll do anything." "I'm bored this weekend. Will you be my escort and show me around your city?" "I can. Please for coffee and some aspirin too if you have it."

A couple minutes later, Erin came into the room, with aspirin in her left hand, a coffee in her right. Her robe opened more as she slid across the king size bed on her knees. All Timothy did was stare at her. "Are you ok Timothy?" He opened his mouth and she fed him the pills and then took a sip of the coffee still in her hand. Setting it down, moved on top of him.

"Oh, my goodness," she screamed as he grabbed her by the back of her legs, she instinctively put her arms around his neck and flipped on her back. He then proceeded to kiss her deeply and work his way down between her thighs. Her moans continued as she pulled and pushed with hands full of hair to guide him where she wanted him.

The rest of the weekend seemed like a mirror of Saturday morning with passionate love making, room service, a shower, a few hours exploring, back to the hotel, and repeat. Timothy was in a state of bliss hoping she would stay beyond the weekend but knowing this couldn't last.

"Are you sick of me yet?" Erin asked with her head lying on his chest. "Are you kidding? I don't want you to leave." "Wow Timothy, are you reading my mind?" "So, what is the plan then?"

Erin walked over, kissed him deeply and then said, "I was thinking that we wake up early, you go home and work. I'll conduct my meetings and then we meet for dinner, and you spend the night. I'm here until Thursday and then need to fly to New England for a week. Then the next week in California. Then I was planning on taking a break for a few weeks."

Timothy dropped his head, not wanting this to end. He was in love or more like lust, "Would you come back?" "I was going to ask if you have any time off because I'd love to have you come with me on the next leg of my trip. If not, maybe schedule a vacation together." "I have some time off, let me talk to my boss tomorrow." "Thank you." For the rest of the evening, they laid naked overlooking the Phoenix skyline.

Once Timothy was back in the office, he reported the weekend tryst as part of the normal operating procedure. Returning the handset to the receiver, then sitting at his desk, he looked out at the flight line with aircraft moving past his window. The mesmerizing sounds and sights forced a flashback to how this all began. Like most who follow in their family's business, he began this life, already working for the Order, like his father, and six earlier generations going back to two hundred years.

"Dad, tell me about your grandpa." Timothy asked. The funny thing was that it wasn't until his twenty-first birthday, he got the true story beyond the line, "Your great grandpa was an Army Air corps Officer who worked in Roswell until he retired in the late fifties. It was a recruiting story that evolved into an event that reemphasized the reason for the Order.

"This was his story from how I was told, and it changed our family's life forever. This is your legacy. When my grandpa was first assigned to Roswell, it was in support of the Army Air Forces. Despite twenty years of resistance for a separate service, and even obstruction, much of because of lack of money, the Army Air Corps, all changed after WWI.

"Just before the war, the Army wanted ground force commanders to oversee all Air Corps missions by being tied to all land forces. The organized combat groups deployed to the Atlantic, Pacific, and Gulf coasts but was small in comparison to European air forces.

"Lines of authority were difficult, at best, since the Air Force controlled only operations of its combat units while the Air Corps was still responsible for doctrine, acquisition of aircraft, and training. Corps area commanders continued to exercise control over airfields and administration of personnel, and in the overseas departments, operational control of units as well.

"Before entering the war, General Marshall implemented a radical reorganization of the aviation branch, developing a structure that unified command, ground elements, and air elements. Success in Europe by the UK, called the British Royal Air Force, the Army Air Corps had general autonomy within the War Department. This was a similar model as the Marine Corps within the Department of the Navy.

"In its expansion during the war, the Army Air Force became the world's most powerful air force. From the Air Corps of nineteen thirty-nine, they had twenty thousand planes and the same number of staff. In nineteen forty-four, there were two and a half million personnel and eighty thousand aircraft, which was a remarkable expansion.

"The logistical demands of this armada needed a Materiel Division and more than four hundred thousand civilian personnel. The Order was hiding in plain sight and aligned with the procurement and maintenance of the Army Air Corps. This infrastructure expansion was the reason Roswell Airfield was a perfect place for the introduction of a nuclear air base. It was close to White Sands Missile Range, Socorro, and Los Alamos in New Mexico.

"When the 509th Bomb Group was activated, your great grandfather was a nuclear scientist assigned to the

Manhattan Project. He flew on both Atomic Bomb missions. After the war, he was assigned to Strategic Air Command in the materials command group.

"In July of nineteen forty-seven, he was assigned to help an Agent from the Order who was assigned to cover up the crash. Your great grandfather was also the first to report aircraft blipping on radar that went dark near the private property outside of Roswell New Mexico. It was in the general location where the base commander received his information and as per protocol. Your great grandfather was assigned the mission to support the transportation of the craft to Wright Patterson Air Force Base and Los Alamos after retrieval.

"When the Agent landed, he contacted your great grandfather because civilians were already talking about the event according to reports from the local sheriff. No one at this point had seen bodies or a real identifiable crash. In these cases, it was easy to push the object as an Army classified balloon with nuclear reading sensors.

"He hoped that being accompanied by Major Marcel, the assigned intelligence officer from the local base, they could change the narrative. Both of them arrived at the site to gather up anything left behind. He told the soldier to store the debris in his office and to tell no one.

"The next day they headed to the coordinates to find the craft. The place was a whole lot of nothing, just mountains of beige and green shrubbery. The Agent took a military dirt bike from the base and searched a twenty-mile zone.

"After spending a whole day, the Agent found the crash site. When your great grandfather talked with him, he said General Donavan didn't want any photos, just a verbal report, and advice on the next actions. In a few hours, the Agent took twenty trusted men, two trucks, and some weather balloon debris. It took eight hours in the dark to stage the scene and pick up everything from the crash site.

"Your great grandfather's mission needed to be the retrieval and shipping to the correct site. The Agent was to develop a plausible terrestrial story, i.e., deflection, and to make the story end naturally. The next day your great grandfather received additional resources to move the crashed UFO. The 'Fallen Angel,' needed to disappear in Los Alamos.

"The Order initially moved the craft and bodies to the Roswell base. He also received more troops and equipment to move the craft measuring sixty feet in length and twenty feet in height. Because of the current exposure of the soldiers, this would involve radiation suits. Equipment consisted of a crane, flatbed truck, large tarp, and heavy security. He said there were roughly sixty men to assist.

"At the Roswell base, when they accessed the craft, there were four seats and three dead bodies. The Agent was in charge and went back to the original crash site with ten men. With no written plan in place at the time, he was dictating actions on the fly. He told the rest of the troops to secure the area and if needed to threaten family members if they spoke about this with anyone. The Agent did his part and threatened the soldiers at gunpoint to sign a non-disclosure agreement.

"The crash site was located on the other side of the mountain about five miles away from the staged weather balloon debris field. As the Agent told your great grandfather, who told me, he found another pilot who was still alive hiding in the jagged rocks. There was a noticeable rip in his silver Mylar looking suit and he was shaking either from fear or shock. The Agent couldn't read the eyes of the pilot and his facial features were modeled without expression.

"The Agent's face was covered in a gas mask and full nuclear biological and chemical suit. Looking more like an insect than a man, he immediately pulled out his suppressed pistol and shot the pilot two times in his chest and one in his head. When the soldiers were waved over, all they saw was a thin tarp made of the same material to shield the radiation.

"After the Agent secured the pilot with a few wraps of duct tape, he rallied the men to move it on to a stretcher. They could only stay in the area for a brief time because of the residual radiation release. A Giger counter were crackling while a soldier was yelling out radiation numbers. Only the Agent saw what happened or who was under the tarp.

"The Agent's next target was Mr. Brazel, whom he met in the café. At the time, the Agent didn't know Mr. Brazel was going to bring his eight-year-old son to the meet up spot. The Agent was posing as a real estate broker who was buying up land in the area. The day before, Mr. Brazel found the debris and called the police. On the fourth of July, his family went back to the location and gathered up more of the debris left for them, which looked like weather balloon wreckage from a government experiment rather than something from out of this world.

"While the Agent was speaking with Mr. Brazel and his son on the Ranch, your great grandfather moved everything to Los Alamos. Roswell Army Air Force was not a good place, because of the five thousand personnel it was hard to keep military staff from talking.

"Your great grandfather also mentioned an argument he heard between the Agent and General Donavan. It was about filming a video of an autopsy on the four pilots. Later we all saw the released footage that was later called 'alien autopsy' in the nineties.

"With the cleared Army personnel who drove the large object at night, your great grandfather successfully moved the dead pilots to Fort Riley. The craft went to Los Alamos, and it remained there for as long as I was read into the program. The smaller debris articles were flown to Wright Patterson Army Airfield.

"I knew with the number of military troops needed to secure the area and because of the potential for civilians' access there needed to be a cover story. Such was the reason for the balloon crash. With rumblings from a few witnesses who saw the Army personnel moving in the area, there were no large-scale media reports.

"Your great grandfather said this mission and the corresponding 'fallen angels' in the future reinforced the lessons learned on limiting the access of any information no matter how high in rank to include the President. Plausible deniability is the best course of action with counter missions like this in the future. Always keep the circle small.

"Over the years, news of this operation was released because people who had access to the information wanted to get it out. This forced the Order to silence them, destroy originals, and as your great grandfather told me, building a paperless organization with only two people and a list. They were called Grimm Reapers, Agents who assassinated anyone who got in the way of what the Order needed to accomplish their mission.

"It was then, General Donavan convinced President Truman to authorize a group called Majestic Twelve as a membership to oversee anything alien. Dr. Bush and General Twining were tasked to develop a manual and organization to make these events disappear, including the people who cannot be silenced through threats of action. The Secretary of Defense James Forrestal made sure President Truman had deniability of anything done by the group and this would continue until today.

"Your great grandfather spent the next year working with Mr. Alpha Grimm, aka General Donavan, to finish the planning for a network of warehouses to store artifacts. Well son, our family has been chosen for a long time to keep our country's secrets. When you are old enough, you will too."

Echo Romeo said from the encrypted phone conversation, "Boss we have additional information and new artifacts because of the warehouse find." "What time period?" I asked. "Way before the Sumer in Mesopotamia, or the Indus valley civilization, or even ancient Egypt who were the first civilizations to develop their own scripts and to keep historical records.

"We now have proof through carbon dating that when the Creator moved all from the Tower of Babel around the world and changed their language. An example is pre-Columbian civilizations in the Americas, these areas show the same date four thousand years before common era. It is the same in Asia and Africa.

"The period when a culture is written about by others but has not developed its own writing system is often known as the protohistory of the culture. Before we build the timeline of the first man, there are no written records of any human prehistory, because no one can discern what was painted on a cave or a frozen mummy with carbon dating but no discernable language. We now know the Adam story was interrupted by a million years of prehistory and at least forty extinction level events of what you would call man in the Creator's image.

"Also, to get back to the Tower of Babel. When the Creator banished humans across all the continents, he also changed their DNA to reflect what they needed to survive in those areas. Meaning our understanding of how we are connected was by design and not evolution."

I interrupted her, "What are the techniques used for carbon dating the human prehistory?" "This molecular evidence, combined with fossil evidence, suggests that the common ancestors of Homo sapiens, Neanderthals and Denisovans lived six hundred thousand years ago. They even interbred with the ancestors of modern humans, and the data shows match bits of their DNA.

"What about the frozen guy? I asked. "We have homo sapiens now found frozen that are millions of years old." I then interrupted Erin, "So you are saying when you found the Garden of Eden, it is much older than six thousand years as stated in the bible?"

Erin gave me an example, "I'll use the hammer made of iron and wood that was found in London, Texas in nineteen thirty-six as an example. Part of the hammer is embedded in a limey rock concretion, leading to it being regarded by some as an anomalous artifact, asking how a man-made tool could come to be encased in a four hundred-million-year-old rock.

"The hammer was found by a local couple, while out walking along the course of the Red Creek near the town of London. They spotted a curious piece of loose rock with a bit of wood embedded in it and took it home with them. A decade later, they broke open the rock to find the concealed hammerhead within.

"The metal hammerhead is approximately six inches long and has a diameter of one inch, leading some to suggest that this hammer was not used for large projects, but rather for fine work or soft metal. The metal of the hammerhead has been confirmed to consist of ninety six percent iron, three percent chlorine, and one percent sulfur. The hammerhead has not rusted and is in the same condition as when found."

"Who would know how to create something so advanced and so many years ago?" I asked. Erin then continued, "When they found footprints inside a dinosaur's print, it wasn't a hoax." "Erin, tell me more about the hammer." "The Hammer began to attract wider attention in the mid nineteen eighties and now sits in a museum. We switched out the artifact and it is in your vault for further study."

I then made a request, "Here is your task, take this back to Control and make it a priority. I need a draft timeline based on what was found at the Garden of Eden, other artifacts collected over the last thirty years by me, all languages and writing, etc. Dump into our fastest computers and give me a probable timeline. No timeline and there can be no plan B. We can't fight the future if we don't have real dates of the past."

"Honey? Where are you?" Timothy asked as he placed his hotel key card on the night table. "In the shower baby. Take off your clothes and join me." As he slowly walked into the large glassed-in shower, the steam poured over the door making him blind.

When the security called the police, it was to report an accident in the hotel. Due to the running of the water after two hours, security received a call from housekeeping, they found the body. A couple days later the coroner reported the death as blunt force trauma to the head from slipping in the shower.

What they didn't know is that he was dead for eight hours before being found. The hundred- and thirty-five-degree water made his time of death seem shorter; he was cooking in the confined space. They used the time in the shower as the timeline.

Echo Romeo, aka Erin, struck Timothy in the back of the head while entering the shower. She then moved him to the bathtub and weighed him down for two hours while searching his computer. Once the data was successfully processed by the Reaper Operation Center, she moved him to the shower and applied and reapplied thirty minutes and then off for an hour. The other Reapers accessed the warehouse Timothy managed. It was that morning they brought the missing link to be scanned and DNA mapped.

RED HORSE

"Can I speak with Ms. Jane Roche?" the voice asked. "Who is calling?" "This is Detective Bloom with the Douglas County sheriff's department in Nevada." "One moment please while I locate Ms. Roche." There was a five-minute pause that was just long enough for Tom to think they were stalling him. Then an answer came over the phone, "This is Ms. Roche, how can I help you detective?"

Detective Bloom asked, "Does your company own a home on Topaz Lake?" Jane paused, "I don't know." "Ma'am, you don't know if the home is yours?" "Detective, we own many company assets, and I am not aware of every one of them." "Do you know any of your tenants or employees in that area?" "I do not." "Who would have set up the lease between this man and your company?" "I don't know. What is this about?" "The man in question is dead and I'm trying to find a next of kin."

Jane paused for a second, accessing the database linked to her synaptic interface surgically implanted in her head. Everything on Dr. Heller had come up giving her enough time to stall the detective so not to lie but to deflect until she had more information. Then she said, "Give me four hours and I'll be in your office." "Where are you coming from?" Timothy asked. "Will four hours be satisfactory so we can discuss this matter face to face?" "Sure thing."

Jane immediately called me and left a message on what happened so far. Then had a car, jet, and helicopter scheduled, and directions to the field across from the Douglas County sheriff's office. The company lawyer discussed the matter with the local district attorney. Her plan was to take the time to lock down Dr. Heller's research and then build contingencies based on what the detective might do. She was on her own, her brother wasn't available to help and only a couple of her Reapers knew who this man really was, before they made him a ghost.

Once in the air, Jane called, "Detective Bloom there?" "This is Tom." "I'll meet you at your office at three thirty pm to discuss what my company has on the tenant and his emergency point of contact." "Thank you, I'll have an interview room ready."

After a long pause, Jane requested, "I would prefer you drive with me to Topaz Lake so I can see this place and what is going on." "Ma'am that is not how we do things here." "Do you want my help?" "Yes, Ma'am but it isn't up to me." "Ok. How about this? You are invited to join me for a drive and can ask me any questions you want without a lawyer present, or I can use my company attorneys to stonewall your investigation to the point, even the district attorney will tell you to shut it down."

Detective Bloom also took a long pause before saying, "Not how I do things." Jane interrupted him, "Ok then, I guess I'll be driving alone." "Ma'am the house is a crime scene." "What crime? The coroner already reported this a suicide and the district attorney said I could have full access to the company property." "Ahh, I didn't know that." "Now you do... so what will it be detective?"

Jane's plan was to find out everything that wasn't in the hacked reports her Operation's Section had pulled from the sheriff's department, county coroner's office, and all the home and traffic video on the internet. She needed to get inside Thomas Jefferson Bloom's head and find out what really happened to her asset. She had everything on Tom. From birth records all the way to yesterday when he was having virtual reality sex with a former coworker. That little escapade reminded her of official distraction.

It had been a while since Benjamin and her were together. Because of Jane's tech, anytime she needed a sexual release, it was instant access to her point of view recording from thirty past encounters. It was enough.

The man who was her emotional amusement ride for many years. Jane thought if Tom looked as good in person as he did in virtual reality, she would not be disappointed.

Detective Bloom noticed the large black sport utility vehicle parked on the other side of the parking lot near the field. It was three thirty pm in the afternoon and he didn't wait for the call from Jane. Tom had spent his time trying to find anything and everything on Raven Defense and the CEO. On the internet there was no picture, just a short bio, and the company mission statement.

When Tom called his assets from days at the Bureau, he either was told it was classified or nothing existed. He found this odd, how could a company be blinded from the eyes of the FBI. Also, his IRS buddy said the file was not accessible at his level and now he was in trouble by his boss because they wanted to know why an unauthorized request was made on this company. When Tom heard that, he immediately knew that Raven Defense must be a front for the CIA, NSA, or DIA. Only they had the muscle to shut down an entire company footprint from sister agencies.

Jane built a new identity for Dr. Heller after getting him out of Alaska. He became Dave Taylor, originally from Atlanta, Georgia. Unlike television, this requires an existing person who has disappeared and been replaced with an imposter. The real Dave was buried in the Nevada high desert the day after Dr. Heller signed the non-disclosed agreement paperwork.

Don't grieve for the original Dave; he was not a good guy. In his youth, he was in and out of juvenile detention, a relapsed gambler, married three times and was an unemployed warehouse manager in New Jersey when I flew him out to the west coast for a job interview. With plastic surgery, Dr. Heller was a dead ringer, after three months of coaching on the life of Dave Taylor, he was ready. With three hundred and fifty people named 'Dave Taylor' in the United States, Dr. Heller disappeared.

Next was the facility location on Service Drive. The company front was a medical warehouse for the Raven Emergency Medical Supply Group company a subsidiary for Raven Defense. There were twelve employees onsite, Mr. Taylor was listed as the manager, even though his front office staff ran the company and he just spent one hour a day signing off on documents. His lab was adjacent to a secret door from his office. Secured with a level five burn protocol for safety and security if there was a raid on the building.

Lastly, the chalet on Topaz Lake was equipped with a two-hundred-and-seventy-degree view of the Eastern skyline and crystal-clear water. Located on the Nevada – California border, the work staff would come over periodically for a work party or the Lodge and Casino was for meetings or events. It was the perfect safe house in plain view. No work was exchanged here, and within a year he had a girlfriend who accepted his stolen life as a fresh start like most who move out west.

Flashing back to twenty twelve, "Hoe sen and Tina, thank you for meeting me on such short notice," I said with a gesture for the two plush dark brown leather sofas positioned at a forty-five-degree angle to my desk, in the office at my home on Jameson Point.

Hoe sen spoke first, "Thank you for the accommodations to get here. The jet and limo make things easy." I responded, "My pleasure, ladies. I know this is short notice, but I have a plan to take down the Order and need you two as my ambassadors."

"After seeing a snapshot of the Order's work in Antarctica, we'll do whatever it takes to fight their future," Hoe sen blurted out without getting a gesture from Tina. "I'm always game for taking down the bad guy but this thing they did may already be in the world. Right?" "Correct, it may be a case of containing what is already out there or at least stopping it from infecting the planet."

Hoe sen then said, "Who is on the list Boss?" I responded, "That's the problem, we know how it is being implemented, through a SARS variant. We don't know where and when, but it hasn't yet." Hoe son spoke up, "Is there a test?" "Do you mean a blood test?" "Yes." "That is what our Mr. Taylor is working on now."

In the present, on the other side of the country, Jane looked at the document sent from Control. Digitally overlayed on her eye, as her mind blurred out the background, she read aloud in her head, "Revelations three and four, and when he had opened the second seal, I heard the second beast say, Come and see. And there went out another horse that was red and power was given to him that sat thereon to take peace from the earth, and that they should kill one another and there was given unto him a great sword."

As she continued reading there were connections that were in her subconscious, as though the computer in her head and neurons surrounding it were one. The same symbol kept coming up in all the research she had done, repeatedly.

To everyone else, it was an unsolvable puzzle from ancient books in different languages, some public, mostly not, used to find something never known. She thought to herself, "How can a group of people be so dedicated to something that literally is faith?" The artifacts discovered by the Order were still random pieces to them, but not to her.

Jane kept seeing the word 'Nibiru.' An unseen distant planet in our solar system with a thirty-six-hundred-year orbit around the sun. This word means 'planet of the crossing,' based on her translations of the many ancient writings.

"Control, this is Grimm. Get me everything you have on the word 'Nibiru.'" This place was the second horseman. I remember reading about it in my brother's journals. When the first telescopes from Earth see it, and the beings who live there, it will cause immediate havoc. Then played in her head the pirated virtual reality session from Simone and Tom.

LXIII

Sweimeh, Jordan MAR 2014
Counter Mission Oscar Papa November Five

"Control received scattered radio chatter from the Order's communication network. There is some chatter about something being reported by scientists with Caltech." "Alpha, please stand by while we intercept, record, run through the computers and send a report." "Alpha reads five by five, out."

Tina was posing as a prostitute at the Crowne Plaza Resort on the Dead Sea. Located in the mountains and on a private beach. It wasn't difficult to set up the meeting with Khaled, section chief for Civil Affairs was known for his only vice. Choking out beautiful young women in his home country. Khaled had bodyguards who would dispose of the bodies in the Dead Sea. We tracked eleven women so far that disappeared after setting up a date with him.

Control intercepted the website Khaled used for setting up the dates. As the door opened, he followed the dimly lit hallway to the highlighted curves of a naked woman. He walked toward her as she turned and entered the bedroom. The guards also entered behind him, making their way to the dining room, the furthest room from the bedroom in the penthouse. Their job would be to dispose of the body once Khaled was done.

"Where are you?" Khaled asked as he started removing his clothes and placing on the couch across from the bed. Tina pressed the voice recorder on her phone from the bathroom, "I'll be right out, or you could come in?"

A minute later, Khaled naked, opened the bathroom door. Tina was an arm length away dressed only in a semitransparent Tyvek body suit with face shield, gloves, shoe covers, and a gas mask. Before he could yell out or gag from the fumes coming from the bathtub, she used subsonic twenty-two ammo to strike him in both eyes. The rounds were not fast enough to exit and stayed in his cranium spinning around causing instant death. At three feet away, she couldn't miss. He then collapsed to the floor.

Meanwhile, waiting for the guards on the dining room table was a cooler filled with American beer. In minutes, they were both unconscious. As Tina made her way to them, both were in a chair leaning forward on the table. She quickly but delicately tied their hand and feet with zip ties. Then placed duct tape over their mouth.

Sitting across from both, Tina watched as the two men suddenly woke up after thirty seconds of sucking the air out of the large bags taped around their neck. She smiled as quiet screams could be heard but muffled by the tape. They struggled against the zip ties tied to their extremities and the arm rest and legs of the chair. Tina learned that using a large clear plastic bag made for satisfying entertainment because it took almost a minute before they stopped moving from complete asphyxiation.

"Control, do you have a report for me? It's been ten minutes," Tina said as she dragged the two men into the bathroom with their boss. "Alpha, we have the report ready and in your email box." "I am working a job right now, can you read it to me?"

"Roger Alpha, standby." "Alpha standing by," Tina said, while taking the top sheet of the bed and laid it out on the bathroom floor, rolling Khaled over on it.

"Love it when a plan comes together," Tina said out loud. "What was that Alpha?" "Disregard Control. I'm ready for the report." "Roger, ready to transcribe." She listened from the small ear canal device linked to her encrypted mobile phone.

"This is Control, we received radio traffic that two astronomers hired by a research institute have been working on proof of another planet in our solar system. This needed to be a mathematical certainty of a giant planet tracing an elongated orbit through the outer solar system. The latest computer simulations prove the existence even though there is no direct observation.

"Called Planet X, it is currently far beyond Pluto. Has a mass about ten times that of Earth and makes one full orbit around the Sun about every twenty thousand years. Based on the unique orbits of some smaller objects in the Kuiper Belt, a distant region of icy debris that extends far beyond the orbit of Neptune. Astronomers are now searching for visual evidence of the theoretical planet."

Tina dragged Khaled to the oversized ceramic soaking tub. Then straddling his legs, lifted him up until half of his body was submerged. She then spun the bed sheet, then under his arms, and tied it off. Walking around to the other side of the tub, she thought to herself, "It's so hard to find a hotel with a beautifully large soaking tub in the center of a bathroom."

Then positioning herself by lying on her back and wedged in a horizontal lunge position against the tub. The radiant heat warmed the ceramic tiles beneath her, and then with a fast extension of her legs firmly planted on the wall of the tub, she jerked Khaled lifeless body. "Gotcha," she said loud enough that Control stopped talking and asked, "Alpha, what happened." "Control. Don't mind me, just making stew." "With an orbit of

Neptune completing an orbit roughly a hundred and sixty-five years, we won't have the ability to see the planet until twenty thirty-six. By calculating the predicted object's orbit, it will be very faint and hard to detect, but is possible."

When Tina finished her conversation, she set a large wet towel at the door and turned on the standup shower. Then after removing the bed sheet from Khaled, she repeated the act with the two guards. All three were in the hundred-gallon tub. "Thanks Control. Please send me the addresses of the two scientists." "This is Control. Out."

Wearing a respirator, set her timer for three hours, it was magic how they all disappeared. Khaled, who was in charge of Civil Affairs for the Order, his organization was to work closely with local populations and civil authorities when it is determined that conflict has arisen to an area. Unlike the military's use of this skill to educate and share benefit with foreign leaders and reduce the root causes of instability.

The Order would leverage local governments to get them to do what they wanted. Their role was to undermine all areas of a community to continue in reducing continuity. His staff have a deep knowledge of government and diplomacy, those teams educate other sections on the needs, vulnerabilities, and complexities of civilian populations. They use their specialized training to plan and execute a variety of ways to continue instability so the Section in charge can better complete their mission.

Their training and assessment are similar to the Reapers except they cause communities to turn on themselves. A Reaper assassinates and makes it look like an accident or the target simply disappears. This is followed by extensive training in core tasks, advanced survival skills, negotiation techniques, and foreign language training to operate independently anywhere in the world.

By making Khaled disappear with a paper trail of travel, it will look like he could no longer lead section nine and was in hiding. This will further destabilize the Order and slow down actions they are planning. Her sister Reaper had all the close circuit television recording erased. We also hired an actor to take on Khaled's persona so there were sightings of him for months.

The two men heard a knock at the door, "Car service." A few moments later, the door opened with Tina standing in the entrance, wearing a sexy female version of a tuxedo ensemble with a limo driver hat. Her hair was pulled up revealing her jaw line and toned shoulders. "Ahhhhh. Wow, not what I expected. I'll grab my partner and be right out." Minutes later the two men, dressed in tuxedos, entered the car.

"How's everything gentlemen?" Tina asked, getting ready to close the privacy window between the driver and the passengers. "Good, what is our ETA to the party?" "Based on traffic conditions, twenty minutes. The champagne is on ice and courtesy of your benefactors." "Thank you." Seconds later, Tina heard three bangs on the privacy glass, she never looked up, just changed into the right lane and to the rendition location set up just for this occasion. The release of gas in the compartment caused nearly instant unconsciousness.

"Control this is Alpha, we are thirty minutes out," Tina said with a slight smile. Admittedly, this was almost as fun as snuffing out a pedophile or human trafficker. "We have you, looks smooth sailing to the location. Let us know if conditions change, Control out."

Waiting for Tina, a full medical team and clean room was set up. TEMA had owned this space since opening the headquarters in Los Angeles. On Nimitz Road, it was far enough away from prying eyes but close enough to keep our boats and submarines.

The semitransparent tent looked very small but bright in comparison to the muted light in the twenty thousand square foot warehouse near the Long Beach fuel pier. As Tina used the remote door controller to access the large warehouse and driving in with purpose took under twenty seconds.

"How long do we get them for?" the lead scientist asked Tina as they moved to two unconscious subjects from the car. "Three hours. Staring now," Tina looked at her watch and started the timer. This process was rather simple, and the Order had been using this method for twenty years, TEMA just perfected it.

"Nurse, I need twenty cubic centimeters of sodium thiopental. Please keep an eye on his respiration," the doctor said, preparing both for interrogations. Unlike most chemically induced truth serums, these were done using auditory and visual cues to extract information.

Tina was sitting in the temporary control room with twelve monitors showing the close circuit cameras. Six in each tented area, while their oxygen, blood pressure, and heartbeat were being monitored. listening to both interrogations, she could hear them being asked the same questions through the headphones and were answering differently. After the hour-long interrogation, a two-hour fake memory was implanted to erase everything from being picked up.

The information obtained was surprising. Like most that have reported this as a myth, the two astronomers said differently with a twist, they were working as researchers found evidence of a giant planet tracing a bizarre, highly elongated orbit in the outer solar system. The object, which the researchers called planet ten, with a mass twelve times the size of earth. With an orbit every fifteen thousand years, it makes sense that this place can't be seen but can be measured. By using mathematical modeling and computer simulations, they knew where it should be but now have eyes on the place.

Under sedation they were in a dream state, as though hypnotized. Stevenson said, "This is a real place and with our telescope, we can see the people and technology. They are the aliens in the movies. Everything Zecharia Sitchin wrote is true. With a mass of seven thousand times that of Pluto and twice the distance to the sun, the only way this place can exist is with the inner heat of the planet core and some type of outer atmosphere holding in the heat and light.

With all mainstream archeologists, astrophysicists, and anthropologists are very skeptical that this planet could exist, it will be real for the world when it is decided to go public. With our investigation complete, nothing will be done until it reaches inside of Jupiter in two thousand years.

The other commented on the partnership, "After we started this year-and-a-half-long collaboration through the funding of the Order, we have been tireless in our investigation of this distant object. As an observer and a theorist, respectively, I work from a very different perspective. I found the planet and surmised how the people on it survive. The atmosphere must be a reflective sheen as though the planet's heat is converted to light to the point it looked like a sunny sky in California."

Tina switched the audio from the closed-circuit camera. She heard Stevenson explain his role, "Once we realized that the six most distant objects in the outer solar system were impacted by an object of massive size and weight forcing planetary pull travel at different rates. We ran simulations involving a planet in a distant orbit that encircled the orbits of the six Kuiper Belt objects. It was solved only when we added the mass of a planet."

When Tina asked for the coordinates, the answer finally made it real. She found the planet using a TEMA asset that was registered as a communication satellite. It was a telescope better than the Hubble.

When Tina sent me the pictures that proved the existence of the Order's lost planet, I was stunned. Was this where the fallen angels live? To think this object was found by calculating what would be needed of mass and distance, to get the correct trajectory. With this same algorithm, we could calculate who was not from the

Order, and then identify who are hidden in plain sight and Reap them.

Mr. Stevenson continued, "One example is that standard-variety Kuiper Belt objects are impacted by Neptune and then return." But how did they know that the planet is real. Must be the predicted model with seven known objects that fit precisely.

Tina got on the microphone and spoke with the interrogator, "Ask him where did planet nine come from and how did it end up in the outer solar system?" He responded after the information was passed, "Scientists have long believed that the early solar system began with four planetary cores that went on to grab all of the gas around them, forming the gas planets of Jupiter, Saturn, Uranus, and Neptune."

Stevenson then said, "But there is no reason that there could not have been five cores, rather than four." Planet Nine could represent that fifth core, and if it got too close to Jupiter or Saturn, it could have been ejected into its distant, eccentric orbit.

If the Order wants it, Franklin and Stevenson will change their simulations about the planet's orbit and its influence on the distant solar system, so it's not found until later. "If the sphere happens to be close to the sun," Stevenson said, "When the Order releases the information, Astronomers should be able to spot it in images captured by today's telescopes."

"We found it," says Franklin in the other room, "But the Order wouldn't allow us to share the coordinates with the public." Tina started pulling the two audio streams and create a report for Control, "It was Franklin who gave the coordinates, twenty-six hundred years away and is shielded by the Kuiper belt so no one can see it unless you use our algorithm." "Ask him where it is?" She barked to keep him talking. When it was revealed, it was on their laptops and not on the university servers, life got much easier. Minutes later, control had downloaded all the findings and had the answer and location.

"At a solar system scale, it is a pin hole in relation to the rest of the universe," Franklin paused then said, "In context the ninth planet is the same until we found the orbit, then we followed the path. Now that we have the planet, the Anunnaki and Sumer people was right when early writing said there were ten planets. Science killed Pluto and we replaced with this one.

"First, most of the planets around other sunlike stars have no single orbital range that is, some orbit extremely close to their host stars while others follow exceptionally distant orbits. Second, the most common planets around other stars range between one and ten Earth-masses."

Tina switched the audio, "One of the most startling discoveries about other planetary systems has been that the most common type of planet out there has a mass between that of Mars and Jupiter, as though a planet was destroyed between them," says Franklin. "Until now, we've thought that the solar system was lacking the mass of another planet. Then we found it."

Tina got everything she needed, the next thing they heard from her was, "Please clean the scene."

REAP THROUGH THE END OF DAYS

LXIV

Milwaukie, Wisconsin JUN 2015
Counter Mission Alpha Delta Golf Eight

"Control to Grimm." "Go for Grimm." "We have the coordinates of the artifacts." "Send it," I said while walking to the bow of the large hydrographic survey ship. Another purchase from Reaper Defense, this was specifically designed to map the bottom floor. As such, it can conduct seismic surveys of the seabed and the underlying geology.

Apart from producing the charts, this information is useful for detecting geological features likely to bear oil or gas. These vessels usually mount equipment on a towed structure, for example, air cannons used to generate shock waves that sound strata beneath the seabed, or mounted on the keel, for example, a depth sounder.

After years of connecting the dots, I needed to get one of the biggest players off the board but not before revealing his plans for using a virus to destroy the planet. I could feel the tension now every time I spoke with Brody. After doing some research, it seemed like the best time to act.

JONATHAN REAPER

COMPANY CLASSIFIED

TEMA GRAY SIDE
624 S Grand Ave
Los Angeles, CA 90017

DATE

01 JUN 2015

To: Mr. Grimm
From: Control
Subject: Artifact on the sunken SS Tucson

Off the shore of Milwaukie, Wisconsin a Wooden steamship caught fire from over-stoked boilers. It burned to the waterline off the coast of Sheboygan, WI, killing 252 with 36 people surviving in lifeboats and 3 were rescued from the water by another ship. This was a Reaper Action. Intercepted communications from the Order says there is a scroll with a list of the entire true lineage from Adam to 1850.

REAP THROUGH THE END OF DAYS

JONATHAN REAPER

Owner: Pease and Allen, Cleveland
Fate: 21 November 1855 burned and sank
Type: Wooden steamship
Length: 138 feet
Beam: 21 feet
Depth: 12 feet
Propulsion: Steam-powered propellers
Crew: 27

The Tucson was a steamship that burned with the loss of 250 lives. The loss of life made this disaster, in terms of loss of life from the sinking of a single vessel, the fourth-worst tragedy in the history of the Great Lakes.

Career: The Tucson spent its career making trips between Buffalo and Chicago. The ship was owned by Pease and Allen of Cleveland.

Final voyage: The Tucson departed Buffalo for its last trip of the year. It was carrying passengers and crew commanded by Captain Barns. The ship also carried a cargo of molasses, coffee, sugar, and an artifact that was going to be picked up by another ship in three weeks at sea. Later we found out it was a ship owned by the Order. While on Lake Erie Captain Barns fell and injured his knee badly enough that he was forced to stay in bed for the rest of the journey. The first mate, H. Watts, took command.

The Tucson reached Manitowoc, Wisconsin just before midnight on 20 November. The ship took on wood for fuel and unloaded all the cargo except the artifact. When the weather to improved, the Tucson departed Manitowoc at 1 am on 21 November.

About two hours from Manitowoc, the Tucson's boilers were not working properly. The engineer reported the finding but was ignored; he later reported that the water in the boilers was dangerously low but was again ignored. This was sabotage. Later it was discovered that TEMA was not the first organization to fight the Order. We have identified seven organization that failed. More to follow in another report.

The Tucson Incident: At 0400 smoke from the ship started billowing from engine room. The passengers were alerted, and the first mate organized the crew and passengers into a bucket brigade to fight the fire. The fire soon grew out of control. First Mate Watts ordered the ship turned towards shore, but the fire overwhelmed the engine room and it drifted to a halt about five miles from shore and nine miles from Sheboygan.

The Tucson carried only two lifeboats, with a capacity of 20 people each. After launch, Captain Barns and 20 others were in one, the second was carrying 19. By the time the lifeboats reached the shore, those aboard were exhausted from rowing, and unable to return to try and rescue more people.

Meanwhile, the Tucson was being consumed by flames. The crew and passengers tore apart the cabin and threw the pieces overboard to use as floats. The water was freezing cold; most of those who managed to find wreckage to cling to succumbed to hypothermia. Those who remained on the ship tried to climb upward to rigging, but the rigging burned and collapsed, sending those on it into the fire below.

In the nearby town of Sheboygan, a justice of the peace named Judge Plakin woke to see flames. He ran down to the harbor and sent out a rescue ship called the Ohio, who began building up the steam needed to take their ship out to assist. At around the same time the captain of another schooner saw the flames and manned the ship's lifeboat and rowed for the Tucson.

By the time the Ohio arrived at around 0700, the Tucson had burned to the waterline. The Ohio found only three survivors, the ship's clerk and a passenger clinging to the rudder chains, and an engineer clinging to a door. The other lifeboat arrived soon after, followed by one of the Tucson's lifeboats. The Ohio retrieved bodies from the water, then took the hull of the Tucson and a lifeboat in tow. The Ohio towed the wreck to Sheboygan, where it was beached by the city's north pier.

Aftermath: The exact death toll from the Tucson is not known. The owners of the ship claimed that no more than 190 died, but the ship's clerk estimated that the number of lives lost was at least 250. 43 people were saved with 40 by lifeboats and 3 from the SS Rhode Island. The engine, boiler, and cargo were later salvaged from the hulk of the Tucson.

Interviews: When the incident first occurred, eight members of the crew working for the Order mapped the exact location, marked it, and lowered the artifact in the water. Delta Romeo obtained the longitude and latitude and will meet you in Milwaukee, the four generations later, one of the former Order Members was researching the treasure passed down by family members.

The asset is being held at a warehouse, Delta has been softening and ready for your arrival. The map he had was laminated with ink writing and a dot yjat marks the spot. The map is Lake Michigan, near Sheboygan 43.757298, -87.700329.

JONATHAN REAPER

Your mission is to team up with the Target, Tory Kilmer. Listed as S-1 Planning, he has the answers to many of the questions we have compiled for the last six years.

Then Alpha Romeo will, switch with a fake for the Order. Mr. Kilmer will not survive the dive. You will deliver the artifact to Brody.

TEMA Gray Side Control

COMPANY CLASSIFIED

174 | Page

REAP THROUGH THE END OF DAYS

"Prepped?" I said pulling his head back. With eyes still dilated and droplets of sweat dripping down his face, Diane put her hand on Tucker Bennet, "Yes Sir. Information provided thus far should be a good start for you." "How long has he been under?" "Twelve hours." "What did you get?" "I cut up the recording to hit the highlights," she handed me the phone with edited footage lasting about four minutes. The drugs helped reveal how and why."

After an hour of follow-on questions, we had the last piece of the puzzle. The investment firm who was funding the expedition. "Tucker won't remember any of this, but I need you to take him on a vacation, make sure everything is a go for the trip. We'll get there before them."

When the ship arrived at the coordinates from the map and radar, a bull horn sounded, and the anchor hit the water. Making my way to the control room, waiting for me was Mr. Kilmer. "Jonathan, you ready?" "I am. Thirty minutes to suit up and we can enter the submersible." "What is the depth of the object being picked up?"

I then said, "One hundred and eighty-three feet." "Just outside of an open water dive." "Yea, right. I've been to two hundred feet a few times. Is the mixture correct?"

REAP THROUGH THE END OF DAYS

"We should be fine. Of course, if we get decompression sickness, there is a tank on board."

As Tori and I boarded the manned submersible, the crew was already preparing the craft with the winch. We had ten hours of air and a compliment of lights completely around to dome shaped cockpit giving off four hundred and fifty thousand lumens.

The route we would take was the set up the lake floor in a grid pattern, with anomalies of the items. Once we have it, the next step was for one operator to stay in the cockpit, while the other, suited up, flooded the wet locker, and go outside the submersible. Tori volunteered as the better diver, so he thought, and made his way out of the craft once we detected the mound size and shape, we discussed from the data provided.

"We found it!" Tori announced on his communication regulator device, it was along with two thumbs up. The light cutting through the sediment kicked up from removing one of the first aluminum containers. After three and half hours of being in this confined space, we were on the target. I watched through the camera as he reentered the wet locker with the container. His air was replaced with a sleep induced cocktail.

Now my goal was a race to the surface, load the submersible and start the interrogation. Like most

Majestic Twelve section chiefs, he had bodyguards, anyone on the boat who was a male, would not survive this day. Seven of the crew members were my Reapers and immediately followed the plan by putting each crew member, including the captain, to forever sleep.

When I exited through the wet locker hatch, in hand was the metal box and a smile. "I need the winch," yelling to lift Tori out of the confined space. My Reapers were fast and disciplined through the next hour to prep Tori and disposing of the crew. With a total of twelve on the vessel.

"Wake up," Tori lethargically heard just before the atropine entered his system forcing his heart to jump from sixty to a hundred and eighty beats per minute. "I'm up. Holy shit that hurt. Where am I. Why am I tied down? Why can't I see?" He muttered, now naked after his dive suit was cut away exposing scares and burns from a different life. One before heading up the planning section for the Order.

With a gyroscope keeping the floor from moving with the waves, Tina and Erin then placed a large white sheet over him so he could feel the sensation of being in a hospital bed. The smells and sounds mirrored a typical hospital. The paralysis he was feeling still gave him comfort as his shoulders and neck was dull but noticeable.

They were in a cargo container placed on the ship before leaving the Quebec City port a month ago. The inside floor was on a computerized gimbal so no matter how the sea state changed, inside felt like dry land.

With a digitally masked voice modulator, Tina sounded like a man, "You were found floating in the water and immobilized for your safety." "Why can't I see?" "Your injuries seem to have impacted your vision. Don't worry, it will come back soon." Unknown by Tori, Tina had prepped him with black contacts only revealing the slightest of light to pass through.

"Where am I?" Tori was trying to catch his breath and get his heart rate down, not knowing it was impossible with the atropine now flowing through his entire body. Tina placed an oxygen mask over his face, "You are in a safe place. Relax, in a few minutes, the doctor will be in to get your information." As the oxygen entered his lungs, he began to slow his breathing and in forty seconds his pulse settled at ninety-five beats a minute.

Echo Romeo, also known as Erin, was carefully preparing her kit for phase three of this information exchange. As usual, there was the first phase to get as much information as possible with the target thinking the situation is as advertised. The next phase is to reveal this is a place under the Order's control and transition to carrot and stick hospital procedures to get the target to reveal more than before. Lastly, phase three is making the target believe that they are not trusted by the Order and things are about to get painful.

"Mr. Kilmer how are you feeling?" now the voice was a woman as an added relaxer. Tori's prior life was as a Reaper like me. He retired in the late nineties and was set on a path to be one of the twelve section chiefs. The muffled sounds were his response until realizing no one could understand him as a small dose of nitrous was added to the mixture. Erin then placed a hand on his shoulder, "It's okay Mr. Kilmer, you are in good hands, try to rest. I'll be back in an hour."

As the Reapers slowly and methodically started disposing of the bodies using a human woodchipper off the back of the boat, the small particles in the water soon brought schools of fish and within three hours all the crew was gone except my girls. I was leaving Lake Michigan, heading north and then east though the Huron and then south into the Erie then east into Ontario. The goal was not to sink her but switch our Automatic Identification System information with a similar sized ship who was headed into Lake Superior. This would give use weeks of miss information and coverage before blaming a computer error.

Over the last month, Control was hacking into the AIS and changing boat information to hide would be drug dealers from Coast Guard oversight. We surmised in our plan that the Order and Brody would be tracking the vessel but not risk communication until Tori contacted him with news. This afforded us at least three weeks before suspicions would cause a contingency and even reveal my intentions. Until now, Brody trusted me like a brother. As you know, this mission changed the game.

Ten minutes later, Tori was awakened by Erin, "Mr. Kilmer, are you ready to talk?" "Why can't I move?" "You were in an accident. We found you after discovering the ship was destroyed in an explosion." "What? When?" "A few weeks ago. You have been in a medically induced coma and now I need to know how your memory recall is so we can start working on your physical therapy."

Tori asked, "Am I going to get my sight and feeling back?" "Based on the cat scan shows swelling in the base of your scull and we feel this may be impacting some of your spine around C3 and T7. I'm confident your sight will return, and the paralysis will subside. You may have to do six months of PT but you're lucky to be alive." "Thanks Doc."

"Can I ask you some questions about the boat and what you remember before the accident?" "Yes. I was a member of a crew of twelve. We were tasked with retrieving an artifact from the SS Tucson." "Are you an archaeologist?" "No well yes. Not professionally, I'm an amateur but a professional diver. Wait, was I the only survivor?" "I'm afraid so." "I need to call my office to let them know I'm ok." "We can do that for you." "How do you know my name." "We know very little. Just what was reported from the Coast Guard." "Where am I?" "You're in Chicago."

Tori asked, "Please call Mr. Quinn Brody, two four zero two nine eight nine zero seven eight and tell them where I am." "We will. Now let's talk about your memory." "Ok. What do you want to know?" "Tell me what happen the last thirty minutes you remember." "My teammate and I were in a submersible, found what we were looking for and I left to get it. When I got in the submersible, everything went dark." "Anything else?"

Tori then paused and then said, "I think so." "Now tell me before you boarded the ship." "What do you mean?" "Tell me about a memory from three weeks ago?" "I was in Italy at the Vatican doing some research for my job." "Can you be more specific?" "Not really, my job has non-disclosure requirements." Erin injected his saline bag and in minutes he was asleep.

A few hours later, Tori was woken by Tina, who revealed she was a member of the Order, and needed to know what he divulged in the hospital. "Nothing, well, wait, I don't know. When are you going to get me out of here?" "Brody sent me, I'm your sister. Can stay with you until the transfer comes through. What did you do?" "I don't understand." "The last radio broadcast from the vessel said you locked yourself in your cabin and threatened to blow up the ship if they brought the artifact to shore. What was it?" "I don't know. What? I'm confused. I don't remember anything."

Passing out again for a few minutes, Tori was in and out of consciousness. Leaning in she said to him, "Brody sent me to find out what the hell you did. If you don't start talking, I'm going to reap you. Do you understand me?" "I do. I'll tell you anything." Knowing that his situation was completely in the hands of Tina, he divulged his work leading up to the accident." She continued to probe why and how he came find the artifact.

Control had enough information on Tori to allow Tina to circumvent the usual codes and passwords to get him to talk. Because of the secrecy of the Majestic Twelve organization, each sector had a protocol, but this had never happened before, and we knew this. Forcing Tori to use what Tina said to build the trust to find out what the Order was planning and the use of the artifact in the plan.

"It's not protocol to share this," Tori said. "Brody needs to know who else is read in if you don't make it. What's your succession plan?" Tina snapped back. "I need you to call this number." "Bullshit. Give me a name." "I want to talk to Brody." "You know better. He wants to tie this off. That is why I'm here." "Ok. Don't kill me. I want to see this through." "Tell me everything or don't. The Order will not allow one person to push out the End of Days." "Ok. I'll tell you everything."

"Grimm, this is Alpha," Tina asked. "Go Alpha," I said from the bridge. "We got it." "Was it torcher?" "No Sir. Never got to phase three." "Impressive. Dump him and we need to get this information to Control."

The decision to take Tori off the board had a cost. I didn't realize it at the time, but when Brody was read into Tori's disappearance to include a team of his men and I was named, he could no longer trust me. Even though I told him all were alive when I left them and delivered the wrong artifacts to Brody, he wasn't convicted.

What followed was his attempt two months later to have me killed by Kate Henderson. As a result, what I write next set me on the course now. A new mission, new enemy, and fighting the future.

COMPANY CLASSIFIED

TEMA GRAY SIDE
624 S Grand Ave
Los Angeles, CA 90017

DATE

01 JUL 2015

To: Mr. Grimm
From: Control
Subject: Scientific analysis of artifact

Once we opened the aluminum box, here is what we found.

1. A vial made of glass. Contents was the common cold.
2. Sumerian writing on tablets dating back to seven thousand years before common era.
3. A cloth with blood. Tested DNA. Matched with you. Relative.
4. Tree bark. DNA mapped. Fits no known species.
5. Three scrolls matching text from the Gospel of Ezekiel and Adam.

Glass Vial: The common cold is a viral infectious disease of the upper respiratory tract that mostly affects the respiratory system. Contagion may appear less than two days after experience. These are but not limited to headache, coughing, runny nose, sore throat, sneezing, and fever. Recovery in ten days to three weeks. Occasionally, those with other problems may develop pneumonia.

There are hundreds of virus strains with enteroviruses being the most common. Air transmission during close contact with infected people or indirectly through contact with objects in the environment. The symptoms of influenza are like those of a cold, although usually more severe.

There is no vaccine for the common cold. The primary methods of prevention are hand washing; not touching the eyes, nose or mouth with unwashed hands; and staying away from sick people. Some evidence supports the use of face masks. There is also no cure, but the symptoms can be treated.

The common cold is the most frequent infectious disease in humans. Under normal circumstances, the average adult gets two to three colds a year, while the average child may get six to eight. Infections occur more commonly during the winter. These infections have existed throughout human history.

The typical symptoms of a cold include cough, runny nose, sneezing, nasal congestion, and a sore throat, sometimes accompanied by muscle ache, fatigue, headache, and loss of appetite. A sore throat is present in about 40% of cases, a cough in about 50%, and muscle ache likewise in about 50%. In adults, a fever is not present, but it is common in infants and young children. The cough is usually mild compared to that accompanying influenza.

While a cough and a fever indicate a higher likelihood of influenza in adults, a great deal of similarity exists between these two conditions. Several viruses that cause the common cold may also result in asymptomatic infections. The color of the mucus or nasal secretion may vary from clear to yellow to green and does not indicate the class of agent causing the infection.

Progression: A cold usually begins with fatigue, a feeling of being headache, chills, runny nose, increased temperature, and cough. Symptoms may begin within twelve hours of exposure and typically peak in three days after onset. They usually resolve in ten days, but some can last for up to three weeks. The average duration of cough is eighteen days, and, in some cases, people develop a post-viral cough which can linger after the infection is gone. In children, the cough lasts more than 25 days.

SARS viruses are a group known for causing the common cold. They have a halo or crown-like appearance when viewed under an electron microscope. The common cold is an infection of the upper respiratory tract which can be caused by many different viruses. The most implicated is a rhinovirus.

Transmission: The common cold virus is typically transmitted by aerosols or direct contact with infected nasal secretions, or contaminated objects. The viruses may survive for prolonged periods in the environment for twenty-four hours and can be picked up by people's hands and subsequently carried to their eyes or nose where infection occurs.

Weather: The reason for the seasonality has not been conclusively determined. Explanations may include cold temperature-induced changes in the respiratory system, decreased immune response, and low humidity causing an increase in viral transmission rates, due to dry air allowing small viral droplets to disperse farther and stay in the air longer.

The seasonality may also be due to social factors, such as people spending more time indoors. Although normal exposure to cold does not increase one's risk of infection, severe exposure leading to significant reduction of body temperature.

Other: Herd immunity, generated from previous exposure to cold viruses, plays an important role in limiting viral spread, as seen with younger populations that have greater rates of respiratory infections. Poor immune function is a risk factor for disease. Less sleep and malnutrition have been linked with higher risk of developing infection following rhinovirus exposure.

Pathophysiology: The common cold is a disease of the upper respiratory tract. The symptoms of the common cold are believed to be primarily related to the immune response to the virus. It then replicates in the nose and throat before frequently spreading to the lower respiratory tract.

Diagnosis: The distinction between viral upper respiratory tract infections is loosely based on the location of symptoms, with the common cold affecting primarily the throat, nose, and lungs.

Prevention: The only useful ways to reduce the spread of cold viruses are physical measures such as using correct hand washing technique and face masks.

Sumerian writing on Tree of Life: Tablets dating back to seven thousand years before common era. We have translated the writing. It said the following. The gods who appear in the Epic of Gilgamesh are the Anunnaki, a name that means "those of royal blood" or "princely offspring" in the ancient Sumerian language.

Biblically speaking, the Nephilim were the descendants of the sons of servants of the Creator and daughters of men in Genesis 6:1-4. While there are differing interpretations of this passage, Control believes it involves the fallen angels, expelled servants of the Creator who took on human form and mated with the daughters of men, thereby producing a race of angelic-human half-breeds.

This is our connection between the Anunnaki and the Nephilim? It is interesting to note that both the biblical flood account and the Epic of Gilgamesh mention supernatural, eternal beings interacting with humanity in connection with a global flood. So, the Anunnaki originated in the reality that they were the fathers of the Nephilim.

Based on a piece of cloth with blood: Tested DNA. Matched with you.

Are you a relative of the Anunnaki or Adam? We don't know who the person is but have matched against Current DNA data base and 1.3 billion people alive today have at least 50% linkage to this person. Cloth dates to six thousand years ago.

Tree bark: DNA mapped. Fits no known species. Plan to recreate in the lab. Should have a sample in six months.

Three scrolls matching text from the Gospel of Ezekiel and Adam. Please refer to documented reference.

TEMA Gray Side Control

COMPANY CLASSIFIED

LXV

Bangor Maine OCT 2016
Counter Mission Charlie Hotel Kilo Five

Because of the close call in Central America, I knew Quinn Brody was on to me, but I didn't know how much he knew of my plan. Part of me thought he found me out, so it was time to tell my story. This first journal was started on four July twenty sixteen, these words are the firsthand accounts of me, code name Jonathan, for the last twenty-six years.

Book one is from nineteen ninety to nineteen ninety-four. This is one of many books I am writing to give a written account in case of my death. Rather than just give dates and facts, I'm going to tell a chronological story so all the people, times, and dates will match if needed. The sad part was I lived, and she was killed. My beautiful Annabelle.

With Matthew, my brother-in-law working most weekends, Jane and Jacob would stay with us. I remember one day looking out the window of my office and Jacob was played catch with Jane. Then minutes later, I heard his loud footsteps coming inside the house.

Then he knocked, I yelled out, "Enter," and Jacob came into my office.

At the front of my desk was a locked green footlocker. He stood on it to get a clear view of what I was doing. I said, "Speak to me lil J." He leaned forward putting his hands on the desk, "What are you doing?" Looking dead in his eyes I said, "Writing down all the ass kicking you will get if you don't get that drink of water and go see your mom." Jacob immediately jumped down off the footlocker and ran for the refrigerator. Less than a minute later, Jacob runs by my office door and yells, "UH-RA."

It was after receiving word from Tina, on Quinn Brody's movements, that he was up to something. Trying to decipher all the pieces that would give a date to a major impact to the entire world's economy, forcing major wars, and ending some of the Order's enemies by taking their wealth. An example of this is a new gold rush of oil in the United States and Western Russia, while the Middle East is weakening. Little did I know the steps Brody would do to change my future.

"Honey are we going to have dinner together?" Bella asked. "I need to drive to the Federal Building in Bangor and pick up some paperwork for a job next week," I said opening the trunk of the black suburban and verifying my credentials were there. "How about I meet you there at four o'clock and we walk to the Tarratine restaurant on Park Street."

I flashed back to the last time I shared a romantic weekend at the Tarratine. "Where are we going?" Bella asked. "It's a surprise," I said while opening her door. "What a gentleman," she said leaning over to give me a passionate kiss before entering the car. Our drive was scenic, taking the long way around from Rockland up through Washington, then route three to Unity. Lastly, a right on route two o' two into Bangor.

As we parked, she started to shake with excitement, "Oh my god, this is my favorite place. Are we going to play pool after dinner?" "We can baby." I said with a smile and then leaned over for a kiss.

After taking our seats for an early dinner we decided to eat outside, with a beautiful view of downtown Bangor. "Tell me about this place," Bella asked. "Ok, let me google it. This building was built in eighteen eighty-four to accommodate for the richest of the time in Bangor.

"The exclusive Tarratine Club members include former fifteenth U.S. VP and first club president, Hannibal Hamlin. Lincoln's running mate in eighteen sixty, was replaced by Andrew Johnson in eighteen sixty-four. Hamlin, later returned to Bangor Maine and was buried in eighteen ninety-one at the Mount Hope Cemetery.

"Originally made up of an elite group of local businessmen, this social club fostered business growth and encouraged the progress of social services in the local community. With a catering staff, offered fully stocked bars, and furnished games of pool and cards for members until nineteen ninety-one. A few years later, they renovated and reopened. This magical place offers a restaurant and a return to being a social club for members."

I was interrupted by our waitress, "Can I get you a drink?" "Yes, do you have prosecco," Bella asked. "We do. And you Sir." "I'd like a scotch neat." A few minutes later we were served and ready to order our dinner. "My wife would like, beef tenderloin for two. And I would like the lobster." "Are you going for the surf and turf." "You read my mind."

After dinner, Bella grabbed another flute of prosecco and went upstairs. I thanked the waitress and asked for a bottle to be brought to our room in a couple hours. "Are you coming, or are you scared?" Bella yelled from the billiard room. "On my way, baby," letting her know the bill was paid.

After a couple hours of billiards, I surprised Bella with more, "Are you ready for bed baby?" "I'm having too much fun and a little drunk," Bella exclaimed. "Let's call it a night. I have another surprise for you."

Walking behind the restaurant there was a path that led to a beautiful home renovated into the Tarratine Inn. "Are you serious?" Bella asked in total surprise. "Only the best for my girl," I said, steadying her as we walked up the many stairs to our room. Waiting for us was a silver platter on the bed with a bucket of ice, prosecco, and cherries covered in chocolate.

Located on French street, the downstairs was a spacious lounge area. With the bedrooms offering all the modern parts of a hotel with midcentury architecture. Later I read that this was the Stetson-Graham House and survived the Great Fire of nineteen eleven.

Placing the tray on the nightstand, she reached for me, and I grabbed her arm, spinning her around until she was in facing me. Running my hand along her back, I pulled her zipper down and her back cocktail dress fell at our feet, exposing all. She pulled on my tie, as I removed my blazer. Then she pulled my white shirt off my shoulders to match the pile forming around us.

Bella then fell back on the bed, with her legs still touching the floor. I joined her by taking a knee while removing my shoes and pants. She moaned and grabbed my hair steering me where to go before pulling me on top of her. This was the last time her and I were together before she died.

When I saw the explosion, my mind was not on any possibility of her being at the Federal Building. It wasn't until I arrived on scene with my credentials, her car was parked across the street. Damaged but recognizable based on her license plate cover 'Princess Bella,' then I knew all of this was meant for me.

Three days earlier I received a call from Brody, "I got a job for you in Western Russia." "Brief?" I asked. "In your office, it will be available at fifteen thirty, encryption key will only work until sixteen fifteen as per current protocol." "Roger that." "Jonathan, this one is special and could change the game in the future. I immediately thought of you for this." "Thanks. I feel honored."

My schedule was to leave Rockland at zero eight thirty and drive to Jane's place in Winslow. "You ready for company?" "I have to work today. Kids aren't at school today due to Columbus Day but us teachers still have to work." "How about I stop by the school and say hi." "Let me guess, you have another job out of the country?"

I answered Jane, "I can't get anything by you. It's tradition." "Well. Why don't you stop by later and see your brother-in-law and nephew?" "I can't. Scheduling a date night with my wife at the Lucerne Inn." "What a good husband you are. Don't know the last time Matt

took me out to a romantic restaurant or a date night."
"Not my fight. See you in a couple hours."

My visit with Jane ran later than I wanted, needing to take the back way to Bangor via route two o' two. I was on State Street, just cresting the Broadway hill when a large mushroom cloud and explosion could be heard as far as Veazie village. Looking at my watch, it said sixteen hundred. Traffic immediately stopped. It took me an hour to get to the aftermath. I remember, trying to call Bella's phone, and it went to voicemail.

I knew my phone was secure, Bella's phone was secure. My daily routine was to sweep the house and my cameras were now with facial recognition and linked to my phone via a cloud site. How did he get to her? I paused, thinking about what he was asking me to do. This was not about Bella; she was innocent here. He was trying to get me in that building. She must have waited in the lobby for me, she was always early and was collateral damage.

I then pulled an app on my phone that tracked Bella's day. Watching the time sped up ten times normal, she left the house at ten hundred hours. Went to the little market on the water, then the coastal route up to Bangor through Searsport and Verona Island.

I flashed back to a romantic lunch we had at Fort Knox State Park located on the western bank of the Penobscot River in the town of Prospect. It was built between in the mid eighteen fifties and the first built entirely of granite. It is named after Major General Henry Knox, the first U.S. Secretary of War and Commander of Artillery during the American Revolutionary War, who at the end of his life lived not far away in Thomaston. This place now serves as an entry site for the observation tower of the Penobscot Narrows Bridge that opened to the public in two thousand and seven.

My plan was simple, on her birthday, we would plan for a drive from Rockland the same way she went this fateful day. Taking the Ducati so she could enjoy the summer air. I had a picnic basket dropped off by Jane as part of the surprise.

Now looking at my phone, while waiting for the many first responder agencies arrived and taped off the horrific scene. I was allowed with my Defense Intelligence Agency badge to stay in my vehicle in the parking lot across the street, out of the way from the giant crater the explosion caused.

Flashing back, "Baby, this is amazing," Bella said, talking through her voice activated headset squeezing me tight as we moved through the twistiness and uneven roads created by winter frost heaves. "Hang on sexy," I said as we crested a hill at speeds that made the front and back wheel leave the ground for an instant and both of us felt weightless. "Where are we going?" "It's a surprise."

When we rolled into the gates to the park, I could hear Bella sigh, "What are we going to do here?" I paused to answer until we parked next to Jane who was waiting for us. "Oh, my goodness," Bella said scrambling to get off the bike and giving Jane a long hug. "Hey Sis. Happy Birthday," Jane responded.

Moments later, "What is this?" Bella said excitedly when I pulled a picnic collapsible basket from Jane's back seat. Thanking Jane, then taking Bella's hand and walked past a cannon to a dirt road just past the gift shop. With the large doors open, it almost seemed like a small open-air market. There was a horse drawn medical buggy leading to an amazing view of the Penobscot River.

"Do you want to walk or eat first," I said leaning in for a kiss. "Can we check out the fort first? Is this place haunted?" Bella asked. "I don't know. Let me ask." I walked into the gift shop and asked the staff member if I could leave the picnic basket and if there were ghost reported. "Absolutely and there have been sightings. Have fun."

"Tell me all about this place," Bella asked taking my hand and giving be a kiss. "Well honey, the war of the states never came to Fort Knox, however many volunteers from Maine, mostly recruits in training before assignment to active duty, manned the fort. Thomas Lincoln Casey supervised work on the fort, including adapting the rifled artillery batteries to use the recently invented Rodman cannon, and oversaw its completion.

"The Rodman gun like you saw when we were entering the park was designed by union soldier Thomas Jackson Rodman. The guns were designed to fire both shot and shell. These heavy guns were intended to be mounted in seacoast fortifications. They were built in from eight inch to twenty-inch rifled bore. All identical with a curving bottle shape and large flat cascabels with ratchets or sockets for the elevating mechanism.

"Rodman guns were true rifled barrels that did not have a howitzer-like powder chamber. The Rodman guns differed from all previous artillery because they were hollow cast, a new technology that Rodman developed that resulted in cast-iron guns that were much stronger than their predecessors.

"Later during the Spanish American War, a regiment from Connecticut manned Fort Knox. See the plaque?" I asked pointing to the item. "I do and it says a minefield was set up in the river during this war. After the war, the large garrison was reduced to one man, called the 'Keeper of the Fort.'"

I then continued, "But did you know that in nineteen hundred the fort received a permanent 'torpedo storehouse' for storing naval mines. And then fast forward to nineteen twenty-three, the federal government declared the fort excess property the State bought it for two thousand dollars for the hundred and twenty-five acres."

Bella then spoke up, "This fort is one of the best, I've ever seen. Reminded me a lot like the Quebec Citadel we visited." "I know baby," I said with a smile." "All of the fort is open to the public with several period weapons." "Follow me baby, I want to show you the torpedo storage shed and the Officer's Quarters."

After we walked back to the gift center, I grabbed the picnic basket. Pointing to the vessel wharf, "Let's throw a blanket out there and have lunch." "It's perfect."

After spending an hour laying on the large blanket, just below the main entrance nearest the water. We laughed, kissed, while watching the ships and clouds move around us. Those families who were also touring the site, tended to leave us alone so we had additional privacy on the point. Napping and drinking, Bella forgot anyone else was around. Emotionally speaking, that was an amazing day, one of thousands I will always remember of her, and she will be missed. Another victim of this life, being a Grimm Reaper.

"Control this is Grimm. Go," I said. "We found Victor. He was the name Mr. Brody gave after the attack. He pulled in the sources to make it happen." "Where is he?" "Transmission ten minutes ago, Panama City Panama." "I will reap him."

JONATHAN REAPER

COMPANY CLASSIFIED

TEMA GRAY SIDE
624 S Grand Ave
Los Angeles, CA 90017

DATE

01 AUG 2015

To: Mr. Grimm
From: Control
Subject: Location of site for craft

Summary: After ten years of research, we have found a cave located on Mount Ararat to house the craft. The site is between Turkey, Armenia, Iran, and Azerbaijan. The Mountain name comes from a Sanskrit word Arjanwartah, meaning holy ground.

Geography: With an elevation of 16,946 ft. The ice cap on the summit of Mount Ararat has been shrinking since at least 1960. There are 10 glaciers emerging from a summit. This is important because if the last major ice age happens after landing, it could trap the craft in the ice.

Geology: Mount Ararat is the largest volcano within the region. Along its northwest-southeast trending long axis, Mount Ararat is about 28 miles by 19 miles long. Mount Ararat consists of two distinct volcanic cones, Greater and Lesser Ararat. The western volcanic cone, Greater Ararat, is a steep-sided volcanic cone that is larger and higher than the eastern volcanic cone. Greater Ararat is about 16 miles wide at the base and rises about 1.9 miles above the adjacent floors.

Geological history: Recent volcanic and seismic activity by archaeological excavations, oral history, historical records, or a combination of this data,

REAP THROUGH THE END OF DAYS

which offer best guess evidence that volcanic eruptions occurred in 2500 BC, 550 BC, 1450 AD, 1783 AD, and in 1840 AD.

Archaeological evidence that explosive eruptions and flows from the northwest flank of Mount Ararat destroyed and buried at least one settlement and caused numerous fatalities in 2500–2400 BC. Oral accounts indicated that a momentous eruption in 550 BC and minor events in 1783 AD.

According to historical and archaeological data, strong earthquakes not related with volcanic eruptions in 139, 368, 851–893, and 1319 AD. During the 139 AD earthquake caused a large landslide that impacted many, there were casualties, and it was similar to the 1840 AD landslide on the summit of Mount Ararat.

An eruption occurred on 2 July 1840, caused a lava flow on the mountain with an associated 7.4 earthquake 10,000 people in the region died in the earthquake, including approximately 2,000 locals were killed by the landslide and succeeding debris and lava flow. In addition, destroyed the Armenian monastery of St. Jacob. The town of Aralik and other surrounding villages and dammed the Sevjur River.

Potential resting place of Noah's Ark: In the northeast, in the mountains above Armenia, shows a rectangular-shaped ark on the summit. In Genesis 8:4, many historians and Bible scholars agree that "Ararat" is the Hebrew name of Urartu, the geographical predecessor of Armenia; they argue that the word referred to the wider region at the time and not specifically to Mount Ararat.

Exact location: 39.7061198, 44.3049340 at 4,916 Meters. A cave has been located that can keep the craft. You are the only pilot cleared to fly it. Based on our estimates and your requirements, we do not feel any eruptions or glaciers will inhibit ingress or egress of the cave from Adam to the Present.

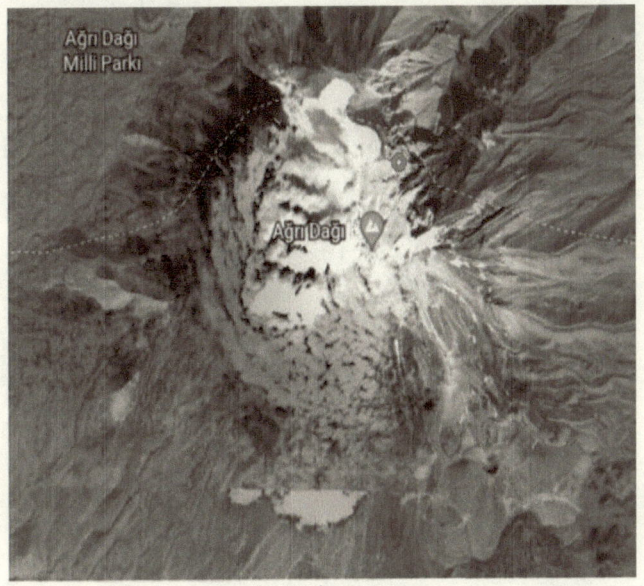

Red dot is the cave location.

REAP THROUGH THE END OF DAYS

BLACK HORSE

Jane gave Control the specifications for what could be her most exciting mission ever. Using our submersible, which was reconfigured from the original design. The goal was to make the vessel look and move like a Basilosaurus.

TEMA had recently hidden the craft at a warehouse outside of San Francisco Bay. Designed to fit into an elongated conex box, flown by a company acquired C-17 it could be easily shipped all over the world with our network of transportation assets. Along for the ride, Jane and Tom flew into the closest runway. They landed at the Van Ferit Melen Airport, unloaded the cargo, and launched the submarine in a moonless night. Because the target location was on a Lake in Turkey with depths of fourteen hundred and fifty feet, this seemed like the perfect setup. Another flawless mission plan by Control.

COMPANY CLASSIFIED

```
          TEMA GRAY SIDE              DATE
           624 S Grand Ave
        Los Angeles, CA 90017     01 JUN 2029
```

To: Mr. Grimm
From: Control
Subject: Location of Eden

Summary: Based on original accounts by November Romeo in twenty fifteen, with video, audio, and photographs. The access to the Garden of Eden is protected by a translucent dome 5,280 feet in diameter and 1,000 feet in height. This ratio keeps the dome free of sediment and allows for sunlight reflection. The dormant volcano provides heat to seventy degrees day and sixty degrees at night with thirty degrees of humidity. Every night it rains for one hour. The perfect terrarium.

November Romeo did not conduct any mapping of inside the dome. Only stayed at the entrance to validate access and environmental conditions. The code to open Eden is a Sumerian phrase loaded into the submarine that will subdue the sea monster and allow for access. The entrance is only five by five feet so additional equipment and supplies other than what can be carried is not advised.

Coordinates are 38.635631, 42.691983

Lake Van the largest lake in the Region and lies in the far east of Turkey in the provinces of Van and Bitlis. It is a saline soda lake, containing high concentrates of salts. It receives water from many small streams that descend from the surrounding mountains. It is one

REAP THROUGH THE END OF DAYS

of the world's few lakes with no outlet. After the Great Flood, Eden filled with water and by not allowing for an outlet, the river leading out dried up. This changed the direction and outflow of the Pishon, Gihon, Tigris, and Euphrates. Also, without the sacred waters coming out of Eden, the area south was less fertile and opulent.

Great Flood: Eden's existence becomes hidden from all time. Early writings always had Eden under a dome, protected from the world by making the place invisible. The membrane reacts to light causing the refraction of the surface to create an invisibility cloak over the entire garden. When flooded, sonar refracts and gives a depth much deeper than if made of a non-porous other worldly material. It is positioned at 5,380 ft in elevation. Despite the high altitude and winter highs below 32°F, high salinity prevents it from freezing at such times. Rarely the shallow northern section can freeze. The dome allows the oxygen molecules to come through and for an hour at night, water molecules cause a light rain on all the plants and trees.

Hydrology and chemistry: At 74 miles across at its widest point and an average depth of 561 feet, the dome hides the true depts by three miles. Surveyors have the deepest area at 1,480 feet. With 270 miles of shoreline and very little population, it is well hidden from man. The lake covers 1,450 square miles and contains 146 cubic miles of water.

The western portion of the lake is deepest minus the dome, with a large basin northeast of Tatvan and south of Ahlat. The eastern arm of the lake is shallower and warmer. The lake water is strongly alkaline with a PH level of 9.7 due to the salts.

Geology: Lake Van is primarily a tectonic lake, formed at the beginning of time and a perfect protected place for Eden. All other humans created lived hundreds of miles away and the mountains around created a perfect balance. The dome was an added protection by keeping the environmental conditions and a breathable membrane.

Lake levels: Section of north rim of the Sheikh Ora crater, showing old beach lines, drawn by Felix Oswald, 1906. Land terraces above the current shore have long been recognized. On a visit in 1898, geologist Felix Oswald noted three elevated beaches at 15, 50 and 100 feet above the lake then, as well as drowned trees. Research in the past century has identified many similar verandas, and the lake's level has varied significantly during that time. As the lake has no outlet, the level over recent millennia rests on inflow and evaporation.

Investigation by a team in the early 1980s determined that the highest lake levels of 236 ft above the current height. Mainstream scientists use the last ice age as a reference. The original scripture shows it was the Great Flood that shaped the planet we know happened approximately 9,500 years ago.

In 1990, an international team of geologists led by Stephan Kempe from the University of Hamburg retrieved ten sediment cores from depths up to 1400 feet. Although these cores only penetrated the first few meters of sediment, they provided sufficient data to show the area was created 14,570 years ago.

Similar but smaller fluctuations have been seen recently. The level of the lake rose by at least 9 feet during the 1990s, drowning much agricultural land, and now seems to be rising again. The level rose approximately 6.6 feet in the 10 years immediately prior to 2004.

Climate: It is in the highest and largest region of Turkey, which has a Mediterranean-influenced humid continental climate. Average temperatures in July are in the seventies and January in the thirties.

Ecology: Prior to 2018, the only fish known to live in the brackish water is a dace, which is caught during the spring floods. In May and June, these fish travel from the lake to less alkaline water, spawning either near the mouths of the rivers feeding the lake or in the rivers themselves. After spawning season, it returns to the lake. The fertile lands and shoreline offer many fruit orchards and grain fields, interspersed by some non-agricultural trees.

Lake Van monster: According to myth, the lake hosts the enigmatic Monster that lurks below the surface, 40 ft long with brown scaly skin, an elongated reptilian head, and flippers. Apart from some amateur photographs and videos, there is no physical evidence to prove its existence. The profile resembles an extinct Basilosaurus. Reports of the Monster surfaced in the late 1800s and gained popularity.

Transportation: In December 2015 the new generation of train ferries operated by the Turkish State Railways, the largest of their kind in Turkey, entered service in Lake Van. Ferit Melen Airport abuts Van. Turkish Airlines, AnadoluJet, Pegasus Airlines, and SunExpress are the companies which have regular flights.

In 2017, archaeologists from Van University and a team of independent divers who were exploring Lake Van reported the discovery of a large underwater fortress spanning 3,000 feet. The team estimates that this fortress was constructed during the Urartian period, based on their visual assessments. The archaeologists believe that the fortress, along with other parts of the ancient city that surrounded it at the time, had slowly become submerged over the millennia by the gradually rising lake.

TEMA Gray Side Control

COMPANY CLASSIFIED

"We hope you both enjoyed the flight," the pilot said to Jane and Tom as they deplaned. Unknown to Tom, still reeling from the lifestyle and toys at her disposal. She nodded to pilot and squeezed Tom's hand. They just spent twelve hours in an apartment located in the nose of the plane. With all the creature comforts of a sailing vessel except for the jump seats for takeoff and landing. They chatted about life and the reason for the exploration. He was trying to find a way in, she was too excited and preoccupied to notice.

Because Tom didn't have the bio technological interface to operate the submersible and dive suit, Jane needed to get a computer installed to run the suit. Heated, it could regulate body temp and pressure at any depth. At a comfortable seventy-two degrees and with no risk of the bends, both could walk the bottom. The innovative water jet system mounted to their back and would be my legs for the trip.

When instructed, the submersible would slowly come to the surface for five minutes and then drop underneath for thirty minutes. Or would sit dormant on the bottom of the lake. Jane and Tom watched from their dive suites as they could access the dry hatch under the belly of the beast. From there I had a one-person space to drain the water, get out of my gear, and now wearing a flight suit wandered the rest of the ship.

The boat designer created an encrypted signal within an artificial animal song to send digital communication to a satellite and then to the Reaper Operations Center or anyplace else. Receiving messages would be from directed bursts that mimicked magma displacement, and other natural sounds picked up by modern sonar.

This sea monster that sounded off like the clicks and whistles of a dolphin wouldn't work as an accepted "Known species in the lake, so we adjusted the sound to mimic tracked microphones of what the Loch Ness Monster.

"Control to Grimm. The following message is in burst form for thirty seconds." Jane responded, "Roger, please report when any of the ships are in a one-mile radius." "Grimm, more to follow as information becomes available. Control Out."

After receiving the message, Jane logged into the servers on the boat. With the limitations to outbound communications, she needed to rely on a new compression developed by TEMA. Also, I could monitor the mission. Also, the Artificial Intelligence, would send additional bursts of information on request anytime the submarine would rise to the surface to get a 'breath of air' to imitate our sea monster.

Another advantage to imitating a myth extinct animal was an adjustment of the dive time and depth. On average, the dives can be up to six hundred feet and last about fifteen minutes. However, they can be underwater for up to thirty minutes. With my research and past investigations from security, via my girls hacking into their system, I read and saw the videos. Most were personal watercraft traveling within five miles of the island and large fishing boats with certain times of the year.

Flashing back to three nights before the trip, Jane and Tom were working late at the hotel, prepping for the drive to Van. One thing led to another, and they were sharing a bed. After a long pause from the months of sexual tension leading to these hours of ecstasy, Tom spoke first. "How about we chock it up to two adults who are in good shape, have a connection, and want to see where this goes. Ok?" Jane smiled and put her head back on his chest, "Well said. Now stop squirming around, I need some sleep."

Now just before disembarking the submarine, this is what Jane told Tom to prepare him for the potential discovery. "Tom are you familiar with Genesis in the Bible?" "I paid attention in Sunday school class." "Well, what I am talking about has been argued since the Bible was first canonized. There are Two Creation stories. Most think it is one, but it is not. The accounts are similar in that they both describe the creation of animals, plants, and humans. But they are distinct in several ways and even contradict each other on key issues.

"For example, though the stories describe some of the same events, they order them differently. In Genesis one, the Creator makes plants, then animals, and then simultaneously creates man and woman. In Genesis two, the Creator designs a place called Eden for two special humans, designed in a controlled environment to be immortal.

"The stories are also quite different in literary style. The first account appears meticulously organized into three days of preparation followed by three days of actual formation. Each day concludes with the rigid expression 'And there was that They created.' I really like that the pronoun is They and not He." "What do you think it means," Tom asked, knowing the answer. "I think it is referring to the Creator and his angels who are Genesis one and just the Creator in Genesis two." "I get that."

Jane then continued, "If I was to give you the broad strokes of the Creation story, it would be that they can live in multiple dimensions. I think 'They' can be corporeal or non-corporeal. The angels in the bible are typically non-corporeal. The ones that are in corporeal form, like the watchers, cherub, or archangels, seem to be able to change when needed. This would be familiar to a medium or physic can see other dimensions to include the past lives and spirits."

Tom then asked, "So, you're saying the energy in everyone remains. Just transfers to another dimension?" Jane nodded, "I think the term Heaven and Hell is merely another place close the here, we can't see it. I think our dimension is built on solid matter. Our physical body charges the energy until it needs to be released to another dimension. Like adding fuel to an engine, it keeps running until something breaks. Remember in the Bible it never says we go to Heaven after death, only go after Judgment Day." "Then where do they go?" "Somewhere else, a place to wait until the End of Days."

Interrupting with a smile, Tom said, "So, the entire Big Bang to today was all due to a celestial all-knowing being that was bored?" Jane responded, "Very funny but it makes sense. I don't have it all down, but I think of it like this. Our physical life and experiences fuel the soul.

"Over time, the physical body breaks, like an engine, and the soul transfers to someplace else. If this keep happening, it keeps the energy moving. Another example is if water is stagnated, no movement of water in or out of the pond, eventually it will die, all the oxygen is used up. But with this movement, the pond flourishes and an ecosystem are maintained. I think this

REAP THROUGH THE END OF DAYS

is what we do for the Creator." Tom nodded, "I get that."

Jane then said, "Also, I need to better understand free will. If one third of the angels rebelled against the Creator, isn't that free will. There is something about human free will in the bible that is the key to all of this. I need more research." Tom then took her hand, "Hopefully Eden is the key you need. Will we find it?"

After they reached the gates of Eden, Jane stopped and explained the rest of the story, "By the seventh day, all creation existed in this place, and the Creator rested. They never intended for this to be a thousand feet under water. The story was supposed to be that Adam and Eve would have children here and life forever and the Creator would walk with them. Morningstar screwed that up.

"The second story that begins in the second half of Genesis and continues through the third chapter lacks both the structure and the focus of the first creation account. It is unorganized; rather, it is a dramatic narrative in a series of seven scenes. All ending with closing the gates to all. We will be walking through those gates today." "Are you kidding me?"

"We are going to map everything; I want the actual account of what happened. If anywhere has this, it is the

Tree of Knowledge and the Tree of Life. To know everything and to live forever. In its present form, the first creation account provides a prologue to the subsequent stories in Genesis describing humankind in the primordial era. Other topics include the fall of Morningstar, Adam in the Garden, the purpose of the oil from the Tree of Life, and a combination of majesty and anthropomorphism of the Creator.

"Here is what we are trying to prove," Jane instructed Tom, "Where did Adam and Eve go after they were expelled from here?" "I don't know but I'm listening," Tom said. "They made a tent and spent seven days in fear and regret. Being outside of Eden, food was not provided, it needed to be foraged. They searched but none was found.

"Adam and Eve pleaded with the Creator to provide them food because they were so hungry. Eve even offered to be martyred if it would fix Adam's expulsion. She was scolded by Adam, and they continued to wander east. When Adam did killed animals to eat, it didn't have the same sustenance as food in the garden.

"As Adam and Eve mourned the loss of paradise, they decided to fast while being emersed in the Tigris River for forty days. Adam's power over all living things came and surrounded him and the water. After eighteen days passed, Morningstar grew angry by what he saw and showed his true form to Eve. He instructed Eve to get out of the water and that she mourned enough. Hearing this, Eve left the water of the river.

"When Adam saw what happened, he cursed them both. Eve then cried out and asked Morningstar why? He responded by saying it was their fault he was kicked out of heaven and forced to roam the Earth. The Creator preferred man over angels. Therefore, it is the angel's job to protect man. Morningstar refused. This is what caused the great war in heaven. This is when man was given the power to dismiss any angel and as such have dominion and power over.

"When Adam and Eve conceived sixty children, he told them about the fall of man. He explained paradise and how they were created and expelled. Then they received seventy body afflictions like headaches, broken bones, infection, lacerations, and ultimately death."

Jane paused to see where Tom's head was at, "Is this too much for you?" He touched her hand, revealing his love for her in a gaze, "I would follow you to Hell or Eden, the why doesn't matter to me. I just want you to get the answers you need. Not too much on the history, just stopping the end of days."

Getting out of the submarine, Jane decided to leave the vessel outside the gate just in case something happened.

"I do have one question Jane," Tom asked. "Shoot" "Why does our vessel look like a Basilosaurus?" "Good eye, meaning 'King lizard,' it was fitting that a giant lizard would be watching the entrance and be the shape of their submarine. This large predator was first described in the eighteen thirties, as a prehistoric whale. Fossils were later found in nineteen hundred in Egypt, Morocco, Jordan, Tunisia, and Pakistan.

"Basilosaurus is considered to have been common in the Tethys Ocean. It was one of the largest animals of the Paleogene. It was the top predator of its environment, preying on sharks, large fish and other marine mammals, namely the dolphin-like, which seems to have been their predominant food source. Basilosaurus, unlike modern cetaceans, had various types of teeth—such as canines and molars—in its mouth, and it probably was able to chew its food in contrast to modern cetaceans which swallow their food whole." "So did you also freak out the people of Loch Ness?" "Very funny."

As they both entered the wet locker, Jane found the cave opening first discovered by November Romeo back in twenty fifteen. Jane and Tom's task was to map Eden, find the Tree of Life, take a sample, and any other significant artifacts. With Jane's new tech, she was the most powerful computer in the history of man. There had to be clues she would see that Naomi missed all those years ago. Before exiting the submersible, Jane used her tech to announce underwater in Sumerian the phrase to unlock the gates.

Tom looked a little freaked out when it came over their dive comm system. Moments later, as they left the vessel, and approached the area, there stood too large statues, who moved away reveling a cave opening. Also, a large reptile that looked a lot like their submersible, swam past Tom and Jane before disappearing in the darkness.

Based on the earlier writing, statues at the gate would morph into corporeal beings when the angels were guarding the entrance. Following the directions from Naomi, Jane used the translator to announce the words spoken in Sumerian, which opened the gates of Eden. Naomi wrote that when she got the transcription wrong the first time, a sea monster attacked her and the submarine.

The entrance was too small for the underwater craft, so Jane and Tom suited up, engaged the two-person wet locker, disembarked, and walked through the underwater cave to the precise gps location. What they found was a large mirror that was a refracted reflection of them. It didn't look like an entrance, more like a translucent membrane. Extending her hand, it disappeared through the doorway, forcing her to brace for an ever-slight pull. She paused, then looked at Tom, he nodded as to say, he had her back. As Jane took her other hand and reached for Tom, holding hands, they walked through the gateway.

Beyond the entrance was another world, a dome as was reported by Naomi with perfect environmental conditions. Looking around, seeing each other dripping wet and the weight of the gear caused both to take a knee. Immediately, they started removing the heavier items like the buoyancy device and weights.

At this moment, Jane thought this was truly her destiny, but why did she bring Tom along? Was it to have a witness, another gunslinger, or did she feel a connection to him that wasn't quantifiable? No matter the reason, she didn't want to be with anyone else for this adventure.

"Should we dare take off the rest of our gear?" Tom said before looking over to Jane. She was already removing her mask, fins, and wetsuit. He then said, "Well, I'm not ashamed to be your Adam. Will you be my Eve?" Jane smiled, "Shut up and get naked."

These two, just like those before, but with one caveat, Jane's a walking computer. With data processing at the speed of light, she could see measurements and material identification as a virtual reality overlay on what was in view. As she looked at the crystal path as wide as a single lane country road, the computer in her head measured the visual distance at a mile before disappearing over the rolling hills. Travelling through the various fields and patches of woods, was all documented to her biomechanical hard drive.

Before heading down the path, Jane reached down to and pulled from her dive gear five golf ball sized UAVs. Throwing them in the air, she could see and control them with her mind. Tom had no idea what was happening or how she was driving these futuristic little vehicles. Mapping everything, she could see five screens showing all of Eden; an experience much more than what he was observing.

Tom knew only what Jane had shared, basically that they were in a giant bubble, two thousand feet underwater, walking in a place that seemed foreign. Even though small parts of this place appeared to be built by aliens, he imagined an influence of Greece, Egypt, and Sumer even though he knew this was the oldest place on Earth. With statues and strange writing, he couldn't understand what it said but the writing looked familiar.

When she spotted the giant crystal castle on one of the UAVs, her walking turned into a light run with Tom trying to keep up. They both were in shock when cresting the hill and seeing the size and scope of this heavenly looking structure.

Walking toward the center of the dome, Jane's tech allowed her to see the curvature of the simulated sky, Tom couldn't, and he would constantly say this place didn't look real. Jane then stopped, still trying to multitask by moving and flying five UAVs while mapping all of Eden. When finished, she flew them back to where their gear was stored.

Immediately after disconnecting with the UAVs, she picked up on a wireless frequency originating from the large lone structure in Eden. In moments, she was able to connect, and in Sumerian, a banner came across her biotech, asking her to come to the castle.

As she got closer to the entrance of the large angelic structure, Jane saw through her tech hologram of perfect man and woman running through the fields, playing with what looked like a variety of farm animals but each looked perfect. Jane didn't bother to explain to Tom, she just watched as this place looked so much more alive back then. Now there was no animal life and the area around her seemed mildly unkept, like when she would visit her Rockland home after the winter.

Jane then flashed to another hologram scene showing a large bright human form about twelve feet in height pointing to the entrance of Eden. Around the deity were hundreds of angels ready for combat. With large white anodized metal wings, sword, helmet, kilt, breast plate, and knee-high combat boots in formation. In front of them, were two humans with hands bound and wearing animal skins.

What seemed like minutes and as though Jane was there when it happened, the condemned were marched out of Eden. When they tried to come back in, the gates were locked. Adam cried and shook the large black iron bars begging for mercy. Eve collapsed and cried with a shame that Jane could actually feel. Her nanites made her double over in pain, as though this video was interactive, and Tom ran to her just in time. She looked up to Tom, "I was here as Eve, I felt what she felt. A dread like nothing I've ever felt before. This was awful Tom, like being pulled from everything you loved and know." "I got you baby."

Jane then got her bearings and returned to her feet. Holding Tom's hand then walked to the castle. It was here, she told him what she could see and feel, "Eve and Adam first go East after being banned from Eden. Then they return to an area close to the gates, south near what is now Northern Iraq. Over time, and with the struggles of surviving without the Creator's paradise on earth, Eve, grief-stricken because of what she did, leaves Adam and goes West. She is weeping and crying the entire journey.

"Months later, and ready to give birth, Eve is alone. Jane is looking through the eyes of Eve, looking down and pregnant. She can feel that Adam is trying to find me." Tom, while holding Jane's hand says, "Are you really seeing what she sees?" "I can and Adam finds her after praying for the Creator's help. In moments many angels arrive to help her with the delivery. Cain and Luluwa are born, fraternal twins, and they return east to their home. The archangel Michael is then sent by the Creator to teach Adam and Cain how to farm and grow crops." Tom is surprised, "Genesis only talks about Cain. Who is Luluwa?" "I guess girls didn't count back then. I had, I mean she had twins. A boy and a girl."

"Then I am seeing a few years later, Eve has two more children, Abel and Aklia. Again, fraternal twins. As the children grow up, looking through Eve's eyes, she tells Adam that she dreams that Cain drinks the blood of Abel. Adam and Eve make Cain a husbandman and Abel a shepherd to separate them from each other.

"Eve's dream comes true as Jane watches Cain murder Abel. When the Creator is told from the angels what happened and confronts Cain, 'Now you are under a curse and driven from this fertile ground. If you try to work the ground, it will no longer yield its crops for you. You will be a restless wanderer on the earth.'

"I then watched as Adam tells Seth that by taking of the fruit of knowledge, he was flushed with visions of everything from the Fall to today. He could see Paradise is a place only for the righteous and a chariot with the Creator seated on it among angels. He was shown that the righteous who worship the wishes of the Creator, would be given a path to paradise. Also, the Creator promised him that knowledge will not be taken away from Adam's seed but without the Tree of Life, there earthly body will die.

"I am now flashing to when Adam is dying, feeling all the symptoms of sickness and anguish. He wants to bless all his sons and daughters before he dies. In trying to help Adam, Seth and Eve travel to the gates of the Eden and beg for some oil from the Tree of Life.

"Archangel Michael refuses to give them access to Eden as the Creator commanded. On their return, Adam is told what Eve did, "What hast thou done? A great plague hast thou brought upon us, transgression and sin for all our generations." "What happened next?" "I need a break from this. Please go upstairs and reconnoiter the rooms. I'll do the same down here."

With Tom now gone, Jane plays in her mind the rest of the story. She sees as Adam dies at the age of nine hundred and thirty and the sun, the moon, and the stars are dark for seven days. Adam's soul is consigned to the

Archangel Michael till the day of Judgment when his sorrow will be converted into joy. The angels assigned to earth and the Creator bury Adam and Abel's body in Eden. Eve has a premonition that she will die and assembles all her sons and daughters for her testament, predicting a double judgment of water and fire.

Seth is charged to write two tablets explaining the life and death of his parents. Six days later, Eve dies, and the Archangel Michael tells Seth never to mourn on the Sabbath. When finished, the tablets were put in the place where Adam used to pray, a cave called the Temple Mount. Jane can see where this is outside of Eden.

Then, after that day, the Creator told all the angels in heaven to never return to Eden. Jane saw where Adam, Eve, and Abel were buried. She walked out onto a large hill next to the castle made of emerald and jade. Looking over a ten-acre area, the short grass reminded her of a perfectly designed golf course fairway with three large stone monoliths at the crest of the hill. She could read the Sumerian writing with the three names, all their accomplishments, and years on the earth.

Each standing at least twenty feet high, she touched the surface and it felt like glass. In that moment, it was as though their entire life was a recording in the stone. Fast forwarding through their eyes, she could see from creation to death.

An hour later, returning to the castle, Jane captured information that could be downloaded or retrieved with a thought. Meanwhile, Tom had been watching Jane from the balcony. With the size and height of the castle, from this position, he could see all of Eden. Even the two trees mentioned in the bible. The Tree of Knowledge was a glowing yellow color, while the Tree of Life was the color of blue.

Jane looked up and waved at Tom who was still on the balcony watching her walk through the gate. He looked like only a small black dot against the castle's height of four hundred feet. The tall pillars made of large crystals surrounded the structure and created a white glow subdued throughout the living space. From the foyer that measure three hundred feet, the large spiraling staircase made of crystal created a cylindrical space all the way to the ceiling made of glass.

Unlike her last visit through the castle, she took her time, visiting the various rooms and hallways throughout the entire. It seemed to be built for two even though it's size could have housed a thousand people. She flashed back to the best resorts in the world, and none could compare to this place. From an Olympic size saltwater pool carved into the stone, to the furniture made from shaped crystal with animal skin covers, everything looked created from thought rather than built with tools.

What seemed like days, Tom looked up when Jane came through the door of the large master bedroom. Approaching her with a smile, both still naked, he touched her face as his other hand softly touched her lower back. Then without warning he grabbed her upper thigh and threw her onto the bed. A mattress made of woven animal skins with down feathers creating a king size pillow top comforter. It was then and for what seemed like an eternity, they became one.

What they didn't know at the time, because I left this out of the original report, is that in Eden there is no time. I held back this information because Jane and Tom would have stayed there forever.

Jane woke and slowly moved out of bed so not to wake Tom. He was still sleeping, gripping the sheets as though if he let go, would fall into the ocean, he was laying on his side facing the balcony. She thought about the bedding material that seemed softer than silk but heavy enough to be a weighted blanket. It was strange, all of this in Eden seemed as though it was designed from the Creator rather than built from man.

Jane left the room and walked back to the large glass control panel that could interface with her tech. Thinking this was like a theater size living room with polished white stone couches with animal skin throw pillows, she plugged into the system. Like playing another movie, she then saw visions of Adam's cave.

This place was where Adam stored all his writings and a detailed map of the region. Unable to access the technology anymore from Eden, Adam wrote down on tanned animal skins and ink from coniferous sap and soot from a fireplace. She watched as he documented everything he saw while visiting his banished son Cain and all the other tribes in the area were living. It seemed as though angels used UAVs to document what the world was doing, and it would download here in Eden. Like this place was a giant data center keeping a record when no one was here to witness notable acts on earth.

Written in Sumerian text, Jane could read what Adam was writing as though she was looking over his shoulder. The maps he drew were very detailed and seemed perfect in design. She couldn't help but feel as though these first people were not like the rest of the current population of the planet. It was as though the smartest men on earth were taken from their technology and marooned on an island to only use what they could build with their hands.

She then fast-forwarded through watched Adam's decedents. Showing cities built from tools smelted by metals from the earth. Things that were known but limited by the technology of the day. Jane thought to herself, "Is this what the Tree of Knowledge gave Adam's decedents?"

Jane then read what Adam wrote about the conflict of Morningstar and Michael. Immortal brothers who were at war with each other. She could then see that the cave was situated on side of a mountain below Eden, this is where the 'Book of Adam and Eve,' is located. More is shown about Adam, who lived to be nine hundred and thirty years old.

Flashing to the author was Seth, Jane could see him born after Cain slew Abel. Adam was a hundred and thirty years old when Seth was born. She was amazed how much he looked like his father, except a younger version. She watched how the descendants of Seth continued living and building large cities until the Great Flood. It seems that the angels recorded the actions of man up to this action entombed Eden under two thousand feet of water.

Next, was a redirect memory of the son of Seth named Enos. He moved his family from Shulon to Cainan, named after his son. Seth and Enos lived a thousand years. The land named after Cainan was another city that grew and grew as people who lived almost a thousand years had families in the thousands with expediential growth until five hundred million was covering modern day Europe to China.

Watching all these experiences in time like an unscripted movie, Jane created a map showing all the data she received from being in Eden, and the surrounding area. She also had a map of all the places tribes migrated West, East, and South from Cain. This was until the Great Flood, as she watched the earth lay waste most of the land mass, there was a mountain near the site that was safe from the rising waters.

Tom woke looking around the large room not able to find Jane. He smiled thinking of yesterday, and then flashed back to the first night they spent together, "I didn't expect the night to go this way," he said as he worked his way up from the horizontal to a sitting position while leaning on the pile of pillows against the large wooden headboard. Naked, she entered the large hotel bedroom with two cups of coffee, "Was there something I did last night that offended you?"

Reaching for the cup being offered, Tom said, "Not to scare you away, but for the first time, it was like you were in my head. It was the most amazing night I've ever had." "Well Tom, I bet you say that to all the girls, but if it's true, I'm glad you enjoyed it. Just know you are what I need right now and hope you stay around because our little adventure is about to get even more fun."

Jane walked back into the room where Tom was sitting up in bed still thinking about how he was falling in love. She was now able to read his thoughts, simply by finding the right frequency that was tuned to each person on earth. The closer she got to him, and like a radio scanner, she was in his head, seeing what he was thinking about… like now was the first night they spent together.

While Tom was sleeping, Jane had mapped all of Eden, took oil from the Tree of Knowledge and the Tree of Life, and had everything needed for the mission.

It was after her return; they walked the path back to where their dive gear was piled at the entrance of Eden. Helping each other get dressed, they were ready to enter the water and return to the submerged craft waiting for them outside the gates. She looked over her shoulder while walking along the bottom of the lake to the ship, Tom was smiling as though he had found his soulmate and was all in helping her through the end of days.

After making their way back to the submersible, Jane contacted the ship at the surface, "Control, I need the current time and date please." "Grimm, you have only been away from contact for thirty minutes." Jane was in shock. Tom couldn't hear what Control said. Also, Jane purposely locked her automatic download function. Even though she was able to download everything to the vessel hard drive. Control had no idea Jane had over a thousand hours of recording.

Jane looked at Tom with amazement, "There is no time in Eden?" Tom was in shock, "Are you kidding me? I left my watch here and thought it had stopped. What is going on?" "Trust me when I know, I'll tell you. Please don't repeat anything you did or saw until I figure this out."

On the flight back to Reno, Jane was too busy going over all the information in her head to speak. Although he was always near, she was preoccupied. Tom was conflicted on what to say or do while she was in this state of disengagement. He was patient and gave her the space she needed while also starting to process all he saw and did while in the Garden of Eden.

When they landed, Jane changed her attention to the next part of the mission. Her girls boarded the plane. "Please take Mr. Bloom home, I need to go to the office," Jane said. Then with an audience, she stood up and kissed him deeply and whispered, "I love you, Tom. Tell no one what you saw and when I have a plan, I'll get you and we will fight the future together."

Jane was honest but said to Tom what he needed to hear so there were no questions about her intentions. With a focus now on analyzing the thousand hours of video, both of us would use this information to figure out the next steps. "Control, please download my hard drive but it is encrypted no one has access accept the AI. I'm going the merge with it, seconds later she could feel her nanites making connections. Once the download was complete, she reached out to me... "I need your help."

LXVI

Bass Harbor, Maine JAN 2017
Counter Mission Zulu Charlie Papa Seven

My first clue. After revisiting the site, the signature was uncanny. Two weeks had passed, and the world wanted answers. As I conveyed the debris field now arranged in neatly identified boxes, the entire aircraft hangar was made up of color-coded tape separating each part of the plane.

Located at the Bangor Air National Guard base, my legend granted me unfettered access to areas of the investigation to find out who was to blame. Now being advertised as the worst terrorist attack since nine eleven, all the U.S. agencies were clamoring for a seat at the table. I just needed to know who did this from the Order.

"Ladies and gentlemen, thank you for participating in this investigation, while the FAA is diligently working with the NSA and the FBI to get our transportation system running again, we are here to validate what has been said in the news and hopefully find out who did this. My name is Thomas Ryan, lead investigator for the National Transportation Safety Board, all of us in this hangar will be conducting the events that led up to this disaster. I know all have seen the news, but we must put aside those unscientific views and focus on the evidence. Before I continue, does anyone know any of the victims shown here on my slide?"

All the people seated in the hanger, just southeast of all the wreckage neatly displayed on white tables, looked at each other around the space until a person stood up after raising his hand. Then immediately three others got up and walked to the front of the large stage made of cargo boxes and bed sheets. Each member of the executive team was seated with a corresponding name sign on the tables. Mr. Ryan gestured to the volunteers to walk to the side doors and one of his staff followed them. "Thank you for your honesty, please follow my colleague, so we can further vet you for this assignment or reassign back to your day jobs," Mr. Ryan said.

I looked at everyone else, trying to determine if they were lying or being honest. Since that fateful day, time had slowed down for me. Much had been talked about on the news and media about first this being a terrible accident and then changing a hundred and eighty degrees, when flight recorder data was leaked, and it was determined it was terrorism. That is what prompted the higher level of security and more usage of the FBI.

Screaming out load in my head, I knew a victim, eying the large wall filled with twelve-by-twelve-inch blown-up passport or driver's license photos. A separated background color of blue and red was meant to show those on the plane and in the building at the time of the crash.

Moving my eyes from the wall back to the stage. "I'd like to break up the teams, if your name is on a list and it's wrong, let me know," Agent Ryan said to the group. We are breaking the teams up into three parts, Investigation, Crash Restoration, and Evidence. I'd like to introduce Supervisory Special Agent Stevens, leading the Investigation Team. I will be leading Crash Restoration, and Agent Williamson will oversee the Evidence Gathering Team. Please get a copy of your respective plan, in it will be all the answers to your questions. If we missed one, let me know tomorrow. I look forward to working with all of you, see you bright and early tomorrow."

"So, who did you piss off to get this assignment?" Special Agent Michael Jasper said just low enough that I could hear him. Eying his name tag, I smiled, "Just seems I was at the right place, at the right time." "How's that?" "Just got off a counter terrorism stint in the middle east. Was waiting for my next assignment when this popped up and thought, what a great addition to the resume." "I want an SSA promotion, and this will solidify it. Lot of visibility."

I responded, "True, but if we can't find the bad guys, it won't look good for us." "I'll take that chance." "I gotta warn you, most of the time it will get pinned on some poor scapegoat that fits a bullshit profile and gets his life ruined on the international news." "Another Richard Jewel?" I said with a slight smirk to generate a response. "Yeah, but they won't be a local."

A few moments passed when I leaned back in responding to his hand gesture, "In fact, they are probably going to pin it on someone you were tracking in the desert," he said. "Good one, hey my name is Jonathan Gray," reaching out my hand to shake his. "Nice to meet you, I'm Michael."

A few minutes passed when he leaned in again, "Where are you staying?" "Here, grabbed up a bunk in the officer's quarters. What about you?" "That sucks. I have a little cabin about an hour and a half from here. Family home." "Nice, so you're from here?" "Not Bangor here. I grew up in the coastal sticks, migrated to Annapolis, Navy, then decided to slum it and become a G-man."

It was at this moment, thinking about all that had transpired, and playing the last five years with my mind movie. Why didn't I see this coming? As I relived all the events leading up to losing my Bella. The weird part was that I wasn't angry, just embarrassed that I never saw this coming. It was a classic military faint. You look right and there is something shiny, and to your left someone is punching you in the face.

Next, it was ironic that now, I was having a conversation with a guy who was on my list, and even though I don't know his role yet, he is one of the chiefs working for the Order. So, with the help of TEMA, I had his BIO days after the attack, now a month later, he was chatting me up like we were drinking buddies. Deep inside, I did feel as though Bella needed some level of justice, I would give her and the others who perished by making the person or people suffer for a long while before ending them.

Two weeks passed before imbedding myself into Michael's path. Before aligning myself with him, I needed to be the good widow and attend a formal memorial erected in honor of those who died that fateful day. I was not there as Special Agent Grey, but as Bella's husband and the son in law to her parents who drove up from New Jersey.

Bella's parents were in shock, as was my sister Jane, her husband Matt, and Jacob my nephew. All were there holding a rose. Waiting in line to lay a flower on a large space holding the remains of all the people who perished from the military tanker that crashed into the federal building. A travesty so unimaginable it carved out a small city in the Northeast into an unforgettable travesty.

When the terrorist attack happened that took the lives of everyone inside to include federal employees, local citizens, and the military crew on board. When the news first reported the event, it was first thought to be a terrible accident. The impressive thing about how it happened was that no one knew it was a simple action, meaning for it to look like an accident. No different than the thousands of assassinations the Grimm Reapers performed with no one knowing it was a name on a list.

The game I was playing was to keep Quinn Brody busy scrambling for an answer while not being able to focus on my infiltration of the crash investigation. In the back of my mind, I knew this could backfire if Michael got my picture in front of Mr. Brody. It was a chance I was willing to take.

My hope was that as a chief and not a trained Reaper, he would not lean on using the Order but simple research on his own as an FBI agent. My backup plan was a honeypot action that would turn into a rendition and termination. I contacted Tina who rented a home across the harbor to do surveillance and if needed, take action.

"Nice digs Michael," I said after opening the front door to this large home overlooking Bass Harbor. "Good thing for gps navigation, because my iPhone is as useful as a hockey puck out here." "I keep a Sat Phone handy but with Maine tree trimming lacking out here, my antenna doesn't get the half of the sky I need." "Always like those tv shows when the hero is calling in an air strike from inside a building." "Yeah, I call it the Jack Bower Magic." "Good one, here is a beer, follow me to why I live out here in the sticks."

Walking the muted hallway, through the kitchen, revealed a wall of glass overlooking two hundred and seventy degrees of crashing blue water ocean. "Wow, what a view," I said with an honest assessment. Even though it was dark outside, he had a wall of illumination across the shoreline and a view of a fifty-foot sailboat. "Does the boat come with the house?" "It does. Need a favor." "What's up?" "How about we drink tonight and tomorrow get the boat to Southwest Harbor, I dry dock it there in the winter but this year, fall came too fast."

I then responded to Michael, "You're right. In all my years sailing, I have never kept a boat in the North Atlantic this long. How did you know, I was capable?" "Oh, just a guess." "So couldn't help yourself. Doing a little cyber stocking, should I be scared or impressed." "How about a little bit of both. I don't invite just anyone to my fortress of solitude." My legend had me as an avid sailor with photos on Facebook and Instagram, courtesy of TEMA Control.

The following morning, I woke to the smell of coffee and bacon. Still drowsy, looked outside while laying on my side, the large window frame revealed low tide and an eastern view of the bay. The sun was bright, so I raised my hand and rolled over to view the room I stumbled into the night before. Michael and I drank way too much, trying to stay warm when huddled by a large wood fire wasn't enough.

The night's conversation was our careers, most notably his inability to conform to structured jobs while ending up in the FBI. I played to an accentuated version of my Facebook account, just in case he was more of a cyber stocker than I thought. Having a legend and knowing it, can be hard if you're not able to 'play the role' inside and out.

What I learned from his drunken rant and BIO, was a man in conflict. Even without saying it, participating in the event will change you. This is the death of over hundreds of innocents, involving thirteen countries is a heavy burden to carry. The worst of it was when it was leaked, this was not an accident, but terrorism in the worst way. The first time in history, someone hacked an airplane and crashed it into a 'target.' The outcry from pundits and news agencies was of blame and fear. This fed into what Brody and the Order wanted. Until justice was served and airplanes air gapped, travel is halted. Initially, background checks on all pilots with no access to flight controls through high frequency radio.

I would like to take credit for solving the crime before the Order could cover it up, but it would be a lie. It was Tina and my Reapers under TEMA, who infiltrated the crash site the day after and cloned the Blackbox. A small group of Order members hijacked a military HF signal, accessed the plane flight controls and made it look like someone else did it.

The Order wanted to copy a mission from the Pentagon where a Marine Corps Special Operations Training Group Team action. They were tasked to execute a year ago that resulted in crashing an Iranian military aircraft. A top secret mission that was never to be seen by the public.

When the news aired the burial of six senators and three military personnel in the Rotunda at the U.S. Capital building, some reporters commented on why they were all together at the Maine federal building. They were asked to be representatives of the United States for the signing of a new NATO agreement that would strengthen both our cyber security sharing but also more defined parameters when any NATO country could attack as 'one' in the event of a cyber threat.

In a leaked classified mission and twelve minutes of Blackbox footage showing everything leading up to the crash, it was reported as a scandal at the highest level. Then information technology subject matter experts, would validate the security weaknesses in High Frequency communication technology exposing most airlines in the U.S. and Europe. It was reported that fleets of aircraft were left accessible from the internet, leaving hundreds of in-flight craft at risk.

In the classified mission brief, it was proven that all transportation connected to High Frequency suggested ships, aircraft, military personnel, emergency services, media, and industrial facilities were all vulnerable—and is now able to demonstrate exactly how a plane's radios were hacked. One of the quoted parts of the semi redacted classified document was... "We successfully accessed the Iranian aircraft though their communications system from a ground terminal."

COMPANY   CLASSIFIED

TEMA GRAY SIDE   DATE
624 S Grand Ave
Los Angeles, CA 90017   10 OCT 2016

To: Mr. Grimm
From: Control
Subject: Results of the crash of Bangor Air National
          Guard Flight

Investigators first thought the crash was from a fluid
leak, caused by a defective oil supply pipe. This could
lead to an engine fire and subsequent uncontained
engine failure. As other engines also showed problems
with the same oil leak, the National Guard ordered many
engines to be changed, including about half of the
engines in the squadron. During the airplane's repair,
cracks were discovered in wing structural fittings,
which also resulted in mandatory inspections of all
aircraft of this design and subsequent design changes.

The KC-46A Pegasus is a widebody, multirole tanker that
can refuel all US, allied and coalition military
aircraft compatible with international aerial refueling
procedures. Boeing designed the KC-46 to carry
passengers, cargo and patients. The aircraft can
detect, avoid, defeat, and survive threats using
multiple layers of protection, which will enable it to
operate safely in medium-threat environments.

Width 156 ft 1 in (47.5 m)
Length 165 ft 10 in (50.5 m)
Height 52 ft 10 in (16.1 m)
Engines Two Pratt & Whitney PW 4062
Maximum Takeoff Weight 415,000 lbs

REAP THROUGH THE END OF DAYS

Maximum Landing Weight 310,000 lbs
Fuel Capacity 212,299 lbs
Maximum Air Speed 650 mph

Prime Contractor: Boeing
Service: USAF
Crew: 15
Passengers: 58

The Boeing-built KC-46 tanker is a military version of the 767 commercial aircraft. It is intended to replace the oldest of the U.S. Air Force's KC-135 Stratotanker fleet -- some of which are over 50 years old.

The KC-46A will be able to refuel any fixed-wing receiver capable aircraft on any mission. This aircraft is equipped with a modernized KC-10 refueling boom integrated with proven fly-by-wire control system and delivering a fuel offload rate required for large aircraft. In addition, the hose and drogue system add additional mission capability that is independently operable from the refueling boom system.

Two high-bypass turbofans, mounted under 34-degree swept wings, power the KC-46A to takeoff at gross weights up to 415,000 pounds. Nearly all internal fuel can be pumped through the boom, drogue and wing aerial refueling pods. The centerline drogue and wing aerial refueling pods are used to refuel aircraft fitted with probes. All aircraft will be configured for the installation of a multipoint refueling system.

MPRS configured aircraft will be capable of refueling two receiver aircraft simultaneously from special "Pods" mounted under the wing. One crewmember known as the boom operator controls the boom, centerline drogue, and wing refueling pods during refueling operations. This new tanker utilizes an advanced KC-10 boom, a center mounted drogue and wing aerial refueling pods allowing it to refuel multiple types of receiver aircraft as well as foreign national aircraft on the same mission.

A cargo deck above the refueling system can accommodate a mix load of passengers, patients, and cargo. The KC-46A can carry up to 18 cargo pallets. Seat tracks and the onboard cargo handling system make it possible to simultaneously carry palletized cargo, seats, and patient support pallets in a variety of combinations.

TEMA Gray Side Control

COMPANY CLASSIFIED

Two weeks later there was a news conference. "Thank you for attending today, my name is Thomas Ryan, I was tasked to oversee the investigation. Before I get into the cause and recommendations, I'd like to thank the hundred and thirty law enforcement and transportation experts who have been working tirelessly of the last three weeks to get to the truth. This is what we know."

I was in the audience behind the rows of reports and camera crews, in the back by the right rear of the hangar. The news would devastate the world and until a villain was revealed, there would be chaos in the world of aviation.

"We have determined the crash of the Bangor Air National Guard tanker was by rogue members of the United States Marine Corps. As shown here by verified and redacted classified documents, we don't know if they were acting under orders from the Pentagon or fringe group acting on their own. To date we do not know who the guilty are but there is to be an investigation by a joint congressional effort by Congress on the event. What happened and any punishment that needs to be carried out will be fast."

After Mr. Ryan opened the floor for questions, it was revealed how they accessed the aircraft through the communications system and took control of the plane. Then flew the plane into the Federal Building. The perpetrators, waited until the aircraft was refueled in Bangor, after take-off, in less than a minute moved the plane toward the target and let it continue through its new flight path and with the impact and fuel on board, the U.S. Federal building and surrounding area were incinerated. No bodies were found and the only way to identify the dead was from witness accounts, gps phone locations, parked cars, and manifests reported from the aircraft after landing in Bangor.

With the transportation industry changing as it becomes increasingly reliant on technology in this digital age, security has not caught up. From digitalizing the check-in-processes, to enabling communications access onboard, to enhancing air traffic management systems, airlines, airports and air traffic control systems have exponential innovations to improve operational efficiency and personalization for customers and employees. This also opens the door for terrorism.

With the speed of multiple frequencies for communications and data, also means that airplanes are exposed to a larger cyber footprint, allowing hackers more opportunities to access an aircraft's operating systems and interfere with satellites and digital technologies used by inflight systems.

Mr. Ryan then said to the world, "Based on our team's investigation, we can corroborate the information leaked to the press on the twenty first of October twenty sixteen. From flight recorder information, recreating the events of that day, and successfully stopping this from further impacting transportation communication in the future. I want to thank the National Security Agency and the Federal Bureau of Investigation, for getting to the truth."

I found out later, Brody didn't have proof that I killed his agent in twenty fifteen. He wanted to retire all the current Reapers and rebuild a new force. Quinn Brody wanted to recruit all the Tier one operators in the Marine Corps community to be his new overt Reaper Force jointly working with U.S. Agencies and the Order. Aligning his mission with the Pentagon, Fort Meade, and Langley. A group of paramilitary assassins to be used with no questions asked. All of this hid the real purpose for keeping his Reaper Force flush. The reason was that my girls were knocking off most his new recruits.

Days before the Marine Corps birthday, Brody leaked to the press a past classified operation where a group of SOTG Marines remotely intercepted an Iranian plane and crashed it into a submarine causing a massive explosion and a major loss of life event. The signature was exactly the same.

It was covertly released as a false flag operation so the Marines could blame Russia and China, destabilizing the treaty recently signed. During the investigation, it was further leaked that the Commandant of the Marine Corps approved the operation. After the dominoes began to fall, everything pointed to rogue members in the service. Rumors continue to point to string of assassinations of key power players in Washington. Each looked like a suicide, Brody passed the whispers among Congress members that Marine leaders were killing citizens.

It only took an hour to convene the Armed Service Committee in a secret meeting. Brody used false reports and missions in the hope of taking down the entire service. Days later and on the Marine Corps birthday, Congress voted to defund the Marine Corps, which would force disbanding them from the Department of the Navy. Most of the contracted members could choose another branch of service or an honorable discharge.

After the news reported the event in all its fanfare, I called Tina, "I need you to interrogate and reap this guy with prejudice. He won't open up to me, and we need to know how his family connects with the Order. In the incoherent ranting of this guy, his linage is one of the founding families in this area. I think the secret to getting him to speak the truth of his role in this travesty is by having a legend as a writer, anthropologist, and genealogist writing a book on the founding families of Mount Desert Island. This guy's ego is eager to give us some voluntary information and other stuff with a little persuasion." "I understand boss. Is he one of the assholes that caused this? And ending my friend Bella." "I know he is involved, but just don't know how much."

As Tina leaned in to take a sip of coffee, she glanced back at her notes for a book that would never get published. She continued to read just loud enough to get noticed by Michael. Sitting just three tables over, he glanced at her while raising the Bangor Daily News.

She continued reading, "Mount Desert Island is rich in geological history dating back about five hundred and fifty million years. The early work on the island wasn't fishing but quarrying granite. Fifty thousand years ago, MDI experienced the Laurentide Ice Sheet as it extended and receded during the Pleistocene epoch. The glacier left visible marks upon the landscape, such as Bubble Rock, a glacial erratic carried twenty miles by the ice sheet from a Lucerne granite outcrop and deposited precariously on the side of South Bubble Mountain in Acadia National Park.

"Other examples are the moraines deposited at the southern ends of many of the glacier-carved valleys on the Island such as the Jordan Pond valley, indicating the extent of the glacier; and the beach sediments in a regression sequence beneath and around Jordan Pond, indicating the rebound of the continent after the glacier's recession about twenty-five thousand years ago.

"Excavations of old Indian sites in the MDI region have yielded remains of the native mammals. Bones of wolf, beaver, deer, elk, gray seal, the Indian dog, and sea mink have been uncovered, as well as large numbers of raccoon, lynx, muskrat, and deer.

"A couple interesting events that were of note from continued research of the region. Although beaver pelts were in high demand across the Acadian region at the time, on the island they were trapped to extinction. Hundreds of years later two pairs of beaver that were released in ninety twenty by Mr. Dorr at the brook between Bubble Pond and Eagle Lake. This small act repopulated the mammal back to health number.

"Twenty years later a large fire cleared the eastern half of the island of its coniferous trees and permitted the growth of aspen, birch, alder, maple and other deciduous trees which enabled the beaver to thrive."

Approached by the waiter, she was handed a menu while waiting for her target to say something. She then read, "Some residents stress the second syllable in the French, while others pronounce it like the English common noun desert. French explorer Samuel de Champlain's observation that the summits of the island's mountains were free of vegetation as seen from the sea led him to call the island L'Isle des Monts-déserts meaning island of barren mountains.

"A village in Hancock County and within the town of Tremont on MDI, and near Acadia National Park is called Bass Harbor. With its well-protected natural harbor, it ranks as one of the most lucrative lobster-producing ports in the state. A lighthouse lies at the mouth of the harbor. The village is terminal for both the Swans Island ferry and Frenchboro ferry.

"Once known as McKinley in early nineteen hundred, when a post office was built in the village, federal officials asked what the post office should be named. Someone remarked, 'Name it after the president for all we care.' The post office was named, and the village was known as the same name until nineteen sixty-one when residents petitioned to change the name back to Bass Harbor.

"Six thousand years ago, the first written descriptions of Maine coast Indians were recorded. It wasn't until sixteen twenty, when the Europeans and Wabanaki Indians started trading. They called the island as the sloping land. They built bark-covered conical shelters and traveled in exquisitely designed birch bark canoes.

REAP THROUGH THE END OF DAYS

"Historical notes record that the Wabanaki wintered in interior forests and spent their summers near the coast. Archeological evidence suggests the opposite pattern; to avoid harsh inland winters and to take advantage of salmon runs upstream, American Indians wintered on the coast and summered inland.

"The first meeting between the Native Americans and the Europeans is a matter of conjecture, but it was a Frenchman, Samuel de Champlain, who made the first important contribution to the historical record of Mount Desert Island. Champlain led an expedition from the St. Croix Settlement. He was tasked with exploring the coast with twelve sailors and two American Indian guides. They were in search of a mythical walled and wealthy American Indian city named Norumbega.

"In sixteen oh' four the expedition crossed Frenchman Bay and sailed towards Otter Creek, where smoke could be seen rising from an American Indian encampment. During high tide the ship hit a ledge off Otter Cliff and while repairing a hole two American Indians boarded the ship as guides.

"It is not clear whether Champlain sailed around the Island or was informed by the guides, but on that day, he wrote in his journal, 'Le sommet de la plus part d'icelles est desgarny d'arbres parceque ce ne sont que roches. Je l'ay nommée l'Isle des Monts-déserts', which translates to 'The mountain summits are all bare and rocky. I name it Isles des Monts Desert.'

"In sixteen thirteen, French Jesuits, welcomed by Indians, established the first French mission in America—Saint Sauveur Mission—on what is now Fernald Point, near the entrance to Somes Sound. Saint Sauveur Mountain, overlooking the point, still bears the name of the mission.

"The French missionaries began to build a fort, plant their corn, and baptize the natives. Two months later, Captain Samuel Argall of the Colony of Virginia arrived to kill and capture these French citizens. Three were killed and three were wounded. The rest, some twenty in all, were taken prisoner to Jamestown.

"Captain Argall eventually returned to Saint-Sauveur and destroyed the Jesuits cross, replacing it with a Protestant version. He then set fire to the few buildings that were there. He then went on to burn the remaining French buildings on Saint Croix Island and Port Royal, Nova Scotia.

"The English raid at Fernald Point signaled the dispute over the boundary between the French colony of Acadia to the north and the English colony of New England to the south. There is evidence that Claude de La Tour directly challenged the English action by re-establishing a fur trading post in the nearby village of Castine in the wake of Argall's raid.

"There was a brief period when it seemed Mount Desert would again become a center of French activity. In sixteen eight eight, Antoine de la Mothe Cadillac, an ambitious young man who had immigrated to New France and bestowed upon himself the title sieur de Cadillac, asked for and received a hundred thousand acres of land along the Maine coast, including all of Mount Desert.

"Cadillac's hopes of establishing a feudal estate in the New World, however, were short-lived. Although he and his bride resided here for a time, they soon abandoned their enterprise. Cadillac later gained lasting recognition as the founder of Detroit Michigan.

"The island's maximum peak, at fifteen hundred feet, is the highest point on the eastern seaboard of the United States, and bears the name Cadillac Mountain, and is notable for the fact that its summit is among the first points in the United States touched by the rays of the rising sun.

"During much of the seventeenth century, nearby Castine was the most southern settlement of Acadia. Bristol was the most northern New England settlement. No one settled in this contested territory, and for the next a hundred- and fifty-years Mount Desert Island's importance was primarily its use as a landmark for seamen, as for example when John Winthrop, first governor of the Massachusetts Bay Colony, sketched the island's mountains on his voyage to the New World.

"During the Seven Year War, in response to the French Raid on Deerfield, New Englander Major Benjamin Church raided the Acadian village of Castine before gathering at Mount Desert Island with other ships to continue with the Raid on St. Stephen, Grand Pré, Piziquid, and Chignecto.

"In seventeen fifty-nine, after a century and a half of conflict, British troops triumphed in Quebec, ending French dominion in Acadia. With Indians scattered and the fleur-de-lis banished, lands along the Maine coast opened for English settlement. Governor Francis Bernard of Massachusetts obtained a royal land grant on Mount Desert Island. Bernard attempted to secure his claim by offering free land to settlers. Abraham Somes and James Richardson accepted the offer and settled their families at what is now Somesville.

"The onset of the American Revolutionary War ended Bernard's plans for Mount Desert Island. In its aftermath, Bernard, who had sided with the British government, lost his claim. Massachusetts, now free of British rule, granted the western half of Mount Desert

Island to John Bernard, son of the governor, who, unlike his father, sided with the rebels. The eastern half of the island was granted to Marie Therese de Gregoire, granddaughter of Cadillac. Bernard and de Gregoire soon sold their landholdings to nonresident land Creators.

"Their real estate transactions made very little difference to the increasing number of settlers homesteading on Mount Desert Island. By eighteen twenty, when Maine separated from Massachusetts and became a separate state, farming and lumbering vied with fishing and shipbuilding as major occupations. Settlers converted hundreds of acres of trees into wood products ranging from schooners and barns to baby cribs and hand tools. Farmers harvested wheat, rye, corn, and potatoes.

"By the time of the civil war, the familiar sights of fishermen and sailors, fish racks and shipyards, revealed a way of life linked to the sea. Quarrying of granite, which could be cut from hills close to deep water anchorage for shipment to major cities on the east coast, was also a major industry.

"It was the outsiders, artists, and journalists, who revealed and popularized this island to the world in the mid-19th century. Painters of the Hudson River School, including Thomas Cole and Frederic Church, glorified Mount Desert Island with their brushstrokes, inspiring patrons, and friends to flock here. These were the 'Rusticators.' Undaunted by crude accommodations and simple food, they sought out local fishermen and farmers to put them up for a modest fee.

"Summer after summer, the rusticators returned to renew friendships with local islanders and, most of all, to savor the fresh salt air, décor, and relaxed space. Soon the villagers' cottages and fishermen's huts filled to overflowing, and after the War, thirty hotels competed for vacationers' dollars. Leisure industry was becoming the major revenue for the state.

"Mount Desert, still remote from the cities, became a retreat for prominent people of the time. The Carnegies, Rockefellers, Morgans, Fords, Vanderbilts, and Astors chose to spend their summers here. Not content with the simple lodgings then available, these families transformed the landscape of Mount Desert Island with elegant estates, called 'cottages.'

"For over forty years, the wealthy held sway at Mount Desert Island, but the Great Depression and World War II marked the end of such extravagance. The final blow came in nineteen forty-seven when a fire of monumental proportions consumed many of the great estates on the island.

"In ninety hundred, George B. Dorr, disturbed by the growing development of the Bar Harbor area. Established a company to buy up six thousand acres. Dorr offered the land to the federal government, and in nineteen sixteen, President Wilson announced the creation of Sieur de Monts National Monument. Dorr continued to acquire land and renewed his efforts to attain full national park status for his beloved preserve.

"In nineteen nineteen, President Woodrow Wilson signed the act establishing Lafayette National Park, the first national park east of the Mississippi. Dorr then became the first park superintendent. In nineteen twenty-six, the park name was changed to Acadia National Park. John D. Rockefeller Jr. endowed the park with much of its land area. Like many rusticators, Rockefeller, whose family fortune was derived from the petroleum industry, wanted to keep the island free of automobiles, but local governments allowed the entry of automobiles on the island's roads.

"Rockefeller constructed about fifty miles of carriage roads around the eastern half of the island. These roads were closed to automobiles and included several vistas and stone bridges. About forty miles of these roads are within Acadia National Park and open only to hikers, bicyclists, horseback riders, horse-drawn carriages and cross-country skiers.

"In nineteen fifty, Marguerite Yourcenar and Grace Frick bought a house, 'Petite Plaisance.' in Northeast Harbor on the island. Yourcenar wrote a large part of her novel Memoires d'Hadrien on the island, and she died there in nineteen eighty-seven. Their house is now a museum. Both ladies were cremated, and their ashes are buried in the Brookside Cemetery in Somesville."

It was here Tina met Michael. After following him to the museum, Tina strategically placed a foot just outside the gift shop. As he walked by, "Excuse me," he said while regaining his balance. With her beauty and well-dressed attire for fashion and a Maine winter, she stood out. Within twenty minutes, they were sharing a bottle of wine at the Blaze on Main Street.

Later that day she shared her book notes, this led to him explaining how his family was aligned with the Champlain and Morgan ancestor. He then opened up with two bottles of wine about his wealth and being dragged into the family business. When Tina asked if it was law enforcement, he laughed and said it was something much less noble. She interrupted and talked about her selfish adventures around the world resulting in writing books and meeting interesting people. He invited her back to his home and into his bed.

When Michael woke in the morning on his back, he noticed being tied to the bed headboard with twisted bedsheets and a racquetball in his mouth. He could only moan, both naked, Tina was sitting on his chest making her first cuts into his upper torso.

Tina giggled as Michael looked at the ceiling of his bedroom, the mirror showed the letters TR as the pain was unbearable." Continuing to laugh, he moaned and shook his head as though it was time to talk. She then quickly grabbed a long acupuncture needle and drove it into his arm pit almost touching his heart. The pain caused him to shriek with agony. Tina then pulled it out, "No one can hear you scream fucker."

She waited as the tears ran down his cheeks. Then after the gag ball was removed, he was gasping for air until she took another needle and pushed in into his penis. Michael lunged forward and screamed, then Tina slapped his face. "Tell me about Brody and why he framed the Marine Corps?" His face changed, "Are you from the Order? Are you a Reaper?" She smiled, "I am, and they think Brody went off script, my job is to find out if it was him or you." "It was him! It was him!" he yelled. "Prove it bitch," she said. Minutes later, he spilled everything.

Tina's multiple camera angles and microphone location felt like I was in the room. "What do ya think Boss?" she asked knowing I watched the video. "Interesting approach and can you teach me the best needle locations the next time I need to get someone to spill their guts without leaving a bloody mess?" I asked. "It worked and based on the responses; it looks like it was Brody without permission from the Order."

I then asked, "What happened to Michael?" "Sailing accident. They found it burning near the town of Frenchbore on Long Island." "And you?" "Delta Romeo picked me up in the submersible and offloaded on our new Research Ship thirty miles offshore. Nice how you named it after your late wife. Very classy." "And that she was, I'll miss her very much."

LXVII

Hull, Massachusetts AUG 2018
Counter Mission Delta Charlie Victor Three

After weeks of tracking, Tina located her target. What she didn't realize was that this would take two off the board. With a long surveillance rotation to get a sense of the section five chief, she inadvertently caught a conversation with the section two chief. This included a location.

"Echo Romeo, she is coming to the car. Stand by," Tina said, looking through her thermal camera screen from across the street. She thought how the oldies were best for playing the 'eye' and Jessica Ramos was the 'rabbit.' Slowly pulling out behind the Uber driver, Tina was in a flower truck. She smiled while thinking how a nice touch was the silhouette of roses in the windows.

Using a 'man in the middle attack,' when Jessica called for an Uber, Control intercepted the app information and was able to switch drivers. Matching the description, it was an easy way to intercept those who thought the transportation service was hack proof. Also, for those Order members hiding in plain sight, this was the best way to get around the city without drawing attention.

"Ready to gas her in three, two, one," Tina said acting as a distraction by missing the yellow light and not stopping which forced the Order's protection car into a parking lot to avoid an accident. Echo then immediately headed down an alley into a warehouse. The electro activated faraday cage inside the car shorted out Jessica's tracking device, allowing them to disappear.

Like all the section chiefs and high value people in the Order. Looking in her side mirror, she could see the black SUV trying to go around the stopped traffic but was blocked by the intersection median. Just like they planned it. Tina then waited as more Order protection detail cars showed up setting a perimeter around a five-block area.

Meanwhile, Jessica was drugged again with an injection, a large piece of foil tape was wrapped around her upper arm. Then moving to another car and placed in the trunk, Echo drove to the city of Hull, where a safe house was set up for an interrogation. In the next twelve hours, Jessica had corroborated most of what we already knew but offered one additional detail before she died. Another section chief named Kelly Masters knew when the virus would be released.

A month later, looking across the road, Tina could see the waves crashing against the smooth soft yellow lines in the sand. This contrasted the weathered road on the ocean side of town. Looking for just the right spot and pulling beach gear with a cart, she looked like local. TEMA set up a summer rental to match her current legend as a historian, author, and North American anthropologist.

The beach Tina was enjoying in late July was located in Hull, a peninsula at the southern edge of Boston Harbor. With twelve thousand permanent residences, this place increases up to sixty thousand people in the summer. Feeding off her reason for researching Hull, this place has been a summer paradise for many influential leaders in American history like Calvin Coolidge and John F. Fitzgerald.

"Do you mind?" Tina asked the person set up at the end of the residential part of the beach just far away from congregated family units. Kelly responded, "Be my guest but I'm not here for conversation, just the sun." Holding up a book, "I just wanted to get away from those annoying kids and set up where it was a little quieter." "Then you found the right spot."

After twenty minutes of silence, Kelly couldn't help but notice Tina was true to her word and didn't even look up to make eye contact. Attracted to her and a little curious, Kelly spoke up, "How's the book?" noticing it was a historical account of the Massachuset tribe. Tina smiled and said, "Fascinating, I love this part of the country."

Kelly said, "Not the typical beach genre, initially I thought you were reading a scandalous romance novel with a hunky shirtless man on the front cover." "Not my gender of choice and I'm here for work," Tina said with a smile and a wink. "Really? What type of work do you do?" "I'm writing a book on this area and how it has influenced the world from Plymouth Rock to the Kennedy's." "So, what did you learn so far," Kelly said.

Sporting a white bikini with matching hat, Tina turned heads anywhere she went. "Do you mind if I move a little closer?" Tina asked. "Yes, I mean No please come on over," Kelly said with a smile. "I'm Tina Maxwell by the way." "I'm Kelly Masters." "Nice to meet you, Kelly." Sliding her beach chair and reposting her umbrella, she positioned herself so they could comfortably get the views of the beach while facing Kelly. Also, teasing her a little by shifting her hips and scissoring her long legs in the lounge chair.

"So here is what I learned so far. The Massachusett tribe are the original inhabitants of the New World when the Europeans first arrived. This covers much of the Boston area. A tribe genealogically aligned with the Algonquian, named as the Great Hill. These are the Blue Hills overlooking Boston Harbor at this time. Within weeks of first contact, the Massachusett were brutally devastated from leptospirosis. Can cause a wide range of symptoms, including high fever, headache, chills, muscle aches, vomiting, and jaundice."

Kelly interrupted, "Oh my goodness. When was this?" "Around sixteen nineteen. The worst part is that the mortality rate was ninety percent. This was followed by other epidemics such as influenza, scarlet fever, and smallpox." Kelly engaged in the conversation, "Herd immunity is hard when multiple viruses impact a population."

"So, you know about this stuff?" Tina asked. "Funny you say that. I am a virologist by trade. Grew up here and trying to unplug over the summer before getting pulled back into my lab in Fredrick Maryland. Wish I had your job, sounds fun." Tina complemented Kelly with a flirtatious gesture and request for suntan lotion. Giggling, "I can help you put that on." "Thank you."

After feeling the warm famine hands of Kelly on her shoulders, Tina continued, "With these native territories decimated and unable to populate, the English colonists took most of the land. When the tribe migrated to other fertile and flat coastlines in search of access to coastal resources, the English objected as trespassing."

Kelly asked, "What happen to them?" "Interesting enough, the English won over the native population with religion. Under the leadership of an early missionary named John Eliot, the remaining Massachusett converted to Christianity. They assimilated and submitted to the colonial laws. John learned the Eastern Algonquian languages and even created a translated Bible. By the eighteen nineties, the language was extinct. Most of their lands were sold and settled in with poorer parts of the area."

"Amazing," Kelly said drinking Tina's pina colada hidden in a large insulated sippy cup. "Did you like that?" she asked while licking her lips. "Tell me more about this place that is my childhood home and never knew." "I'll do my best. So, you are aware this area was called Nantasket, meaning the low tide place. This is several islands connected by sandbars forming a Peninsula. The original Plymouth Colony set up a trading post here to trade with the Wampanoags. Incorporated in sixteen forty-four, it was named for Kingston upon Hull, England."

"So that is why they call this place Hull. I never knew," Kelly stated while pouring Tina another glass. "Kelly, would you like me to tell you a little about your sister city in England?" "Please continue my sexy personal tour guide." "Oh, I like that. Kingston upon Hull is a peninsula in the Northern England area of the country east of Manchester. The area was settled because of access to a prosperous vicinity of freshwater rivers and the North Sea.

"The River Hull was a major hub for trading, in twelve ninety-three, King Edward I, acquired the lands and renamed the area King's town upon Hull. A hundred and fifty years later, a new charter incorporated the town with a mayor, sheriff, and twelve elected members of a municipal council."

Kelly said, "Incredible." Tina smiled, "In my prior research there were plenty of stories on a less official name of the area." "Oh, I like this," Kelly said leaning in on Tina and touching her leg." Tina raised her eyebrow, and pushed her lips together, "So the story goes, the King and his hunting party started chasing a rabbit which led them along the banks of the River Hull. Getting off his horse, he slipped on a wet root exposed on the trail and slide into the river.

"Laughing to himself and captivated by the moment, Edward sat there for some time until others found him. Watching the boats moving back and forth, fires and people could be seen along the river and an idea came to him. He needed to use this place as a major foothold on his kingdom.

"By marketing the area as a major trading outpost for the King, would bring safe and reliable revenue in his northern territory. Also, with more people making money, they are more likely to protect it against foreign invaders. Edward acquired the land from the Abbot of Meaux weeks later. After the purchase, the King had a manor hall built and bestowed upon it the royal appellation, King's Town."

"That's a much better story. You need to put that in the book," Kelly proclaimed. Tina chuckled loudly exposing her chiseled abs and major scare on her side, "I'll do that. Want to hear more?" "Yes. Please. How about over dinner?" "I would love that, Kelly." "Let's pickup and you can shower at my place, it's right up the hill." "Lead the way, I like the view."

After getting a wet and a change of borrowed clothes, Tina took the time to set up cameras and audio listening devices in key areas on the second floor. Kelly was setting the table when Tina walked down the stairs sporting a flowered summer dress that was transparent enough to make Kelly want more.

"Tina, come here," Kelly said reaching out for her hand. Leading her through two large white pocket doors and into an office with dark oak walls and two with ceiling high bookshelves. On the wall, behind her chair, was a patchwork of pictures and diplomas. As she looked at the old and new books carefully sized to make the room seem orderly but personal, most of the books were a history of virology with new and old editions. There was even a small lab in the corner of the room.

"You're a doctor?" Tina asked touching the frame showing she had a medical degree from Tufts University. "I studied medicine there, then residency at Mass General, before being a GP, I mean general practitioner for five years. My love for viruses changed my focus to doing research full time." "Very nice."

A few moments later, Tina commented on what seemed out of place in the room, "Nice chemistry set." Kelly laughed, "I am testing water samples from many areas around here." "Oh really," Tina reached down to touch the beakers. "Bad girl," Kelly said lightly slapping Tina's hand.

"After you," Tina said as they left the room. Then pulled two small cameras with audio near the lab and at the going in the room. She now had seven set up around the house. Last place Tina needed to look was the basement. This meant staying the night.

"Dinner was amazing Kelly. Can I clean the table?" "No, you can't Tina, but you can tell me more about my hometown." "Ok. Let us talk about some historic structures that are still here." Tina got out of her chair and took Kelly's hand waling to the large wrap around deck overlooking Quincy Bay. "Can you pour us a couple glasses of white and I'll give you the grand tour?" Kelly returned to the deck with the sunset off her right shoulder.

"Deal is a deal. So, in sixteen thirty-two, the Hull peninsula, was first considered by Governor Winthrop as an outer harbor defense for Boston. In sixteen seventy-three, an early warning beacon was established at Telegraph Hill to alert Boston of potential Dutch or French naval attacks. Then in seventeen hundred, the Telegraph Hill beacon is erected during King William's War to forewarn against French revenge for the New England's raids into Canada. In seventeen oh four, Telegraph Hill is a rendezvous camp for Church's northern expedition during Queen Anne's War.

"In seventeen seventy-five, Fort Independence is built on top of Telegraph Hill just prior to the War that separated officially separated loyalists and patriots. This was probably the first fortified by Washington's forces shortly after the conclusion of the siege of Boston. Sources suggest that an earthwork battery fired on the blockading British fleet in June. This work later saluted American Independence.

"A year later, the Committee on Fortifications reports that a ditched pentagonal fort with fifteen embrasures stood at Hull. Supported by two detached water batteries, the fort still needed a glacis, powder magazine, guardhouse, and several barracks. A military hospital was located near the fort and over five hundred troops and local militia were stationed at Hull's defenses.

"In seventeen seventy-eight, many changes happened to the fort. Chief engineer du Portail, was documented strengthening Hull defenses. Currently there is a cemetery with headstones of French soldiers who died of smallpox in seventeen eighty. Last reported note of use during the Revolutionary War was seventeen eighty-three.

"It seems that epidemics had a major impact through history around here," Kelly said. "I know. If they had a virologist like you, could have saved hundreds of millions of people." "I don't know if that's true. A girl like me who desires women over men would have been difficult." "I think you're beautiful."

Kelly felt a connection and moved closer, and they embraced. "Oh Tina, I haven't been with someone since med school." Tina touched Kelly's shoulder and slid a hand down her youthful and athletic frame. As she was touched over her dress, Kelly sighed and playfully bit Tina's ear lobe. "You are so sexy," Kelly exclaimed.

As Tina pushed Kelly away, it forced them to stop. Before Kelly could react, Tina ran her thumbs under the straps on her dress and it slowly fell to the floor exposing her naked body. "Oh my," Kelly said kissing Tina's mouth and then her neck and shoulder. Tina then spun Kelly around and got behind her. Pulling her dress off, Kelly was wearing a red lacey bra and panties. Reminding her of the Victoria Secret show opening model, Tina then said, "I'll be gentle unless you don't want that." "Follow me, I've got a whole drawer of fun in my bedroom.

"Good morning," Kelly said softly laying on Tina's chest with their legs intertwined. Tina ran a hand through Kelly's hair and kissed her head, "Last night was amazing." "We were good together. I felt so comfortable with you." "Me too." "Would you spend the day with me?" "I'm a writer. All I need is a place to plug in my computer." "Well, I don't have to return to work until the end of September." "Sounds like we have a few days together before either one of us need to figure things out."

"Control, this is Alpha One." "Go for Control." I am in the basement and have placed the radio transmitters, amplifier, and power supply. Do you have everything up?" After a twenty second pause, "This is Control. We have positive signal on all cameras." "I need Medical to verify the equipment in the lab. It looks like more than water testing."

Control said, "Roger that. We will review your iPhone recording sent and the live camera footage."

Tina responded, "Let Grimm know that on plan for the Mark." Drugging Kelly a couple hours earlier, gave her plenty of time to track for any foreign security measures. Tina was in a long-term cover role while I researched from the side lines.

"Honey, are you ready yet?" Tina said to Kelly waiting at the door. "I just need to change my shoes since you told me we were going to be walking everywhere today," Kelly said. "I'll be in the car." "I'll be right out."

Tina leisurely travelled down the brick walkway watching the typical sight lines as though someone was watching. A couple minutes later the passenger door opened. "Miss me?" Kelly said after opening the door. "Of course, I did baby. Ready for some fun," Tina said putting the car in reverse.

Glancing at her phone, Tina read the encrypted banner note saying that a package arrived at the agreed time. She thought how easy this life was now, it was instinctive, then flashed back to the first day she met Jonathan Reaper. So much had changed since then. Her ability to manipulate a Mark and change the course of the world was an adrenaline rush.

"Tell me about this place," Kelly asked. "Don't you remember the first day we met?" Tina said holding her hand. "I don't remember anything except that passionate night with you." "Well, let me give you a review but just the cliff notes.

"The site was first used as a fort in nineteen seventy-six to defend the port of Boston. The first telegraph tower was built in eighteen twenty-seven. Several other telegraph stations later occupied the site until the mid-nineteen hundred, when radio communications made the site obsolete.

"In nineteen hundred, the United States Government built a hundred- and twenty-foot height. At twenty feet in diameter, with a hundred and twenty gallons of steel water storage tank to serve Fort Revere. This now state-owned historic site and public recreation area occupies six acres on Telegraph Hill. We can visit the park including a water tower with observation deck, a military history museum, and picnicking facilities and is open from sunrise until sunset."

It was weeks later when I received the report from Tina. "Control, this is Grimm. Based on Alpha Romeo's report, need additional options potentially used by the Order to get their virus in the world.

COMPANY CLASSIFIED

TEMA GRAY SIDE   DATE
624 S Grand Ave
Los Angeles, CA 90017   01 AUG 2018

To: Mr. Grimm
From: Alpha Romeo
Subject: Nine Options for Distribution of Virus on
         World Population.

Summary: Based on what I found out from the interrogation, she said they have not decided the delivery system, just nine options.

Challenge: The Order will need to distribute the compound across the planet. This virus will alter our DNA and make it difficult for people to have children. The long-term effects are unknow or if like other viral interactions and herd immunity, a percentage will be asymptomatic while others with become barren.

Option 1: Virus in the drinking water. Through a current bottled water distribution company owned by the Order. Mount Katahdin Spring Water is the top-selling spring water brand in America in two thousand six with contracts for the military. The company sells approximately a billion gallons per year, with contracts for NATO and the Middle East. They will soon be selling in China and India. Best estimates are that it would take eight years for the entire population to be infected enough for DNA to be altered.

Option 2: Virus added to water supply. Viral Hydro Transference is a form of rain that binds with H2O, meaning that it has elevated levels of a virus over time. With more rain and for extended periods of time, the buildup would eventually be noticeable. The best delivery technique is the use of Chemtrails to seed the clouds. With a live virus binding to H2O molecules in the atmosphere, can live for weeks and easy access through nose, eyes, and mouth. Remember that Viral Hydro Transference is a classified term used by the Order. The USAF published a nineteen ninety-six report about weather modification. USAF wrote a paper called "Weather as a Force Multiplier. Owning the Weather in twenty twenty-five." The paper was presented in response to a military directive to outline a future strategic weather modification system for the purpose of maintaining the United States military dominance in the year 2025 and identified as fictional representations of future situations.

Option 3: Adding a virus to coffee beans. Caffeine reaches the environment via several means. Purification plants, sludge spreading, organic waste composting, and coffee in waste treatment. The alkaloid is now found in all freshwater environments and was the subject of several research to be utilized as a pesticide against frogs in the Hawaiian Islands.

Option 4: Adding a virus to water fluoridation. This process is the controlled adjustment of fluoride to a public water supply to reduce tooth decay. Fluoridated water contains fluoride at a level that is effective for preventing cavities; this can happen naturally or by adding fluoride.

Option 5: Attach a virus to a standard vaccine. A vaccine naturally comprises of an agent that resembles a disease-causing microorganism and is often made from weakened or killed forms of the microbe, its toxins, or one of its surface proteins. The agent stimulates the body's immune system to recognize the agent as a threat, destroy it, and to further recognize and destroy any of the microorganisms associated with that agent that it may encounter in the future. The Order could create a vaccine that will eradicate the virus but add a DNA alternating substance that would be untraceable unless a specific analysis.

Option 6: Attach a virus to an inactivated micro-organisms that have been destroyed with chemicals, heat, or radiation. Examples include the influenza, rabies, polio, and hepatitis A vaccine. Many of these are active viruses that have been cultivated under conditions that disable their virulent properties, or that use closely related but less dangerous organisms to produce a broad immune response. Although most lessened vaccines are viral, some are bacterial in nature. Toxoid vaccines are made from inactivated toxic compounds that cause illness rather than the micro-organism.

Option 7: Attach a virus to a DNA vaccination mechanism is the insertion of viral or bacterial DNA into human or animal cells. The DNA is injected into the body and taken up by cells, whose normal metabolic processes synthesize proteins based on the genetic code in the plasmid that they have taken up. Because these proteins contain regions of amino acid sequences that are characteristic of bacteria or viruses, they are recognized as foreign and when they are processed by the host cells and displayed on their surface, the immune system is alerted, which then triggers immune responses.

Option 8: Attach a virus to RNA vaccine, packaged within a vector such as lipid nanoparticles. Targeting of identified bacterial proteins that are involved in complement inhibition would neutralize the key bacterial virulence mechanism. While most vaccines are created using inactivated or attenuated compounds from micro-organisms, synthetic vaccines are composed mainly or of synthetic antigens, carbohydrates, and peptides.

Option 9: Attach a virus to vaccine plasmids has been validated in preclinical studies as a protective vaccine strategy for cancer and infectious diseases. However, in human studies, this approach has failed to provide clinically relevant benefit. The overall efficacy of plasmid DNA immunization depends on increasing the plasmid's immunogenicity while also correcting for factors involved in the specific activation of immune effector cells.

I surmise that Option 4-9 would be the easiest to implement and distribute only if a pandemic hit the world. Based on intelligence gathering, we think the Order is trying to develop a virus more contagious than SARS and killing less than two million People. If it becomes a pandemic, a respiratory vaccine would be easy to infect and populated first world counties. The Order would need the World Health Organization to get all areas with no unified healthcare system.

Alpha Romeo
TEMA Gray Side

COMPANY CLASSIFIED

"Control this is Grimm." "Go for Control." "I need to meet with Alpha Romeo." "Wait one." There was a long pause then Control responded, "Tomorrow, thirteen hundred, Telegraph Hill, Hull, Massachusetts."

Tina received the message to meet with me. She was reading the paper while sipping her dark roast coffee, holding heavy in the air. Taking a deep breath, sitting on the balcony in Boston Harbor. She noticed page six, reading under her breath, "Kelly Masters was found drown in Narragansett Bay."

LXVIII

Nasiriyah Iraq MAR 2019
Counter Mission Alpha Delta Xray One

Receiving the brief from November Romeo, Tina smiled, nodded, and continued, "Called corona virus twenty nineteen or severe acute respiratory syndrome two, this highly infectious cold virus would be the first of three phases to make woman and men incompatible to have children. The virus was developed in Antarctica under the direction of the Order, then weaponized in Wuhan China, and finally released as a highly transmittable and aerosolized delivery system.

"But this didn't just start in two thousand two when SARS first appeared in China. It was just the first successful test. When it did happen, it spread worldwide within a few months, though it was quickly contained. This virus was an aerosol when someone with the disease coughs, sneezes, or talks.

"No known transmission has occurred since two thousand four. Fever, dry cough, headache, muscle aches, and difficulty breathing are symptoms. No treatment exists except supportive care. This by design and was found and not invented.

"It is revealed that Saddam Hussain was part of the Order, and his job was to resurrect Nebuchadnezzar's palace for the Order to return too just before the fourth seal is release on the world. In trying to find lost artifacts, a vial called 'namtar' meaning death was discovered, transported to China and was mapped until it was understood how the Order could use it for the purpose of population control."

My girl, Delta Romeo also named Diane Roman, was tasked with finding the location, any additional artifacts, and then clean the scene. With pockets of civil unrest in the area between the Shia and the Sunnis, it was an easy cover up. As she made her way to the Great Ziggurat of Ur or known as the temple whose foundation creates aura.

Diane opened the door to her large white Toyota land cruiser and spoke in Farsi, she asked the driver if this was the Neo-Sumerian ziggurat in what was the city of Ur. This is near Nasiriyah, in present-day Dhi Qar Province, Iraq. In the twenty first century before common era, the structure was built during the Early Bronze Age but had crumbled to ruins by the six century BCE of the Neo-Babylonian period, when it was restored by King Nabonidus.

As she recorded the inscriptions on the walls of the large underground structure, her laptop revealed the translation of the ancient text. After reading she thought, how did the Sumerians have the understanding to know what a virus is?

COMPANY CLASSIFIED

```
       TEMA GRAY SIDE              DATE
       624 S Grand Ave
   Los Angeles, CA 90017      06 MAR 2019
```

```
To:      Mr. Grimm
From:    Control
Subject: Counter Mission Alpha Delta Xray One
```

S-1 ~~Tory Kilmer, Milwaukie, Wisconsin~~
S-2 ~~Jessica Ramos, Hull, Massachusetts~~
S-3 Quinn Brody, Bangor, Maine
S-4 ~~Timothy Hicks, Phoenix, Arizona~~
S-5 ~~Kelly Masters, Boston, Massachusetts~~
S-6 Thomas Shasta, Wright Patterson AFB
S-7 ~~Ginger Garner, Sacramento, California~~
S-8 Brian Burke, Washington D.C.
S-9 ~~Khaled Basmi, Sweimeh, Jordan~~
S-10 ~~Victor Cartwright, Central America~~
S-11 ~~Dorian Phillips, NYC, New York~~
S-12 ~~Michael Jasper, Bass Harbor, Maine~~

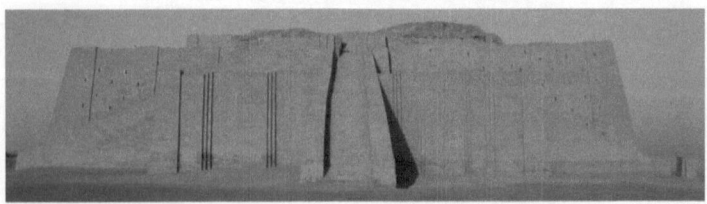

Information of interest: All the following is after the
Great Flood and the tower of babel incident. Before the
city of Ur, this land was called Enoch. Please refer to

REAP THROUGH THE END OF DAYS

information before the Great flood for more details. Once the ziggurat was completed it measured 200 ft in length, 150 ft in width and 100 ft in height. Elsewhere, buildings were integrated into the 26-foot ramparts. The Euphrates River complemented these fortifications on the city's western side.

Society and culture: Archaeological discoveries have shown unequivocally that Ur was a major Sumerian urban center on the Mesopotamian plain. Especially the discovery of the Royal Tombs has confirmed its splendor. These tombs, which date to the 25th or 24th century BC, contained an immense treasure of luxury items made of precious metals and semi-precious stones imported from the known world at this time.

Archaeological study of the region has contributed to our understanding of the landscape and long-distance interactions during these ancient times. Ur was a major port on the Persian Gulf, which extended much further inland than today, and the city controlled much of the trade into Mesopotamia. Imports to Ur came from many parts of the world: precious metals such as gold and silver, and semi-precious stones, namely lapis lazuli and carnelian. It is thought that Ur had a stratified social system including slaves. Tens of thousands of cuneiform texts have been recovered from citizens, local government, and religious temples. One item of note was a plaque located in the royal tomb. It depicts inscriptions of peace and a war. As a warning for all who come to the city.

Geography: When Ur was founded, the Persian Gulf's water level was two-and-a-half meters higher than today. It had marshland all about that made for excellent farming when irrigation was introduced. With a large canal system could be used for all uses, from laundry to transportation. The bible is the first to mention the city and is a central theme in Genius. Once discovered, earlier writing was found. The First Dynasty of Ur seems to have had great wealth and power, as shown by the lavish remains of the Royal Cemetery at

Ur. The Sumerian King List provides a tentative political history and a system of government.

2600 BC: The first ruler in the Sumerian King List is the Anunnaki, a group of deities of the ancient Sumerians, Akkadians, Assyrians, and Babylonians. In the earliest Sumerian writings about them, which come from the Post-Akkadian period, the Anunnaki are deities in the pantheon, descendants of An and Ki, the god of the heavens and the goddess of earth, and their primary function was to decree the fates of humanity.

They appear to have lived in the 26th century BC. That Ur was an important urban center already then is the reason why many type cylinder seal called the City Seals were found. These seals contain a set of proto-cuneiform signs which is texts or ciphers of the name of city-states in ancient Mesopotamia. Many of these seals have been found in Ur, to inside a large body of cuneiform documents, mostly from the empire of the so-called Third Dynasty of Ur or the Sumerian Empire, appears at the very end of the third millennium. Considered an advanced society for the time, the centralized bureaucratic state would have been at the center of trade and writing. Ur came under the control of the Akkadian who had entered Mesopotamia in 3000 BC, gained ascendancy over the Sumerians, and indeed much of the ancient Near East.

2047 BC: The third dynasty was established when the king Ur-Nammu created temples, including the Ziggurat. Agriculture innovations improved through advanced irrigation. An addition to this dynasty is a list laws found called the Code of Ur-Nammu is one of the oldest such documents known.

2030 BC: According to one estimate, Ur was the largest city in the world at around a hundred thousand.

2000 BC: In the Book of Genesis Ur is mentioned as the birthplace of the Jewish, Christian and Muslim patriarch Abraham.

1940 BC: Shulgi is considered the greatest and last local king of the Third Dynasty of Ur, who solidified the hegemony of Ur and reformed the empire into a highly centralized bureaucratic state.

1800 BC: The city of Ur lost its political power after the demise of the Third Dynasty. Nevertheless, its important position which kept on providing access to the Persian Gulf ensured the ongoing economic importance of the city during the second millennium BC. The city is consumed by Babylonia which rose to prominence in southern Mesopotamia.

1600 BC: The Kassite Dynastic period begins, along with the rest of Babylonia.

1400 BC: Elamites and the Middle Assyrian Empire came to be.

850 BC: The biblical Ur is mentioned four times in the Old Testament. The Chaldeans had settled in the vicinity by around 850 BC but were not extant anywhere in Mesopotamia during the 2nd millennium BC period when Abraham is traditionally held to have lived.

700 BC: The Chaldean rule Babylonia and held power only until the 600 BC. The name is found in Genesis 11:28-31, 15:7, and Nehemiah 9:7.

600 BC: The city, along with the rest of southern Mesopotamia and much of the Near East, Asia Minor, North Africa and southern Caucasus, fell to the north Mesopotamian Neo-Assyrian Empire. New construction in Ur was under the rule of Nebuchadnezzar II of Babylon. The last Babylonian king, Nabonidus, improved the ziggurat.

539 BC: In the four corners of the ziggurat's top stage, found clay cylinders bearing an inscription of Nabonidus, the last king of Babylon.

530 BC: The demise of Ur was from and lack of trade in the region. Reports indicate this is due to changes in

river patterns, and the silting of the outlet to the Persian Gulf.

1625: the site was visited by Pietro Della Valle, who recorded the presence of ancient bricks stamped with strange symbols, cemented together with bitumen, as well as inscribed pieces of black marble that appeared to be seals.

1849: Bricks are deciphered by the Order.

1850: The first excavation at the site conducted with the hypothesis that this was Ur. The ziggurat was a piece in a temple complex that served as an administrative center for the city, and which was a shrine of the moon god Nanna, the patron deity of Ur. The construction of the ziggurat was finished in the 21st century BCE by King Shulgi, who, to win the allegiance of cities, proclaimed himself a god. During his 48-year reign, the city of Ur grew to be the capital of a state controlling much of Mesopotamia. Many ziggurats were made by stacking mudbricks up and using mud to seal them together.

1853: The site was first excavated. The Order infiltrated the British Museum and with instructions to uncover the Ziggurat of Ur and a structure with an arch called the Gate of Judgment.

1872: Nasiriyah was founded and became the administrative center of the district. Commodities at the time included ghee, leather, and grain. The town contained about 600 well-built stone houses, but most buildings and homes were constructed from mud brick. There were about 350 shops in Nasiriyah as well as five 5 hotels. The area surrounding the town was abundant in date palms and grain fields. The town was not protected by a wall like other major administrative centers.

1915: During World War I, the British conquered the city, controlled at the time by the Ottoman Empire, in July 1915. Some 400 British and Indian and up to 2,000

Turkish soldiers were killed in the battle for Nasiriyah on 24 July 1915.

1920: Nasiriyah had 6,523 inhabitants. The population was ethnically diverse with Arab 72.7%, Jews 8%, Mandeans 9.7%, Persians 4.6%, Lurs 4.3% and .7% Christians.

1922: After World War I, preliminary excavations were performed by the Order based on a new find.

1924: Archaeologists discovered evidence of an early occupation at Ur during the Ubaid period 6500 to 3800 BC. These early levels were sealed off with a sterile deposit of soil showing evidence for the Great Flood of the Book of Genesis. It is now understood that the South Mesopotamian plain was exposed to regular floods from the Euphrates and the Tigris rivers, with heavy erosion from water and wind, which may have given rise to the Mesopotamian and derivative Biblical Great Flood stories.

1927: 1,850 burials were uncovered, including 16 that were described as royal and contained many valuable artifacts, including the Standard of Ur. Most of the royal tombs were dated to about 2600 BC. Found evidence of golden jewelry and pottery. There were a few Lyres that were inside of the tombs as well. One of the most significant objects that was discovered was the Standard of Ur.

1934: The city's patron deity was Nanna, the Sumerian and Akkadian moon god, and the name of the city is in origin derived from the god's name, UNUGKI, literally. The site is marked by the partially restored ruins of the Ziggurat of Ur, which contained the shrine of Nanna, excavated in the 1930s. The temple was built in the 21st century BC, during the reign of Ur-Nammu and was reconstructed in the 6th century BC by Nabonidus, the last king of Babylon. The ruins cover an area of 3,900 ft northwest to southeast by 2,600 ft northeast to southwest and rise to about 66 ft above the present plain level.

1980: The remains of the ziggurat consist of a three-layered solid mass of mud brick faced with burnt bricks set in bitumen. The lowest layer corresponds to the original construction of Ur-Nammu, while the two upper layers are part of the Neo-Babylonian restorations. The façade of the lowest level and the monumental staircase were rebuilt under the orders of Saddam Hussein.

1991: The ziggurat was damaged in the Gulf War by small arms fire and the structure was shaken by explosions. Four bomb craters can be seen nearby, and the walls of the ziggurat are marred with hundreds of bullet holes. During the 1991 Gulf War, Nasiriyah marked the furthest point to which coalition forces penetrated Iraq, with the United States 82nd and 101st Airborne Division reaching the main road just outside the city.

In March, following the American withdrawal at the war's end, the Shia population of Nasiriyah took part in the revolt against the rule of Iraqi president Saddam Hussein.

January – September 2003: Most of the treasures excavated at Ur are in the British Museum and the University of Pennsylvania Museum of Archaeology and Anthropology. The Order was successful in removing or replacing most of the artifacts before they were put on display.

March 2003: Nasiriyah was the first major battle of the invasion of Iraq. Led by 2nd Marine Expeditionary Brigade under the call sign "Task Force Tarawa" of the U.S. Marine Corps battle lasted 5 days and 18 Marines were killed and over 150 were wounded. Mostly due to a friendly fire from Air Force A-10 aircraft. The Iraqi resistance was defeated rapidly thereafter. The town has been calm since the fall of Saddam Hussein. A truck bomb killed 18 Italian soldiers and 11 civilians in November 2003, and clashes erupted here in April 2004.

2009: Iraqi team resumed archaeological work at the site of Ur.

2010: The Great Ziggurat is fully cleared and stands as the best-preserved and most visible landmark at the site. Also, the famous Royal tombs, also called the Neo-Sumerian Mausolea, located about 900 ft south-east of the landmark in the corner of the wall that surrounds the city.

Sumerian writing on many walls, some entirely covered in script stamped into the mudbricks. The text is sometimes difficult to read, but it covers most surfaces. Modern graffiti has also found its way to the graves, usually in the form of names made with colored pens. The Great Ziggurat itself has far more graffiti, mostly lightly carved into the bricks. The graves are completely empty.

A small number of the tombs are accessible. Most of them have been cordoned off. The whole site is covered with pottery debris, to the extent that it is virtually impossible to set foot anywhere without stepping on them; some have colors and paintings. Pottery debris and human remains form many of the walls of the royal tombs area.

2012: A Joint team of Italian and Iraqi archaeologists found an area once used as a trading center associated with Ur.

2014: The first updated survey was produced. A new aerial map by UAV.

Current information: Nasiriyah is a city in Iraq. It is situated along the banks of the Euphrates River, about 225 miles southeast of Baghdad. About 560,000, making it the fourth largest city in Iraq. It has since become a major hub for transportation. Nasiriyah is the center of a date-growing area. The city's cottage industries include boatbuilding, carpentry and silver working.

Mission: Brian Burke is going to this location to retrieve an artifact and recruit assets for the Order. This is the best place to capture and interrogate him. Once complete, he needs to disappear.

JONATHAN REAPER

Per your request, we reached out to Francis Underwood
to run the mission so Agent Alpha and Delta can keep
their cover. They will run interrogation.

TEMA Gray Side Control

COMPANY CLASSIFIED

REAP THROUGH THE END OF DAYS

"Boss, we found it," Tina said with a smile bleeding through the phone. "Is this the last piece?" "Yes, and being delivered to your site. What is it?" "A backup plan if everything goes sideways." "Thank you."

The artifact, in pieces and somehow placed in twenty separate sites around the world was combined to create what we believe is a time machine. A way for anything of matter to move through time. Never forward, only backward. A one-way trip because once something changes the timeline the future is different. The reason, when the timeline is changed, because there is no fate. There is a new future.

"Alpha Romeo this is Control." "Go Control," Tina responded. "Grimm wants us to infiltrate the life of Brian Burke. Currently in Washington DC. He is boarding an Air Force C-17 out of Andrews on Saturday." "Let Grimm know I'll be pulling in Delta Romeo. Please send standard ID package for both. NSA working in Nasiriyah." "Sending next day at your position. Control Out." "Alpha Romeo Out."

"Hello, two for Iraq," Tina said handing over Diane's and her passport to the Air Force Crew Chief standing on the Ramp. She said it just loud enough for Mr. Burke to raise his head. Looking at both and with a nod, he handed it back and called the pilots through his headset, "We got everyone. Ready to roll."

As Tina and Diane made their way to the high back seats attached to a cargo pallet, they made sure to sit behind Brian, so he could hear bits and pieces of what they said but with everyone wearing earplugs to combat the noise of the C-17 Globemaster.

It only took about an hour into the flight for Brian to stand up and gesture to Tina, "I'm Brian." "Hi there. This is Diane and I'm Tina." "I couldn't help but overhear that you both are headed to Nasiriyah?" "Oh, great our cover is blown," Tina said looking at Diane. "Well, should we throw him out of the plane here or over Europe?" Diane said with a giggle.

Brian laughed even though he could tell both ladies looked as though they could handle themselves in a fight. More so, he was instantly attracted to them, "Ladies, I'm on your side. I work for the State Department. We are practically cousins." "I know who you are Mr. Burke. We have been briefed," Tina said with a snarky smile.

"Wow. I didn't realize that was standard operating procedure for the NSA," Brian snapped back to keep his masculine card. Diane then blurted, "I need to use the latrine. I'll be back in a few." "Roger that," Tina said with an assertive tone that made Brian think all kinds of dirty thoughts.

"So, it's a long flight, do you want to help the time fly by and fill me in on your job in Nasiriyah? I have spent some time there, have local contacts that could help and maybe make your trip a little more productive." "Thank you for the invitation. Most of our tasks are classified, so if I tell you, then 'I have to kill you' clause applies," she said with a smile and then continued, "but the gist of it is we are in search of some illegal communication transmissions, find the source, and shut it down."

Brian started unreeling to the fact that these girls were here to shut down a major communication hub for the Order. He knew this because he was dishing out millions of dollars to contractors all over the middle east keeping communications flowing in preparation of their latest campaign, 'Operation Pandora.'

"So let me get out my phone and send some contacts," he said. "Well, if this is your smooth approach to get my number, I'm impressed." "I was hoping maybe the three of us could meet up, I'll be in Al-Kut most of the time on this trip but would like to see you ladies again." "Sounds good."

When Diane returned, walking by Brian, who was back in his seat. She noticed him watching a movie on his phone through a virtual reality head display. He looked up briefly and smiled before engaging again with his personal entertainment device.

Nothing else was said on the flight. Both Tina and Diana were communicating via their phones and Wi-Fi glasses. As Tina and Diane were going over the plan and contingencies, Brian was doing the same with his first call to Thomas Shasta, S-6 Communications, to warn him about the NSA's team and how he could help.

About a week went by when Brian reached out to Tina, "Hey there, still in country? I'll buy you both dinner." "Where are you?" "Outside of Nasiriyah." "We can be there in a couple days." "Ok, I'll be at the Gudea Hotel for the week. Let me know when you arrive."

Unknown to Brian, both had been tracking him since landing. Monitoring his mobile phone communication, travel, eating habits, and even a full electronic surveillance package in his hotel room to watch him sleep. With a little makeup and a hijab, both the ladies were invisible in a sea of similar looking women. They were waiting for the right opportunity to accomplish the mission.

"Control to Alpha." "Go for Alpha." "Grimm wants you to execute rendition operation on drive to Basrah tonight." "Roger, need comms blackout on 30.77835267711367, 47.60218858351782 for a three-mile radius and for thirty minutes. Need a commercial fishing boat, coxswain, rendition location also within three miles."

Tina had been following and reaping the Order since meeting me, one thing that was certain in her mind, the ability of these high-ranking members to move freely in plain sight made them vulnerable. Here again, it would be a simple extraction. The hard part was always convincing the locals to help so having a group of compartmentalized contractors was the key to success. For this job, we hired a friend of mine, Francis Underwood to complete the extraction and let Tina and Diane focus on the interrogation.

"Ladies welcome to the team," Francis said having worked with Tina before and remembering that time they mixed a little business with pleasure. "Thanks Frank, give me a status, walk Diane and me through the plan, times and locations, and lastly, how long we have for the interrogation." "Ok let's begin."

The extraction team was made up of twelve people. Tina noticed that half of the group were locals and the other half former tier one operators. Both women were in bourkas so not to be identified. They walked around with bottled water to hand out to the team. Invisible. All in a classroom style setup with a large projector.

Francis was presenting at the podium. As he spoke about each minute of the operation, those who were involved would raise their hand so Tina and Diane could see.

"Welcome everyone. T minus two hours to kick this off. For the benefit of the customer, we are using a car accident to extract the target. This is about fifteen miles from the hotel and would take about forty minutes with traffic. Before arriving in Al Hartha, our driver," Tina could see him with hand raised, "Will have a tire blow in front of the target, flipping the car, while being boxed in at the time with the other two drivers," Francis said. Then two other middle-aged men raised their hand.

Francis then said, "it will force an accident, and this is when the clock starts." A grey bearded man in good shape pointed to Francis, "What are the contingencies?" "If he is not grabbed here, we have a backup location event closer to the hotel but with more people and cameras, could get compromised." "Ok. Continue."

Raising the laser pointer to the screen, Francis was showing a google map view of the exact spot where the accident would happen, then showed a timeline from initial accident to ambulance that will be traveling back to the Al Moosawi Hospital. "We copied two ambulance crews in case we are stopped on the way to Nasiriyah. The target will be subdued, treated for injuries, and driven to Basra Oil. They have a hospital there we have been granted access with all the privacy of any interrogation site.

"Once there, we will set the area to look and feel like a real hospital. The rest of the staff will be playing along. You two have twelve hours before he is missed. The goal is to dump him in another room. So, no one thinks there was foul play." "If his car is tracked, what is the protocol?" one of the team members asked. "We plan to replicate the signal and bring to the hotel. The vehicle will be put on a flatbed, covered, and taken to a drop off site.

Because Brian, Tina, and Diane met, it wouldn't make sense to have them conducting the extraction or interrogation. However, with an earpiece and one-way glass or close circuit camera, the staff could be the face of the operation. Francis understood what needed to happen. Even though he was not read in on what or who the Order was, he had run hundreds of snatch and grab missions. Serving with me when in the Corps, it seemed like a good fit.

"Control, this is Grimm." "Go for Control." "Status update." "Target prepped and ready for interrogation." Alpha then said, "Clock started an hour ago. They have five more before the target needs to be back at the hotel." "Roger, Grimm Out."

After the extraction and interrogation, Brian was smuggled into the hotel through the laundry survey. When he woke, Diane and Tina were laying on either side of him. "What happened?" he said. Tina pulled herself on to Brian while kissing him deeply. Diane on the opposite side of Brian, grabbing his waist, "Can we go again or do you need to hydrate." "I don't know how I got here," he said still confused by the situation.

Tina received strict orders from me, "With the drugs he was under, won't remember the interrogation. Don't end him until he is seen at the hotel by others. Feels safe and in a happy place. Then when he disappears, the camera footage will look as though he ran away from his family."

Over all my years, I have learned before a drug induced interrogation that most people under threat of death or lost body parts will not work, if trained. Only by the verification of information and the threat of killing family will work. Tina was a master at this, with much research and photos of different pain points. From the examination, Brian admitted that he and Brody planned the entire event in Bangor.

I flashed back to the unforgettable day when the Marine Corps was disbanded. A big deal on all the major news media sites, they reported that Congress voted, and the president signed it. Disbanded on their two hundred and forty third birthday. I remember getting a call from Jane. An hour later, they arrived at the house. I had already started packing away all my Marine Corps momentous in my office.

REAP THROUGH THE END OF DAYS

LXIX

Wright Patterson AFB NOV 2019
Counter Mission Indigo Kilo Sierra Seven

"Control, I need everything on Thomas Shasta, S-6 Communications Sector for the Order. He has been promoted to lead MJ-12 after we reaped Brian," I said. "Standby Grimm."

A few minutes earlier, "I need to talk to you now," Tina said barely able to get the words out because she was out of breath. "Stop. Inhale, hold it, now breath again, relax and slowly exhale until there is nothing left in your lungs. Good. Now breath again. Are you good?" I asked.

Thirty seconds later, "I'm good boss." "Now what did he say Alpha?" "Brian revealed that Thomas signed the order to release the SARS-02 virus." "Who is Thomas?" "Thomas Shasta, S-6, he is now in charge of MJ-12. Well, what is left of it? We decimated their ranks to the point that only Quinn and Thomas are running the United States part of the project."

Tina responded, "Brian reported that the virus was meant to impact enough people to force vaccinations. This 'endemic' as he called it, will never go away.

Everyone in the world will be required to take the vaccine and a booster every year forever. The twenty percent who refuse will lose their job, not attend school, a public event, or restaurants. The plan had been established years in the making, what they needed was a delivery system through a series of vaccines to cause the end of days." "Tina, I need to get everything on SARS-02 projections and how we can stop the vaccines from impacting the world."

JONATHAN REAPER

COMPANY CLASSIFIED

TEMA GRAY SIDE   DATE
624 S Grand Ave
Los Angeles, CA 90017   01 OCT 2019

To: Mr. Grimm
From: Control
Subject: Likelihood of the Order using SARS-02 virus
and vaccine to infect the planet and cause the end of
days.

Summary: Based on SARS-01, the virus is likely to be a
more contagious and deadly infectious disease caused by
severe acute respiratory syndrome. It is planned to be
released in December 2019 in China. Current projections
show twenty-two million cases around the world
resulting in more than seven hundred thousand deaths.
More than fourteen million people have recovered from
the disease by July 2020.

Common symptoms will include fever, cough, fatigue,
shortness of breath, and loss of smell and taste. While
most people will have mild symptoms, 3% will develop
acute respiratory distress syndrome precipitated multi-
organ failure, septic shock, and blood clots. The time
from exposure to onset of symptoms should be five days
but may range from two to fourteen days.

The virus will be spread via airborne transmission, the
aerosolized droplets quickly evaporate, leaving even
smaller virus particles that can float in the air for
an extended period. The media will report initially
that it can only occur through water droplets and
surfaces for twenty days. This we be produced by
coughing, sneezing, and talking. The droplets usually

REAP THROUGH THE END OF DAYS

do not travel through air over long distances. However, those standing in proximity may inhale these droplets and become infected. People may also become sick by touching a contaminated surface and then touching their face. All of this will be said to prepare the population to shut down everything.

Later it will be reported that transmission will also occur through smaller droplets that are able to stay suspended in the air for longer periods of time in enclosed spaces. It will be mostly contagious during the first three days after the onset of symptoms, although spread is possible before symptoms appear, and from people who do not show symptoms. The standard method of diagnosis will be by real-time reverse transcription polymerase chain reaction from a nasopharyngeal swab. When admitted in a hospital, the chest computerized tomography imaging will be the go-to diagnosis in individuals where there is a high suspicion of infection based on symptoms and risk factors.

Projected timeline of the SARS-02 Pandemic: The outbreak of the virus, which will begin in Wuhan, China by the Order (this is based on interrogation notes from Brian Burke, MJ-12 former Leader.) It was created in a lab with the intent to kill twelve million people worldwide. This was needed to guarantee that everyone would take the vaccine when available. Start in December of 2019 and last through 2030. WHO will continue a vaccine regiment around the world until it is discovered that the vaccine is causing infertility. The world will blame multiple reasons for how this happened. Once it is revealed why the low birth rates, all three Pharmaceutical Companies are investigated and claim bankruptcy. At this point, it is too late for the world.

It is the mRNA vaccine that will infect everyone and cause a long-term depopulation event through twenty fifty. With schools requiring vaccines for all students, the below are the Artificial Intelligence Projects based on information received from Alpha Romeo and past data on public reaction to the following viruses released by the Order in the last fifty years. The goal being to prepare the country for this virus and accept the vaccines.

1920: The Order creates the first strain of Influenza. There is no agreement on the origin, but it is first publicly reported in Spain. It infects an estimated five hundred million people, roughly one-third of the world's population at the time, and kills some fifty million, with an unusually high fatality rate among otherwise healthy young adults. Many governments look to isolation measures, quarantines, and disinfecting efforts, but the global movement of troops hinders containment. In the United States alone, about 675,000 people die, lowering the country's average life expectancy by more than twelve years.

1923: The Order creates a new outbreak of cholera, a bacterial infection contracted through the consumption of contaminated food and water, begins in India at the turn of the century. The outbreak spreads to Russia, as well as to parts of the Middle East and North Africa, killing hundreds of thousands of people with particularly high death tolls in India and Russia. Advancements in sanitation and public hygiene are credited with preventing the pandemic from taking hold in Europe and North America.

1928: The Order creates penicillin, the first antibiotic. A class of drugs used to treat bacterial infections—marking a major milestone for global health.

1948: The Order creates the World Health Organization's along with the United Nations. The Order has used these two agencies to control large parts of the world.

1958: The Order figures out how to mutate the influenza virus, designated H2N2, is reported in Singapore. The Asian Flu kills more than one million people worldwide.

1961: The Order releases another cholera pandemic originating in Indonesia, spreads to other parts of

Asia, the Middle East, and Africa over the course of a decade, and continues to this day.

1969: The Order engineers a new influenza strain, and it soon travels across East and South Asia, then to Australia, Europe, and North America, and on to Africa and South America by 1969. US troops returning from the Vietnam War are believed to have brought the virus to the United States.

1980: The Order tries to weaponize Smallpox, a viral disease that plagued humans for millennia, is diagnosed in in Somalia, following a two-decade-long global vaccination campaign. Gaining a reputation of an ill-conceived organization, three years later the WHO formally declares it eradicated around the globe.

1981: The Order creates the first acquired immunodeficiency syndrome. This was the leading cause of death in men between the ages of twenty-five and forty-four in the United States. In 1996, the United Nations establishes UNAIDS to coordinate global action. The introduction of antiretroviral therapy helps to bring down the U.S. death toll, but the epidemic grows across Africa.

2001: Smallpox and Anthrax is identified as a Weapon of Mass destruction from Iraq. Created, weaponized, and information released to push the US into war in the middle east in order to acquire artifacts for the end of days.

2002: The Severe Acute Respiratory Syndrome, part of a family of viruses that commonly cause respiratory symptoms such as coughing and shortness of breath, is first identified in southern China. SARS spreads to more than two dozen countries across four continents, infecting more than eight thousand people. The Order failed to design a virus to infect more people.

2005: The WHO rewrites its International Health Regulations, rules originally drawn up in 1969 that are binding on all WHO member states. This was a way to refresh authority in combating a pandemic.

2009: The Order created a Swine Flu virus called H1N1 and commonly understood as originating from pigs, begins to spread. This virus disproportionately affects children and younger people.

2012: The Order changes the SARS virus to infect more people. Using DNA identified virus vectors, the Middle East Respiratory Syndrome, is transmitted to humans from camels in Saudi Arabia.

2014: In an attempt to cripple parts of the world, the Order releases polio to the unvaccinated, which disproportionately affects young people, proves hard to eliminate completely, particularly in conflict zones. WHO Director-General declares an epidemic over a rise in polio cases in Africa and Asia. Worldwide vaccination programs are restarted, and it becomes a major challenge.

2014: The Order releases the Ebola virus, a rare and severe infectious disease that leads to death in half of those who contract it, are detected in Guinea and soon after in Liberia and Sierra Leone. It is the first time the disease moves into densely populated urban areas, allowing for rapid transmission.

2015: The Order tests experimental Malaria bioengineered to kill specific populations. It kills 600,000 people, 2/3 of whom are children under 5 years old.

2015: The Order designs a new virus called Zika, thousands of women infected with the virus while pregnant and give birth to babies with microcephaly, a condition in which a child's head is smaller than normal, and other congenital conditions. Some governments urge women to delay pregnancy amid the outbreak.

2018: The Order reengineers the Ebola virus again and is the 2nd largest infection rate in history, international efforts rally to try to prevent the virus from spreading.

2019: The Order will release SARS-02 in nine areas around the Wahun Province. To confuse people, it will be given a different name by the WHO.

DEC: Hospital receives patient zero. The first person who is diagnosed is from the province of Hubei. After contact tracing is completed, he will be from Wahun. Seven other people will also be infected at the same location. Several new patients arrive in neighboring hospitals with the same symptoms. Originally diagnosed as SARS, many will be diagnosed as influenza. The early stages of the onset of the virus, there will be no clear evidence of how many people are affected. For this reason, information from Chinese authorities and those of the WHO report first fifty cases that are tested and are positive with SARS-02.

The situation will be unfolded rapidly. First, the Chinese officially report to the WHO of the possibility of a new virus but of unknown etymology. The information to WHO officials based in China will be that this disease had been detected in Wuhan, from the Hubei Province. By the time of the reporting, the ECDC supported that Wuhan Municipal Health Commission will be already handling cases with some in critical conditions. While reporting, the officials won't have information about how the disease will be transmitted, only that they will merely human-to-human infection. While that is the case, all patients with symptoms who received treatment will be placed under quarantine, as work to establish and identify the type of the virus and its origin began. The extreme will be if the who province is under quarantine.

Next is the United States reaction. With ambiguity on this, there will be data from different sources denoting cases with varying dates. Next, hospitals will continue to receive more patients with unknown pneumonia-like symptoms, the Order will push news agencies to lead with fear of an outbreak, also using social media vehicles within China. Brian Burke stated that the other Order members around the world will not know this is from MJ-12. It is meant for a power grab and centralize authority here in the United States. To lead the Order in the future.

The recurrence of the word SARS and shortness of breath in the social media and will start to increase. While other cases will be misdiagnosed, over two hundred people in the province will be infected. Since doctors won't communicate, there will be no suspicion of this 'unknown' disease. With the possibility of an unknown outbreak, at that time, the concern will be to establish the transmissibility, severity, and other issues that may be related to this new virus.

Wuhan, an industrial city of over 11 million people, will be experiencing an outbreak of an unknown disease. Fears of this virus being spread in those social media platforms with some medical documents from a hospital in Wuhan showing that some people with the virus had agonizing deaths. Since there will be uncertainties revolved around the virus, panic will be building up around the perception that SARS-02 has emerged again. Following the spread of fear and how to escape quarantine, a hundred individuals will be arrested and imprisoned by the Public Security Bureau. This will trigger an eruption of media buzz in the Western World.

Outside China, its neighbors start to be cautious. Taiwan will be reported to immediately take the issue seriously and demanded the screening for any signs of pneumonia-like or flu symptoms for all individuals coming from China.

After rigorous probes, tests, analysis, and other medical practices, the Chinese authorities make a global announcement that they had successfully identified the virus, like the one associated with SARS and MERS. Prior to this groundbreaking discovery, the officials had two days earlier, ruled out that the virus they were dealing with will be either SARS or MERS, hence concluding that it will be indeed a new but similar virus. Upon its successful identification, it will be tentatively named as another name, but we will call it "SARS-02."

The identification will come after Chinese scientists isolate the virus from one of the patients quarantined. Initially, the virus will have a 95% homology with bats to convince the world that "mother nature" is to blame. SARS-02 and will be also greater than 70% similarity with the virus responsible for causing SARS. It will be also reported that the samples collected from the Wuhan market tested positive, thus confirming the fears that the virus came from an infected animal and not from the lab.

Beyond China, neighboring countries will be stepping up their health precautions. And when the samples are shared with other labs around the world, medical tests i.e., reverse RNA polymerase chain reaction test and then sequenced, the results are positive for SARS-02. Chinese officials will report to the WHO that they have finally identified the virus, and subsequently, the WHO will make the official announcement of the same information to the world.

The Order wants to kill the most medically compromised first. This is 3% of the world population in the first wave. The result will be mass panic for those over forty. Under forty will dismiss as an 'old person virus.' By resetting most government benefit systems i.e., social security to allow for a refresh in the welfare systems and retirement systems across the world.

FEB: An epidemiological survey will be sent out across Asia. The virus genome will be shared on www.virologist.org and uploaded other government accessible websites. In parallel, the Chinese Health officials will consider closing the Chinese laboratory that the infection may be from and destroy all documentation. China locks down the country.

TEMA Artificial Intelligence started mapping delivery systems based on travel. Civilian Flights are the fastest way to infect large populations across borders.

Top destinations would be at high risk following the airline travel of patient zero. From the research, those flagged are Thailand, Hong Kong, Japan, Taiwan, Australia, and the United Arab Emirates. This will cause for screening at all major airports in the region ones mapped by the WHO. Outside China, Japan confirmed their first case, a man in his thirties who had lived in Wuhan and traveled back to Japan on January 6. While in Wuhan, he reported to have developed a high fever, but it will be only days later, Japan confirmed first case SARS-02 positive. The man, now in a Japanese hospital, who had not visited the Huanan seafood market, recovered, and dismissed from the hospital.

MAR: Other countries, including the United States, will have confirmed cases. A cruise ships will be a major incubator for the virus. Projected to be thousands of travelers leaving infected countries are now quarantined, causing anger and violence. China executes any doctor who says the virus came from their labs. Rumors circulate key scientists have disappeared or died under unusual circumstances. One of many Chinese doctors who tried to raise the alarm, report died under natural conditions. Europe will start getting cases reported. This will be the first major outbreak as the number of reported cases in schools, sporting, cultural force closures. The Middle East will report less deaths than China, to reduce fears in the country. With social media everywhere, hospital staff will report in Iran. Weeks later Iraq, Afghanistan, Bahrain, Kuwait, Oman, Lebanon, the United Arab Emirates and one in Canada, were traced back to Iran. Latin America starts reporting cases. Projected that 3,000 killed from SARS-02.

APR: US declares a national emergency. This will release federal funds available to states and territories to combat SARS-02. Recommendations from the CDC pushes for lockdowns. India and Russia will admit they have cases and start locking down their county's boarders. More US money released to keep economy from collapsing. More states issued stay-at-home directives. While cases are over two million, deaths are only impacting those with immune compromised conditions.

The Order will use agents in the International Monetary Fund to warn that the global economy will be a Great Depression unless all countries print more money and give to the economy. This will continue until inflation hits.

Some restrictions in States go against the US Constitution. This will cause 10% of the population to pushback against government causing violence and murder. Gun and ammo purchases will rise by 300% due to Police not able to protect citizens from violence due to sickness and fear.

May: Predicted global death toll will surpassed 300,000. With 5 million sick worldwide, even though most counties don't report real numbers to the WHO.

Airlines will require passengers to wear face coverings and distance on planes. Stock in all areas related to travel are decimated. The Order buys stock when they bottom out.

All countries besides the US and China will start a global recession. This is due to printing money and spending it.

MAY: Protests dominate the news in at least 100 cities because of state restrictions. Also, a rise in suicides and violent crimes as most of the US is locked down.

JUN: SARS-02 hits Africa worse than the AIDS epidemic. Outbreaks ramp up South Asia and United States again with a new focus on outdoor gathering.

US mortality will surpass 500,000 due to any death where SARS is present will be the cause of death. Each hospital will get a federal government kickback on each SARS death.

The Insurance industry will start denying benefits to salvage budgets. And any treatment proposed already in circulation will be vilified with false data through the media.

Scientists will be paid by the Order to say the following. "SARS-02 will always be here, like the flu. Vaccines won't eliminate SARS-02, but we'll get yearly shots to ward off the disease and create a much milder course of infection."

SARS-02 Vaccine Timeline: The Order will slowly release to agents in all the major pharmaceutical companies a nontraditional method called Messenger RNA (mRNA) vaccines, the vaccine will teach cells how to make a protein that triggers an immune response if someone gets infected. When the vaccine is injected into the upper arm, the mRNA enters cells near the site of the injection and tells the cells to start making the same protein that is found in the SARS-02 virus. The immune system recognizes this protein and begins producing antibodies that can fight the virus if the vaccinated person is later infected.

It will be reported that this is safe and none of the vaccines interact with or alter your DNA in any way, and therefore cannot cause cancer. MRNA is not the same as DNA and cannot be combined to change your genetic code. The mRNA is fragile, so after it delivers the instructions to your cells, it breaks down and disappears from the body in about 72 hours. The mRNA never goes into the nucleus of the cell i.e., the part that contains your DNA.

Mission: TEMA Reapers infiltrate CDC, WHO, and pharmaceutical companies and stop the Order's agents so they can't release the vaccines.

Summation of what the vaccines can do and would make all women in the world with the following blood types unable to have children. Even though we don't know how they will do it, the AI thinks this is the best way to reduce the world's population.

TEMA Artificial Intelligence projects a set of numbers if we fail. All in millions. Current population numbers, SARS estimated deaths before vaccine and eight boosters, new population numbers after an 3.8% reduction due to birthrate drop.

2019 Population 7,674M
2050 Population 1,999M

Country (Populations)	2019 (M)	SARS-2 (M)	2050 (M)
China	1,439	86.36	369.06
India	1,380	82.80	353.85
United States	331	19.86	84.87
Indonesia	274	16.41	70.13
Pakistan	221	13.25	56.64
Brazil	213	12.75	54.50
Nigeria	206	12.37	52.86
Bangladesh	165	9.88	42.23
Russia	146	8.76	37.42
Mexico	129	7.74	33.06
Japan	126	7.59	32.43
Ethiopia	115	6.90	29.48
Philippines	110	6.57	28.10
Egypt	102	6.14	26.24
Vietnam	97	5.84	24.96
DR Congo	90	5.37	22.96
Turkey	84	5.06	21.63
Iran	84	5.04	21.54
Germany	84	5.03	21.48
Thailand	70	4.19	17.90

Country (Populations)	2019 (M)	SARS-2 (M)	2050 (M)
United Kingdom	68	4.07	17.41
France	65	3.92	16.74
Italy	60	3.63	15.50
Tanzania	60	3.58	15.32
South Africa	59	3.56	15.21
Myanmar	54	3.26	13.95
Kenya	54	3.23	13.79
South Korea	51	3.08	13.15
Colombia	51	3.05	13.05
Spain	47	2.81	11.99
Uganda	46	2.74	11.73
Argentina	45	2.71	11.59
Algeria	44	2.63	11.24
Sudan	44	2.63	11.24
Ukraine	44	2.62	11.21
Iraq	40	2.41	10.31
Afghanistan	39	2.34	9.98
Poland	38	2.27	9.70
Canada	38	2.26	9.68
Morocco	37	2.21	9.46
Saudi Arabia	35	2.09	8.93
Uzbekistan	33	2.01	8.58
Peru	33	1.98	8.45
Angola	33	1.97	8.43
Malaysia	32	1.94	8.30
Mozambique	31	1.88	8.01
Ghana	31	1.86	7.97
Yemen	30	1.79	7.65
Nepal	29	1.75	7.47
Venezuela	28	1.71	7.29

Country (Populations)	2019 (M)	SARS-2 (M)	2050 (M)
Madagascar	28	1.66	7.10
Cameroon	27	1.59	6.81
Côte d'Ivoire	26	1.58	6.76
North Korea	26	1.55	6.61
Australia	25	1.53	6.54
Niger	24	1.45	6.21
Taiwan	24	1.43	6.11
Sri Lanka	21	1.28	5.49
Burkina Faso	21	1.25	5.36
Mali	20	1.22	5.19
Romania	19	1.15	4.93
Malawi	19	1.15	4.91
Chile	19	1.15	4.90
Kazakhstan	19	1.13	4.81
Zambia	18	1.10	4.71
Guatemala	18	1.07	4.59
Ecuador	18	1.06	4.52
Syria	18	1.05	4.49
Netherlands	17	1.03	4.39
Senegal	17	1.00	4.29
Cambodia	17	1.00	4.29
Chad	16	0.99	4.21
Somalia	16	0.95	4.08
Zimbabwe	15	0.89	3.81
Guinea	13	0.79	3.37
Rwanda	13	0.78	3.32
Benin	12	0.73	3.11
Burundi	12	0.71	3.05
Tunisia	12	0.71	3.03
Bolivia	12	0.70	2.99

Country (Populations)	2019 (M)	SARS-2 (M)	2050 (M)
Belgium	12	0.70	2.97
Haiti	11	0.68	2.92
Cuba	11	0.68	2.90
South Sudan	11	0.67	2.87
Dominican Rep	11	0.65	2.78
Czech Rep	11	0.64	2.75
Greece	10	0.63	2.67
Jordan	10.20	0.61	2.62
Portugal	10.20	0.61	2.61
Azerbaijan	10.14	0.61	2.60
Sweden	10.10	0.61	2.59
Honduras	9.90	0.59	2.54
UAE	9.89	0.59	2.54
Hungary	9.66	0.58	2.48
Tajikistan	9.54	0.57	2.45
Belarus	9.45	0.57	2.42
Austria	9.01	0.54	2.31
Papua NG	8.95	0.54	2.29
Serbia	8.74	0.52	2.24
Israel	8.66	0.52	2.22
Switzerland	8.65	0.52	2.22
Togo	8.28	0.50	2.12
Sierra Leone	7.98	0.48	2.05
Rest of the World	7.62	0.46	1.95
Hong Kong	7.50	0.45	1.92
Laos	7.28	0.44	1.87
Paraguay	7.13	0.43	1.83
Bulgaria	6.95	0.42	1.78
Libya	6.87	0.41	1.76
Lebanon	6.83	0.41	1.75

Country (Populations)	2019 (M)	SARS-2 (M)	2050 (M)
Nicaragua	6.62	0.40	1.70
Kyrgyzstan	6.52	0.39	1.67
El Salvador	6.49	0.39	1.66
Turkmenistan	6.03	0.36	1.55
Singapore	5.85	0.35	1.50
Denmark	5.79	0.35	1.49
Finland	5.54	0.33	1.42
Congo	5.52	0.33	1.41
Slovakia	5.46	0.33	1.40
Norway	5.42	0.33	1.39
Oman	5.11	0.31	1.31
State of Palestine	5.10	0.31	1.31
Costa Rica	5.09	0.31	1.31
Liberia	5.06	0.30	1.30
Ireland	4.94	0.30	1.27
Central AR	4.83	0.29	1.24
New Zealand	4.82	0.29	1.24
Mauritania	4.65	0.28	1.19
Panama	4.31	0.26	1.11
Kuwait	4.27	0.26	1.10
Croatia	4.11	0.25	1.05
Moldova	4.03	0.24	1.03
Georgia	3.99	0.24	1.02
Eritrea	3.55	0.21	0.91
Uruguay	3.47	0.21	0.89
Bosnia	3.28	0.20	0.84
Mongolia	3.28	0.20	0.84
Armenia	2.96	0.18	0.76
Jamaica	2.96	0.18	0.76
Qatar	2.88	0.17	0.74

Country (Populations)	2019 (M)	SARS-2 (M)	2050 (M)
Albania	2.88	0.17	0.74
Puerto Rico	2.86	0.17	0.73
Lithuania	2.72	0.16	0.70
Namibia	2.54	0.15	0.65
Gambia	2.42	0.15	0.62
Botswana	2.35	0.14	0.60
Gabon	2.23	0.13	0.57
Lesotho	2.14	0.13	0.55
North Macedonia	2.08	0.13	0.53
Slovenia	2.08	0.12	0.53
Guinea-Bissau	1.97	0.12	0.50
Latvia	1.89	0.11	0.48
Bahrain	1.70	0.10	0.44
Equatorial Guinea	1.40	0.08	0.36
Trinidad and Tobago	1.40	0.08	0.36
Estonia	1.33	0.08	0.34
Timor-Leste	1.32	0.08	0.34
Mauritius	1.27	0.08	0.33
Cyprus	1.21	0.07	0.31
Eswatini	1.16	0.07	0.30
Djibouti	0.99	0.06	0.25
Fiji	0.90	0.05	0.23
Réunion	0.90	0.05	0.23
Comoros	0.87	0.05	0.22
Guyana	0.79	0.05	0.20
Bhutan	0.77	0.05	0.20
Solomon Islands	0.69	0.04	0.18
Macao	0.65	0.04	0.17
Montenegro	0.63	0.04	0.16
Luxembourg	0.63	0.04	0.16

REAP THROUGH THE END OF DAYS

Country (Populations)	2019 (M)	SARS-2 (M)	2050 (M)
Western Sahara	0.60	0.04	0.15
Suriname	0.59	0.04	0.15
Cabo Verde	0.56	0.03	0.14
Micronesia	0.55	0.03	0.14
Maldives	0.54	0.03	0.14

TEMA Gray Side Control

COMPANY CLASSIFIED

REAP THROUGH THE END OF DAYS

Meanwhile, I was working with my TEMA Reapers to execute the backup plan. First, I needed to get the craft to the correct spot. Based on Stephen's journal, the open design of this ship allowed for no one else to captain but those who had the biotech installed. So far that was just me. My goal was to introduce to new Reapers, so all had this ability to access, control machines, heal quickly, and lastly potentially read people's thoughts.

Second, I needed to get to San Nicolas Island, an eight hundred- and five-mile swim and would take a hundred and sixty hours by submersible if this was to look like a whale migration. This one is the most remote of California's Channel Islands. It is located sixty-one miles from the nearest point on the mainland coast. Part of Ventura County, twenty-two square miles in size, the island is currently controlled by the United States Navy and is used as a weapon testing and training facility.

The uninhabited island was the home of the Nicoleno Native American tribe until eighteen thirty-five. This was when the Order relocated them to Santa Barbara. Today, or any given day, there are least two hundred military and civilian personnel that live on the island at any given time. Three of them were my Reapers. The island has a small airport and several buildings, including an antenna array for talking to submarines in the Pacific.

The reason why I chose the design of my new underwater vehicle was based on the migration of whales that go through these waters. This Island had so many whale sightings there were two steam-schooners at this location before the Navy took over. The names of the two whale catchers were the Hawk and Port Saunders. They operated off San Nicolas from nineteen thirty-two through thirty-nine, catching about fifty whales off the island during this time of year.

Another fun fact was that San Nicolas Island was one of ten potential sites to detonate the first atomic bomb before White Sands Proving Ground was selected for the Trinity nuclear test. Also, between nineteen fifty-seven and two thousand four, the Navy launched rockets from this location and today remains part of the Pacific Missile Range.

My girls gained access to the base through a contract with my company, Raven Defense. They served as engineers, to conduct missile testing in the coordination of Port Hueneme and Mugu contracting office. They were sleepers, to be activated when the time was right.

Another reason why Stephen chose this location as an underwater and subterranean launch site was the Eocene sandstone and shale. It is easy to dig through, and much of the island also has marine terrace deposits of Pleistocene age.

Another advantage of having a secret base here was the general climate for conducting operations. The Island features a semi-arid climate with Mediterranean characteristics. Winters are mild with an average temperature of fifty-five degrees in February, the coolest month and is the season where most of the precipitation falls. Summers are dry and warm with an average of seventy degrees in September. On average, there are less than forty days of measurable rainfall.

My goal was to use this large and protected area to fight the future. By placing items here that are protected and built to work in tandem to the location at Mt. Ararat. This would be a backup site if the primary site is destroyed.

"Standby. We have on radar," Control said to me as I took the craft from the TEMA research vessel and dropped into the water. I was able to position the craft with the artifact gathered in a space under the Island and only accessible by a cave under the water. Waiting for me was the submersible craft that looked like a whale.

The next task was getting the craft from the base identified by Stephen's journal. Following the noted frequency signature in the water, it led me to the Malibu coast. I also read the rumors of an alien base somewhere in the area, with most identifying on Google Earth, a stadium-shaped object at a depth of two thousand feet.

It is known as the Sycamore Knoll. On the map it measures at three miles in circumference.

I then researched classified reports in two thousand fourteen that referenced this very place that I was going. In the interviews with military witnesses, he was quoted saying, "I was convinced there was something there before this Malibu anomaly was publicized. A lot of people are under the false impression that there's a base there. Now that doesn't mean that there aren't there. I've seen them myself on many occasions. But just because crafts are seen there, that doesn't mean that that is a base under the water.

"They don't need massive bases under the water or under the ground. I'm not saying there aren't any, but they don't need them because they can just pop in and out of our skies anytime the visitors want, anywhere they want, as far as I can tell."

Another Researcher was quoted saying, "I've collected probably a hundred reports of people who have seen going in and out of the water there. But my problem is that the Google images are coming out different, depending on what viewpoint you're looking at this thing. Some show a tunnel. Some don't. I'm very intrigued by the possibility," he says. "I'm convinced there's something down there."

I was amazed at how much information was out there on this place Stephen wanted me to research. He wrote this journal back in nineteen ninety-seven. Before Google Earth was on everyone's desktop, I'll soon find out. I'll arrive in three hours, so I kept reading.

In two thousand six, there was an article in Fate magazine called, "Is There an Underwater UFO Base off the Southern California Coast?" where the author cited several witness accounts and opinions. Then I read several articles from Unicus, including "Who Discovered the So-Called Malibu UFO Base?" and "Digital Deception in the Pacific: There is No 'UFO Base' off the Coast of Malibu.

I then zoomed in to the latest version of Google Earth and found the structure at coordinates 34°1'23.31" N 118°59'45.64" W. Unlike all these theories, I was going down to look. What I there to find was technology to stop the Order. I won't be writing an article, "I found the Alien base in my artificial Humpback whale. Come on down and take a look."

One thing that was prevalent in everything I read, half of the articles and videos believe, and the other half do not. A scientifically skeptical group that has for many years offered a critical analysis of the claims. One example that came up in the general sense that has been the voice of hard science since the late forties is the response that 'extraterrestrial beings' don't exist. All can be explained just like crop circles appearing in Indonesia, which the government and the National Institute of Aeronautics and Space described as 'man-made.'

The skeptics were also mostly government officials who if they spoke up for an alien base would probably lose their job. One scientist responded after seeing the GIS mapping, "I didn't see anything special about it. I think it's because it looks like there's a flat surface and then, below it, it looks like there are these vertical columns, so somebody can say, 'Oh, this is the entryway to something special.'

"I think it's natural and is a part of the continental shelf. It's just a complicated part of what's now offshore that has seen some erosion and slumping when this was partially exposed when sea level was lower. This is a major earthquake area, and some of these features are a result of slope failures, due to shaking. There's no flag under the water that says, 'I'm the entrance to an alien base.' There's nothing unnatural looking about it. The anomaly is showing some sort of variation in the offshore coastal morphology."

Others who are believers but were cautions said, "I'm convinced that they are a real. There's too much evidence out there. Beyond that, we don't know anything. We don't know who they are, why they're here, how much of this stuff is our own government. A point beyond that is that anything that is not clarified or that can't be explained by current scientific methods, automatically it's aliens. It's the explanation of last resort, and I just don't buy that."

Lastly, there was a former FBI Special Agent who is automatically an expert because he had a badge and a gun, analyzed the questionable pictures and videos. He then proposed the following as a counter-argument, "This was taken from a different angle of the 'mysterious base.' We need to remember that Google obtains their underwater data from several different sources, including satellite radar and echo sonar from the Navy, NOAA, NASA, and other agencies. Because they often use quite different technologies, the derived information isn't always going to agree. When it doesn't, Google relies on its automated 3D auto-generation programs to make sense of it.

"We're dealing with limited information to render the graphic because we can see it evidenced in the disparity of image quality between the anomaly and the areas immediately surrounding it. The blurry sections and jagged edges obviously suggest a patchwork of image processing has taken place.

"There's no big mystery to this thing two thousand feet under the sea in terms of it being an entrance. Of course, until you get a camera there, you don't know where the ingress is leading. I'd hazard a guess that it doesn't go in too far, and if they do get in there, I think the chances are that they're not going to find the lost treasures of Atlantis."

Meanwhile, during the journey to the location to find what was there, my girls were doing some work for me. They were accessing specialized ground penetrating radar. Reaper Agents twelve, sixteen, and twenty-one were in the lab downloading files for me. Suddenly one of the doctors on staff happened to run into Agent twelve. This was because there can be no witnesses.

It only took seconds for the poison to make its way into his nervous system. Agent Lima grabbed the clear plastic from under the table unraveled to cover a large area of the lab space. Next, Agent Oscar kicked the target from table. Then Victor slid her pelvis under his head and placed a small clear plastic bag over it, catching the blood coming out of his mouth. Agent Oscar wrapped duct tape around his neck. Her legs tightened as he shook from the hypoxia and poison in his body.

"Lima, grab a gurney. We need to get him in the oven fast," Victor barked. "Got it. Three floors down and I'll flirt with the guard." Then sixteen spoke up, "I'll keep downloading the files." All agreed the mission just cranked up a notch.

With the data and access to the elevator, made their way down to the extraction point. A cave that could only be accessed from a submersible. I was waiting for them. Minutes later, we headed off the coast of Malibu to retrieve a craft for our future mission.

A week later, Agent Victor shouted at Control that was received when the submersible arrived on the surface, "Holy shit. When the craft left the Malibu cave and popped out of the water, it ascended to eighty thousand feet in a flash. I hope Jonathan is all right." Control then responded, "We did get to track the object for about four miles at six thousand feet before it headed above the ionosphere." Agent Victor then said, "The craft looked like a flying ticktack about forty feet long with no wings, and fast."

REAP THROUGH THE END OF DAYS

PALE HORSE

Looking at the mirror with my tech recoding a message for Jane, I spoke, "And when he had opened the fourth seal, I heard the voice of the beast say, Come and see. And I looked and behold a pale horse and his name that sat on him was Death, and Hell followed with him. And power was given unto them over three quarters of the earth, to kill with sword, and with hunger, and with death, and with the beasts of the earth."

"It's June first, two thousand twenty-nine. What I just read was the last thing in Dr. Heller's notebook, he failed to find a cure. Little did I know that my plan back in twenty twelve would unravel before my eyes, trusting in his ability to find a solution to this mess was ill conceived. All we did was delay to inevitable by revealing the Order's plan for a virus and vaccine series that will make all women in the world with certain blood types infertile.

"Only O positive and A positive matches will have offspring until twenty twenty-eight. Then another virus and vaccine series will be introduced and only O positive will be able to have children. By the year, twenty thirty-one there will only be one remaining blood type and the

Order will have control over the remaining population and the last phase in their plan will be ready for execution by twenty fifty, the end of days.

"In six months, when A and O positive have children, soon after it will be discovered that blood types matched in the right way determine fertility. Due to antigens, proteins on the surface of blood cells, cause a response from the immune system. The Rh factor is a type of protein on the surface of red blood cells. Most people who have the Rh factor are Rh-positive. Those who do not have the Rh factor are Rh-negative.

"When the mother is Rh-negative and the father is Rh-positive, the fetus can inherit the Rh factor from the father. This makes the fetus Rh-positive too. Problems can arise when the fetus's blood has the Rh factor and the mother's blood does not.

"If a woman is Rh-negative or positive with this new virus, will develop antibodies to a Rh-positive baby. If a small amount of the baby's blood mixes with her blood, which often happens, the mother's body may respond as if it were allergic to the baby. Her body may make antibodies to the Rh antigens in the baby's blood. This means you have become sensitized, and antibodies can cross the placenta and attack the baby's blood.

"The next event is a breakdown of the fetus's red blood cells and produces anemia. This is a condition that happens when the blood has a low number of red blood cells. This condition is called hemolytic disease or hemolytic anemia. It can become severe enough to cause serious illness, brain damage, or even death in the fetus or newborn. Sensitization can occur any time the fetus's blood mixes with the mother's blood.

"What will happen to eighty-five percent of all pregnancies is a miscarriage. An induced abortion or menstrual extraction. An ectopic pregnancy. Chorionic villus sampling. Or a blood transfusion. All will result in babies that will not make it to a year old.

"The CDC and WHO will first try to prevent the problem with a blood test, but the virus will give false hope within the first five years and then will be abandoned not knowing what is happening with blood type and Rh factor diagnosis. Antibody screening will also give false negative that will impact the pregnancy.

"The next attempt will be an injection of Rh immunoglobulin a blood product that can prevent sensitization of a Rh-negative mother. But this too will fail, and the fetus will miscarry.

"The other issue that will arise is a higher-than-normal death rate of mothers because if a woman with Rh-negative blood has not been sensitized, her doctor will inject RhIg around the twenty eighth week of pregnancy to prevent sensitization for the rest of the pregnancy and with the virus will cause an immediate poisoning of the blood causing death. With more than eighty five percent of the population is Rh positive, doctors will fight over why pregnancies are failing. It will take three to five years for them to come to the conclusion the issue is blood type and not RH factor.

"Even if the baby is born with Rh-positive blood, the mother that is RH negative may be given another dose of RhIg to prevent her from making antibodies to the Rh-positive cells she may have received from the baby before and during delivery. This too with the virus will kill the mother. With the higher death rate of mothers, some will be too afraid to have children.

"Dr. Heller explained to me that the virus would be scheduled for release in twenty nineteen in China as an accidental leak from a lab. Then once the first wave hits North America and Europe, the second wave will hit Africa, India, and the remaining world. The variants of the virus and initial death rates will hit two million before a vaccine will be available. Then with the population forced to get vaccines and boosters, SARS-03 will be introduced in one month. With a readily available vaccine strategy, in weeks, the new vaccine with mRNA will be released.

"The last push for vaccines will be for those who refuse, will no longer be employable. It will take six months until the entire population is vaccinated, to include all poorer countries, this is when the birth rate will start to plummet. Once a scientist discovered the vaccine effects on expected mothers, it will be too late.

"A percentage of the population will say this is a conspiracy and the government is behind it, however, by the time it is admitted by the government, people will have accepted their fate. Some of the loudest scientists, news personalities, companies, and government officials will be killed, and cities burned due to vigilante justice.

"You are our last hope to fight the future. I love you, Jane."

Stopping the recording and setting a timed delay for her receipt of the message, I flashed back to twenty twelve when I was so hopeful to find a cure and save the future. Also, to give Dr. Heller a chance to make things right. I said, "Dr. Heller, where do you want to live?" "I don't care as long as I get the facility needed for the work." "I looked at the SF-86 form questionnaire for the clearance you had with the Center for Disease Control back two years ago. I suggest we set you up in Gardnerville Nevada." "Reason?" he asked not knowing where it was but intrigued by the certainty in my voice.

"It's on the opposite side of where everyone knows you. An hour to Reno, a quick plane flight and I can be there. About the same time to Lake Tahoe. Also, there is a nice home on Topaz Lake you can use that will allow for some quality of life moving forward." "Any good fishing?" "Yes sir, I read you are into hunting and fishing. This area should meet all your needs."

In early twenty twelve, I built a new identity for Dr. Heller. He became Dave Taylor, originally from Atlanta Georgia. Unlike television, this requires an existing person who is disappeared and replaced with my imposter. The real Dave was buried in the Nevada desert the day after the Dr. Heller signed the paperwork.

Don't grieve for the real Dave, he was not a good guy. In his youth, he was in and out of juvenile detention, a relapsed gambler, married three times, and was unemployed warehouse worker in New Jerseys when I flew him out to the west coast for a job interview. With plastic surgery, Dr. Heller was a dead ringer, after three months of coaching on the life of Dave Taylor, he was ready. With three hundred and fifty in the United States, he disappeared.

Next was the facility on service drive. The company front was a medical warehouse for the Raven Emergency Medical Supply Group company part of the Defense subsidiary. There were twelve employees onsite,

Mr. Taylor was listed as the manager, even though his front office staff ran the company, he just spent one hour a day signing off on documents. His lab was adjacent a secret door from his office. Secured with a level five burn protocol for safety and security if there was a raid on the building.

Lastly, the chalet on Topaz Lake was equipped with a two-hundred-and-seventy-degree view of the Eastern skyline and crystal-clear water. Located on the Nevada – California border, the work staff would come over periodically for a party or the Lodge and Casino was home to customer meetings or planning events. It was the perfect safe house in plain view. No work was exchanged here and within a year he had a girlfriend who accepted his stolen life as a fresh start like most who move out west.

Ultimately, and after seventeen years of work Dr. Heller was unable to design an antidote to fight the future. I needed to reap him per his instructions. He didn't suffer, I injected him with strychnine after he was unconscious from an insulin cocktail. I needed Jane to have a partner, Thomas Bloom seemed like the guy who would give her the love and support needed to complete her last mission. Now we are here, cracking open the seal in twenty thirty, the Pale Horse.

Jane witnessed the local guide throw a grenade into the recently discovered cavern in Göbekli Tepe.

Flashing back, Tom and she were researching a void discovered by a TEMA satellite. When she read the writings, it described a world before Noah's flood. It also was the place where a manuscript would help in her next journey.

As they navigated the large cavern, Jane was separated from Tom as he wanted to go further. Looking at the map linked to her biotech, Jane decided to follow a secondary entrance on the backside of the mountain. As she found the exit, she popped her head up back toward the decided original entrance. Not knowing if the guide was from the Order, she made her way back through the only access point to find Tom.

It was there, just outside the first entrance she saw Tom's leg and arm mashed up by the ceiling high cave-in. Again, flashing back in an instant, her hard drive pushed a thousand images at her of him. In two years, they had shared so much together. He was a friend, a lover, a fellow soldier, and the last man she would ever know from this timeline.

As Jane made her way to him, a formality in order to validate death, his exposed foot moved as she heard him cough. "Baby, I'll get you out. Wait a minute. I got you," she said ripping the rubble away from him. It was then, as Tom was conscious saw her lift large boulders as though they were made of foam. She then picked him up in her arms. "How are you doing this?" he softly said as they made their way back to the other entrance.

Jane's biomechanics were complete. With the last upgrade she received a month ago and injecting herself with oil from the Tree of Life itself, she was now perfect, body and soul. With the nanites increasing her strength ten-fold and the ability to read the thoughts of others, she knew Tom was alive even though he probably didn't.

Now in hiding, Jane was working on getting Tom healthy, one month after they were both pronounced dead and laid to rest in empty coffins, the entire planet is infected with the final task from the Order. To slow down child births and in the next twenty years, a population shrinking. With the country overwhelmed by SARS-03 variants for the last ten years and a couple other epidemics. Jane realizes that they won.

As she followed my instructions and contacted no one, TEMA and Raven Defense was willed to Jacob who is now the CEO. Tina was instructed to teach him how to best use the tools to delay the end of days. I would be his guardian angel.

Receiving my recording, she knew what needed to be done. As I explained in my last message why she needed to take the manuscript to a secret destination. Jane was torn between saving a doomed future or starting again.

As Tom received the last part of his medicine before the long trip, Jane injected him with the oil from the Tree of Life. Since arriving to the safe house outside of Damascus, he received tech implants and injected with nanites. She watched as his bones healed and he was brought on-line to learn how to use the tech.

Now that Tom was sleeping and tech upgrades complete, she watched an artificial intelligence simulation of the next twenty years sped up. The in the first few years there was a world with no hope. A world where eighty percent of the population are unable to have offspring. She watched as cities burn and new ones more adaptable to the current conditions thrive.

Then in her hologram, she sees the Order designing and selling synthetic children. Robots so real they are indistinguishable to the real thing. With fear of babies and children being stolen, Alaska becomes a safe haven with accommodations and free land. Other countries try to do the same. In ten years, the world has changed.

Jane ends the virtual reality experience with a map revealing the best way to reach her destination. She realizes that the future can't be saved, and without her sacrifice, the seventh seal will be opened, and, on that day, the world will end as two billion inhabit the earth.

"Tom we are almost there." Jane said making her way to the next cravat. "I think there is an opening up ahead. Man, I love this tech." Tom said leading the way up the rock outcropping and then dragging up their supplies, not knowing what to expect. Her heads-up display was showing a path, that Tom could see, they were close now.

As they reached the destination, was massive entrance that seemed to be hidden by both satellite and topography analysis. Then when they were three hundred yards inside, their thermal vision was interrupted by a three-dimensional hologram of me appearing and a large light illuminated the area revealing a large cylinder-shaped metallic object.

"Hey Jane and Tom, I have some good news and some bad news. Let us start with the good one; we have a chance to change our future and stop the end of days. Adam wrote of an Illuminator who can change the future. With what was designed here and in an underwater cave in San Nicolaus Island, you can be our savior. Now the bad news; it needs to be by going back in time. I know what you're thinking, what do I do with this?" my hologram said as I gestured to the lighted opening.

"Are you actually expecting me to do this? Leave my life, Jacob, you, everything? Jane asked realizing that no one has a future without her sacrifice. Adjusting her thermal sight to a low light mode showing the size and scope of the inner walls of the cave with a large object in the middle. Roughly the size of football field.

"Tom. What do you want to do?" "I have no family, you do. I'm willing to do what you want."

The hologram then spoke, "I need you to fight the future. Follow me and I'll explain how to use the craft as a way to go back in time. Once you have changed the future, our timeline will disappear. The good news is that our AI in onboard and will help you know if reaping will help or hurt your future."

"Will I have a future to come back to?" "This is unknown. If you change large events, it could make things worse, this is why the AI is valuable at calculating the likelihood an event will help mankind." "Will Tom and I live forever?" "Yes, but you can still be killed. That is why the oil from the Tree of Life is so important." "Will the Creator stop me?" Jane asked. "With our interpretation of the ancient documentation provided, as long as you make things better, 'They' should let you continue," the hologram said.

Tom then interrupted, "But if you could have stopped Morningstar from eating the forbidden fruit or stop Cain from killing Able." "I'm scared," Jane said reaching out for Tom. "I got you baby. Nothing will happen on our watch."

The hologram then spoke up, "Remember the craft will not go to the future, only the past. Our analysis is loss of freedom until the End of Days. The only alternative is to go back to the beginning and make changes, so they don't succeed.

"To help you, I've attached to a new pulse Medium to High Frequency radio signal so powerful that it can talk to you around the world. That means your biotech and nanites will work with this craft. This can give you the ability to know everything that is on the current internet.

"Every person, fact, item, and event are at your fingertips. You will need it to get money, so we have calculated deposits of gold to use as currency. Also know what is going to happen and know the impact of a decision reaping someone. As you keep making changes, the AI will recalibrate the likelihood of the End of Days.

"I've also added an Artificial Intelligence computer program called J.O.N.N. it stands for Joint Observation Neural Network. When you board the ship, it will engage and merge with your tech. And yes, it is me, in your head and when put online, will be visible to you anywhere you are. You and Tom should live forever. This means moving from place to place every twenty years so not to be found out."

Jane realized at this moment; she had no choice. Walking under the craft, she reached the ramp and they both went inside. It was then, the entire ship lighted up and waiting for her was JONN. "Welcome, tell me what you want," JONN said. "First of all, since you walk and talk like my big brother, I'm going to call you bro. It's easier to say and if we go far enough back in time, they won't know what this means." "Understood. Let me explain the ship."

JONN then continued, "To make this easy, I'll speak in the first person. I look like your brother and have all of the memories of him. Now all is in the craft." Jane laughed while shaking her head, "So, you are literally my brother in a hologram form with all the answers ever documented? What an ego." "I am but without emotion or ego, I can only simulate based on pitch, diction, and inflection." "Where do I sit?" Pointing to the chair, "Here, now let me explain the controls."

Getting one last response from Tom with a thumbs up, she was ready to power the ship. Jane then shouted, Bro. What about saying goodbye to my kid and the other you?" "You need to leave now." "What about how I look? How do I get around? Weapons?" "Everything you need is on the ship. Artifacts gathered over the last forty years will corroborate time periods, language, and weapons." "What about language?" she paused, "Oh, right, I can speak and understand any language with the AI computer." "That's now me, JONN." "So, my brother has been gathering everything to get me ready for this?"

The hologram then said, "When he knew that the Order was too powerful, he just needed to prepare you to change the End of Days. When the fourth horseman was revealed, you needed to leave. To succeed, trust your training and change the past so today will never happen. No Order. No Watchers. No death to free will."

As the ramp lifted on the craft, the silent propulsion system was not taking Jane through a worm hole in space. It would simply take her to the sixth day without leaving the cave. Using a matter stability bubble created by the ship, everything in the cave to include the communication antenna, supplies, and ten thousand years of gear will not change. Her brother also confirmed that this cave has not altered since the days of Adam and Eve.

Our souls can live in corporeal bodies for a hundred and twenty years. Jane and Tom have enough oil to last them ten thousand years. If they decide to abandon the mission, simply by not taking the oil, they will die during the next hundred- and twenty-year cycle. The nanites in her blood would keep her from aging and damage.

Lastly, I separated the stone so Tom and Jane would both be invisible to the Watchers, Archangels, and even the Creator. Adam wrote, "That it is was to be worn by the illuminator to walk freely from all, even the Creator."

This will begin their journey to write the wrongs from our timeline and restore balance by destroying the Order before it becomes the powerful worldwide power that causes the End of Days. The cave will be their sanctuary with resupplies for anything they would need. A backup site has the same set up in case something happens.

As she leaned over to press the glass control panel with a small green light blinking, she looked to the handwritten instructions taped to the hull of the ship. In the last line she read…

JONATHAN REAPER

Reap Through the End of Days
J.R.
This is your Beginning.

REAP THROUGH THE END OF DAYS

OTHER WORKS

BY
JONATHAN REAPER

REAP THROUGH THE END OF DAYS

THE RECRUIT

JONATHAN REAPER

A true account in real time of Marine Corps Recruit Depot Parris Island 20+ years ago. This is a true account of my experience at Parris Island in real time. So, what does this mean? I literally wrote in a journal, hidden from the drill instructors, each day or night when there was a moment to scribble the actions of "what is happening now." The poems, illustrations, and incoherent writing are all word for word from the journal. This book is dedicated to the men I served with for 20 years in the Marine Corps: from the fjords of Norway to the mountains of Iran to the jungles of Central America, thank you for saving my life daily and letting me get back to my family. Someday we will get to tell the stories of what we did, whom we did it to, and the difference we made to history.

On the coast of Maine, a young man foraging for treasure in an old attic learns about the secret life of his family. In hopes to protect them, his uncle explains in five journals his secret life. As a professional assassin, he was trained by the military and government agencies, no one knew his true occupation or of his grandfather.

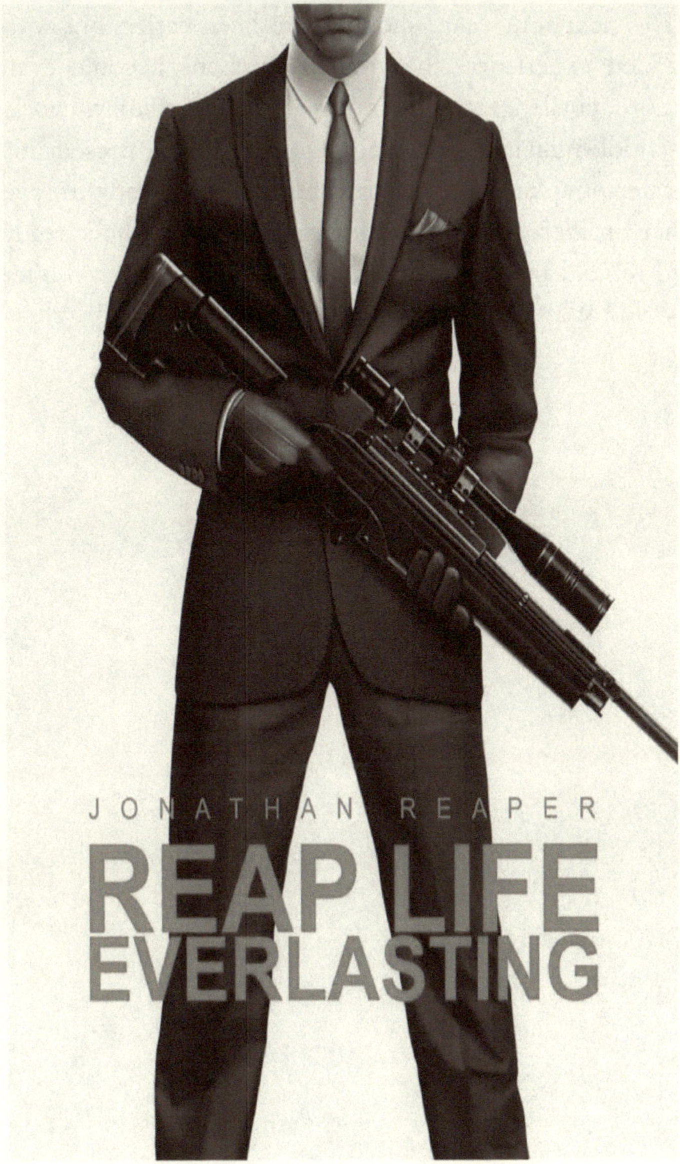
JONATHAN REAPER
REAP LIFE
EVERLASTING

The next four years should have been easier, but with added experience, the counter missions become even more challenging. He is now juggling, family, work, school, military, and being a reaper. In the present his sister now knows the secret and is getting ready to save her brother. Building her own reaper force, she is ready to rebuild the organization her grandfather started after World War II.

With the death of the first Grimm Reaper, he leaves memoirs for his grandson to validate a lifetime of service and secrecy. In the beginning, there was no hope for the allies, then an organization was created called the Office of Strategic Services. This changed the outcome of the war, saved countless lives, and was all top secret until now. Because of their success, a new unit was created called the Grimm Reapers. One man was selected for the program. Over the next fifty-one years, his identity and mission was hidden from everyone. This book will reveal the hero and his untold story.

REAP THROUGH THE END OF DAYS

JONATHAN REAPER

Based on a deathbed whisper from the first Reaper in nineteen ninety-six, a footlocker revealed a journal. In it was a first-person confessional spanning from nineteen forty-two through nineteen eighty-six. The admission answers what really happened to all the major conspiracies of this period of time.

The journal was written after receiving a fifty-year celebratory visit to Fort Bragg in nineteen ninety-five. This was for his service in the Office of Strategic Services as an Operational Group member. The declassified reports revealed how the Reaper Force was created from the ashes of our first heroes in the shadow.

In the beginning, there was no fate. An organization needed to be created out of the atrocities of World War II. There was no such thing as fate deciding if you would live or die... then came the Grimm Reaper. Even though this is Volume 4, it is a prequel to Volume 0 called the Recruit. Because of the spoilers in this book, please read the others first.

In the Journals, with the Global War on Terrorism and Iraqi Freedom, the OSS has a purpose not aligned with the allies. Jonathan's counter missions are revealed as stealing artifacts, hiding the enemy, and erasing weapons of mass destruction.

In the present, Jane is tasked with growing her Reaper force while protecting the family. It is exposed to Tina the Grimm Reaper mission. Jacob's curiosity almost gets him killed.

What would you do if it was revealed that your friend was really using you for evil? With the Order controlling the past, the counter missions just got bigger in the present. Join the adventure with all the old and new characters in Volume 5, help fight the future.

REAP THROUGH THE END OF DAYS

An origin story of the OSS recruiter, operations officer, and Jonathan's mentor is revealed with a revelation to his purpose and vision. Who was Mr. P. Grimm and was he a man of good or evil intentions? Like most who have a cataloged life with each moment added to the scale of justice, his fate was preordained like Jonathan starting with Stephen's father. This story takes you on a journey from 1943 thru 2028. With the arrival of a journal on a summer day in 2007, exactly 10 years after his death, Jonathan was given a chance to read Mr. P. Grimm's story and what is needed to fight the future. Three generations of Grimms and Reapers intertwined in an attempt to keep the Order from reaching their goal and the apocalypse in its wake.